LORD OF THE RIVER

LORD OF THE RIVER

BERNARD CLAVEL

TRANSLATED BY ELIZABETH WALTER

LITTLE, BROWN AND COMPANY
BOSTON   TORONTO

FIRST AMERICAN EDITION
FIRST PUBLISHED IN FRANCE UNDER THE TITLE
Le Seigneur du Fleuve
T 01/74

Library of Congress Cataloging in Publication Data

Clavel, Bernard, 1923–
  Lord of the river.

  Translation of Le seigneur du fleuve.
  I. Title.
PZ4.C6155Lo3 [PQ2663.L325]   843'.9'14   73–12800
ISBN 0-316-14706-0

PRINTED IN THE UNITED STATES OF AMERICA

Clavel

To
HERVÉ BAZIN
in memory of La Croix du Meunier
and in friendship

CONTENTS

PART ONE

The Mists of Dawn

※ ※

In all the lands bordering the valleys of the Rhône and Saône, autumn had set in well before the end of summer. Some years autumn is ushered in prematurely by rain and cold winds, but in the year 1840 the sun was dominant. It seemed as though the heavy storms at the end of July had emptied the sky for good. There followed a long blazing August, with interminable days when everything sizzled as if on hot coals, and stifling nights without a breath of wind.

The water-level had dropped, the freshwater lagoons bordering the Rhône had dried out. The mud cracked. Thousands of creatures died. Leeches, small worms, water snails, fish and freshwater mussels. Flocks of birds had rejected this morbid offering, then, finding neither food nor water, had taken wing for lands where perhaps the sky still had something other than fire to pour down upon the earth.

This void had been felt first by the country people and the river folk; it finally affected the town-dwellers also, who are less given to glancing at the sky.

Lyons, whose effluents and sewage emptied into the Rhône and Saône, suffered the stench of decay. It had crept over the cat's-head cobblestones, along the alleyways, up flights of steps. Then it invaded the *traboules*, the dark passages running beneath the houses from one street to the next. There, it underwent a slow change, becoming impregnated with the damp freshness which continued to seep out of the old stones despite the drought. It was rather as if the interior of every house, at the foot of the spiral staircases, had coldly sweated out a bad fever. Towards the middle of August the smell had reached the wide modern avenues and squares.

On the left bank of the Rhône, where lay the fields, marshes and thin woodlands of the alluvial promontories, the earth had dried out and hardened. The grassy paths had gone yellow and were covered with a whitish-grey dust. At the beginning of September the trees began to turn, then swiftly shed their first leaves. And these were not the golden leaves of normal autumns, but shrivelled, brittle leaves, the colour of overbaked bread.

To the south of the new road which ran from the old bridge and crossed the district of La Guillotière, construction work had ceased. The river was too low for boats to carry stone and sand. A further misery was added to the distress which for years past had driven the silk-weavers out of the city to take refuge in Givors, Tarare, L'Arbresle or Limonest. In these little towns where the duty was lower, weavers could more easily acquire a patch of ground to cultivate and were less fearful of the fluctuations of the silk markets. That year, however, they had seen their few crops wither. Those who had banded together to work at silk-weaving, utilizing the waterfalls to make their looms clack and their winders turn, had had to stop work when the flow of water dried up.

Navigation had not ceased on the Saône, which was slower and deeper than the Rhône, but since only one barge at a time could risk it downstream from Lyons, the traffic in goods was insignificant. So there, too, there was unemployment and want.

When the boatmen ceased work, all the lesser men whose living depended on the port – porters, unloaders, checkers, counting-house clerks, commission agents – found themselves out of work too. Some turned to the railway stations linking Lyons to Saint-Etienne, others sought employment with the overland carriers. But the stations, like the staging-posts, had men to spare and rioting had broken out.

There was also sporadic fighting along the waterfronts of the Rhône, where out-of-work crews got drunk and became enraged while arguing politics. Those who were for Monsieur Thiers did not know what they had against Guizot; Guizot's supporters had no idea why they favoured his policies; but both sides exchanged insults and came to blows. It was due to heat and unemployment rather than to politics, which were only an excuse.

Fighting also broke out between the barge crews and the sailors or mechanics of the steam vessels, but there were reasons for that which everyone thought he understood. But the only men to fight were those who earned just about the same working for the new companies as they would have with the masters of the horse-drawn barges. The barge-masters never fought with the financiers and those responsible for the steam vessels. Yet it was money that was the real issue on both sides. Of course, since a steamer needed fewer men than a train of horse-drawn barges, the barge crews might have been seeking a quarrel with the employees of those who wanted to rob them of their living. In reality, it was mainly pride that goaded them, and an attachment to their harsh way of life.

And then there was the heat, which frayed the nerves, set them on edge, and built up a rage in the body which brought into play the brute strength no longer needed for work.

So long as a man has work to keep his mind and body occupied, so long as he and his children are well fed, he has neither the time nor the inclination to take an interest in other people's business. He goes his own way, and when that way is a river as turbulent as the Rhône, he has enough to do just keeping an eye on its moods. But that summer and the fiery autumn which it trailed behind it had not allowed life to pursue its normal course.

And then, on the evening of October 25, a great hope sprang up in the valleys. Heavy clouds had gathered behind the slopes of Sainte-Foy.

Since they were coming from that quarter of the sky, they must have arisen over the sea. Huge, purplish, ready to break, they had to be heavy with rain. But they did not break. And as the sun went down they looked as if they were heavy with fire, not water.

They were very beautiful clouds, but they went on their way without halting.

The river folk, like the country folk and the townsfolk whom the sudden shade had drawn to their windows, talked among themselves.

'What's going to happen?'

'What's up now in that accursed sky?'

'We ought to light candles.'

'Have a big procession with the bishop.'

'If only we had guns to fire at those vile clouds!'

'We'll end up without a drop of water to drink.'

'And no wine either. The vine hasn't borne anything this year, and if this goes on, it'll die.'

A great hope had sprung up, then drifted away towards the east. So the people retired to bed in houses where the heat of the day came in at evening to crouch in the corners of the rooms till morning broke.

And while the inhabitants of towns and villages stretched out on their beds, in the barges moored along the banks of the Rhône the barge crews had gone to sleep beneath the canvas deck-tents. Some of them had been there for weeks, like sailors caught in the ice by a never-ending winter. In their case it was the summer which held them prisoner, a summer which was devouring the autumn and quenching its thirst by drinking up their river.

Dawn was still far distant. Christian Merlin realized that as soon as he awoke. Thick night pressed down upon the canvas of the deck-tent. Christian raised himself on his elbow and cast about for what had wakened him. His two hundred pounds of bone and muscle made the webbing of his bunk creak.

He listened a moment.

Nothing.

Nothing but water brushing past between the planks of the barge and the stones of the quay. The level of the river had not altered. The eddy which formed beneath the first arch of the bridge of La Guillotière still faded out against the prow, maintaining the same rhythm. It was the breathing of the Rhône in this stretch of its course. Like a big dog dreaming of a fight, the river growled for as long as it took to count five. The eddy came into being at the apex of the triangle of water bounded by two embanked piers. It deepened, gathered momentum, then rose to the surface and spread out. And the wave bordering the eddy began to curl as it described its first circle. At that point there was always a hesitation, a wondering whether it would remain fixed like this, or disappear, or open out still further into an enormous peony. Invariably, during all the centuries that the bridge had stood there, successive eddies were born in order to die downstream in the gathering speed of the current or against the quays. The only variation was in their language, livelier, more abrupt, shriller in tone when the river was low; slower, heavier and graver as the level rose.

Four, five, six . . . You could count the waves which were raised, only to spread outwards as they were drawn downstream. They receded into the distance, and, well spaced out, slapped into stillness against the stones.

Christian had fallen asleep listening to the river's breathing. He found it unchanged, and it was the sign that the water-level had not altered an inch. He repeated this to himself several times, while telling himself that something else must have made him uneasy while he slept.

In order to hear better, he had been holding his breath, lungs half empty. In one gasp he expelled this air which he had retained too long and which was making the blood pound in his temples, and then drew in a great gulp. He exhaled it quickly, but then drew in the air in little sips, testing it with his nose and palate. It was no longer Christian Merlin, barge-master, who stretched his big frame on his bunk; it was a hunting animal. Pointing for a few moments, he ceased to listen.

There was a mist. That much was certain. And it must even be a very thick one. There was no need to see clearly to know that it was seeping in under the awning at the level of the gunwales and trickling its murk between the bunks. As always, the mist carried a mixture of several smells. That of the river to start with, permanent and predominant. A good smell of water constantly on the move, of water-licked stone, of mosses soaked a thousand times and dried and soaked again, of sand washed then grilled by the sun.

The smell of horses, of course. Twenty-eight horses stabled in the barge moored downstream from the one in which Christian slept with his son Claude and his prowman, Honoré Baudry. These two were also distinguishable. Sweat, breath, boots, tobacco, farts, wine. But these were no more than the normal elements of the atmosphere in the deck-tent.

And tonight there was something else.

Ill at ease, Christian got up. When his bare feet touched the floor he realized that the mist was even thicker than he had thought. The boards were as slimy as a quay beside the muddy Saône. Water must be pouring off the deck-tent as after a downpour. Christian's hands fumbled through the thick darkness and found his velvet trousers, which he put on. The drenched material was icy and stiff.

Left hand in front of him, he groped as far as the canvas screening the entrance and thrust it aside. As soon as he was outside, he felt himself surrounded. He shivered. His bare body, his face, his arms, were plunged into the cold vapour, almost palpable, which bore down upon the invisible river.

Nothing. It was impossible to see a thing. Night had blotted out the river and swallowed up the town.

Christian took three steps and stopped short. He knew his boat. He raised his right foot, which found at once the top of the bulwark, where he rested it. What Christian was inhaling was so cold that smells were no longer even recognizable. He had wanted to go too fast and the whole of his inside had seized up. He restrained himself, breathing more slowly through mouth and nose. The air was thick. It was as much to be savoured as breathed. Outside, the night lacked the scent of men. The scent of horses was stronger. It was good to catch it, because it made one think of the pleasant warmth of the stable and of clean dry straw. Christian had a sense of well-being, which vanished as soon as he discovered what had awakened him. Beyond the good smell of the beasts, fainter because more distant, there was the stench of smoke.

Coal!

Drowned in the mist, dampened, distorted, but identifiable through it all, it was her all right. It was that disgusting filthy plague of all the devils!

Oh God, it was the *Triomphant*!

Christian let out a roar. It seemed to him that this terrible thickness of the night in which he had just detected the smell of burning coal was sticking in his throat.

He swore more loudly. He spoke without knowing what he was

saying, as if he wanted to spit to clear his throat, to sweep out the whole of his interior, in order to rid himself of the poison he had just breathed in.

He no longer felt the cold or the weight of night. One thing remained, heavier and more oppressive than mist and darkness combined: coal.

He came back under the deck-tent where the other two were still asleep. His hands went at once to the sides of the bunks, which he shook, crying:

'Baudry! Claude! Up quick! The weather's changed and that damned steamer's going to beat us. Get up!'

There was a movement, the creak of the wood and webbing of the bunks, bumps, the heavy thud of the awning thrust up by a head and falling back with all its weight of water and night. The others were getting up. Stupefied with sleep, grumbling, scraping their throats, fumbling for their clothes and boots. They had no idea what was happening, but when Captain Merlin bellowed, no one asked questions.

By the time Christian had struck a light, taken down and lit the lantern, Claude and the prowman were already dressed.

'You sleep like logs,' the captain grumbled. 'Didn't you smell anything?'

Even inside, the air was murky, already laden with humidity. The prowman sniffed several times. He coughed again and asked:

'No, what?... The mist.'

'Coal,' yelled Christian. 'That devil's filth, can't you smell it?'

The prowman thrust aside the flap of canvas which closed the deck-tent and took a step towards the night. In the hesitant light of the lantern which Christian had just hung high on the mast supporting the canvas, mist flooded in. The light tinted it, giving its milky trail the appearance of a sleeping river on a rosy evening. The men's every movement, every gesture, touched off a shimmering in this sluggish flood.

Baudry let the canvas flap fall. There was a displacement of air which hollowed out the mist, then, very rapidly, everything was still. As if stuck fast in this light where only shadows seemed transparent, the three men stood motionless. Silence returned. Not so complete, however, but that the river's regular breathing was very real.

Baudry's square face, invaded by the red undergrowth of his beard which was never trimmed, turned towards the captain. His animal's eyes, glinting with gold and filled with uneasiness, looked questioningly at him.

'You think it's the *Triomphant*? Isn't it more likely from the forges?'

Christian did not hesitate. 'It's her, I tell you.'

'But the river looks no different,' Claude observed.

Silence.

They stood in silence. The three men and the lamp, and its opaque glow, and the canvas heavy above them. Each of them had spoken once, as if reluctantly. They allowed two eddies to form and fade, gazing fixedly towards the interior, all their senses hanging on what the current's sighs might tell them. They waited. They seemed to be listening more with their eyes than with their ears, around which the lamplight glowed, reflecting the gold rings which were the sign of their calling.

Claude Merlin, tall as his father, stood beside and slightly behind him. At twenty-three, he already had Christian's broad shoulders. The same long muscles, the same wrists where the skin was taut over outsize bones and the veins ran like living cords, the same large, thick hands. They were both equally sunburnt. Only, jutting out above his big leather waistbelt, the curve of the father's belly was more marked than that of his son. They both had black hair, but the father's was coarser and more abundant. Beneath his stiff, close-trimmed beard was a band of light-coloured skin which seldom saw the sun. The difference was not because Christian was forty-five; he had always been hairy as a beaver and had a slight paunch.

The prowman was smaller than the two Merlins, but broad, squat, bull-necked. Deep-chested, his arms bulging with muscle, his hands stubby, he seemed to be holding his sledge-hammer fists half clenched. He was the shortest of the twenty-three men comprising the crew, but he was quite possibly the strongest. At twelve, he had signed on as a deck-boy, and Captain Merlin, seeing his red hair, had immediately christened him Petit Roux. The nickname had evolved into Tirou and stuck.

During all the years that they had battled together against the river, they had learnt to understand one another. Naturally the captain remained the captain, but when a man wanted to voice his opinion, he did so without embarrassment. And Christian listened because he recognized that all his men knew the river and their calling. They were not given to wild talk.

This morning, however, something restrained them from saying what they thought. Several times the prowman let out a sigh. He was going to speak. No. He tightened his lips. His red beard moved as if he were chewing his tongue. He cleared his throat.

Still silence, and time passed, measured by the eddies. And then suddenly, at a word from the captain, they all three began to talk very fast, perhaps to frighten the silence.

'The Saône,' said Christian. 'The Saône must have risen.'

'The storm yesterday?' the prowman asked.

'Impossible,' Claude said. 'It came straight from the west. If it got as far as Switzerland, the Rhône would have risen.'

'It could have changed course.'

'Or broken over the Jura.'

'It was certainly big-bellied.'

'And very weird.'

'Didn't you notice how it was veering?'

'That's right. At one point I even thought it was going to break over there. And I swear there was water in those clouds. It wouldn't take long to come down, but it would be heavy. I swear there was water. And plenty of it.'

'Well, if the rise can be felt here already, it can't have fallen far off.'

'And to think we were fast asleep!'

'Perhaps they stationed a man on the banks of the Saône to keep an eye on the water-level.'

'Or else the rise hasn't reached here yet, and their company's notified them from Chalon or Mâcon.'

'My God, those bastards are organized.'

'And there we were like school kids...'

Silence. They looked at one another. It was the prowman who had just spoken. And Christian thought: No, not you. Me. Me alone. He thought it and he said it. Because it would not be right for his prowman to share the burden of this fault.

'I'm to blame. I ought to have thought of it.'

'We all ought,' the prowman said. 'But that's water under the bridge. What's he planning to do with his smoke-factory? Nothing. Suppose the Saône's sent down a foot, or even eighteen inches, what does that amount to after the confluence? One drop.'

Christian knew it. All this had been going round in his head for the last minute. But he needed to turn against himself the anger born of that poison he had inhaled.

'It might be just enough for us to get down,' he said. 'But not her, with her speed and draught. At the first shallows she'll go aground.'

'Then what are they stoking up for?' Claude asked. 'They're crazy.'

Without answering, Christian unhooked the lantern and went out. The other two followed.

The cold enveloped them, but they no longer bothered about the cold.

On the deck of loose planking the orange flare did not carry more than a couple of yards. The mist formed a wall, but a wall which advanced ceaselessly, slowly built up of wavering drifts. The men felt it brush against their skin with a thousand icy fins.

'There's a very light wind from the south,' Christian observed. 'It's only the tail-end blowing here. Or else it's blowing higher up and there's virtually nothing at ground level. It's just as we said. The storm must have gone upstream and broken over the Saône. And we slept on like fools.'

'I've known Monnier for fifteen years. Becoming captain of the *Triomphant* won't have made him any more intelligent. But he's a night bird. He's always liked to hang around the inns that are open at night. He'll have got back late, and if he sniffed the wind...'

The prowman said no more. For a moment they stood watching

the river of mist move slowly upstream above the river of water, which continued to flow down musically.

'What if it's from the forges?'

'The forges start at six. It's too early for them.'

'Besides, we'd hear the forges.'

'I don't know, with this mist...'

'No, even if they were working, they're too far to our left; it would need an east wind, and a strong one, for us to smell them here.'

They went on worrying and reassuring one another.

Almost in spite of himself, Christian joined in this game, and then, with a sudden change of tone, he growled: 'That'll do. Whether we go downstream or not, we've got to be ready.'

He turned and went back into the tent. He hung up the lantern, which clinked as it struck the mast. The flame quivered, and for a moment everything danced beneath the deck-tent, where the mist now seemed slightly less dense.

While pulling on his shirt and buckling the skein of rope belts round his waist, the captain gave his first orders. His voice was crisp and cutting, but without anger. Now that the action was starting, there was no longer any place for emotional outbursts. Nor for banter.

'Claude, run down to the Saône and see what's happened. On the way back, try and get a close-up of their outfit . . . But don't show yourself.'

As soon as the father said 'run down to the Saône', the young man took off his wooden-soled boots. At the last word, he was already pushing aside the canvas flap, which fell back with a sodden thud. Christian heard the patter of his son's bare feet on the deck, then nothing. He had leapt on to the quay. Christian turned to his prowman.

'Tirou, you wake everyone up. Get the horses ready, the men on the tow-lines, so that we're ready to set off downstream.'

Baudry had finished buckling on his belt, into which he thrust the handle of his axe. He lit a lantern and went out.

Left alone, Christian listened to his prowman's wooden soles clattering over the deck. The steps receded. There was a pause, a shout, then the same steps on the stone of the waterfront.

Christian folded up the blanket on his bunk, then he in turn went out and let the sodden flap of canvas fall behind him. Motionless, drawing in deep breaths of mist, he stood like a blind man to listen to this night which had at last begun to come alive.

There are nights which astonish the world. Nights which surprise the creatures and things of earth, and make ready such mornings as men no longer dared hope for. But it is only in the moment of waking that men know surprise, whereas all that continues to live intensely after sunset feels the earth undergoing change.

It was a terrific storm which had broken beyond the confines of the city. Hustled by a sudden wind from the south which had sped through those higher regions of space which the sun's rays traverse but never warm, the clouds had changed direction. The storm, needled on its right flank, had tried at first to sink towards the earth. But at night the over-baked earth cast back the heat of the day, and slept beneath this sultry air which formed a burning vault overhead. The clouds had therefore moved obliquely northwards. But the wind which had driven them here from the western seas was still at their heels. Harried from behind and crowded from the right, they had run into one another. Caught in the pincers in which the wind's wrath was squeezing them, shot through with lightning, they had ended by settling on the vines of Beaujolais.

Water had cascaded down, soaking the earth and carrying down torrents of mud. A strong scent of damp dust and crushed leaves had flowed towards the Saône, spreading as far as the vast flatlands of the Dombes and Bresse. All the ponds sick with thirst had breathed in this scent of water. The meadows and ploughed fields had quivered with that life which slumbers beneath the surface but awakens at the slightest change. A great spontaneous rejoicing had flowered in the darkness, shaken by a wind which smelt pleasantly of long-awaited rain.

Cut off by their wood and plaster houses from this rejoicing, men had missed the celebration. Only the carters lying in ditches had sensed that something was afoot. And the bakers, whose ovens had suddenly begun to roar more gleefully, had come to the thresholds of their bakeries for a breath of air. The south wind had raised a dense covering of mist over the sea, in which the whole of the Rhône valley had been blanketed from midnight on.

And as the mist moved northwards it became denser, closer, thicker, as though fattening on its progress. It clung to everything that made the earth bristle like an upturned harrow. Poplars, steeples, the jagged ruins of crumbling towers, chimney-stacks, the stone pillars which carried the ferry cables from one bank to the other, the tall new piers of the suspension bridges which Monsieur Seguin had begun to sling across the river.

And at this point the blanket had grown so heavy that the wind finally let it drop. Still shaken, slow to halt, it spread outwards.

In Lyons there were so many spires, gabled houses, narrow lanes and odd corners that it had halted its advance. The stones of the quays and the tiles on the roofs were refreshed by it.

The river pursued its course, but its ripples sang less clearly against the embankments of the bridges. In the stones of the bridge piers, in the cracks between them, beneath the moss half dead with thirst, there was still life. A life dragged forth from torpor by these myriads of delicate droplets which were infiltrating everywhere. The rats came to the mouths of their runs tunnelled underneath the banks to breathe in this air which carried the smell of food. For them, this night so different from its predecessors held promise of a feast.

The townspeople, kept awake so many nights by the heat, felt no surprise. Breathing more easily, they had sunk deeply into sleep, never suspecting that they would waken to a world for which the night had given birth to hope.

Admittedly, in the districts where the storm had broken, some people had wakened. Once the first fear was past, they had stayed glued to their windows, their bare feet resting on floorboards still warm, to listen to the rain coming down and the gurgling of the gutters as they carried down to the streams the water that would revivify the world.

In this tail-end of night there was the life of the mist and the life of the barges. And for the boatmen, the mist and the river were one. They told themselves it must be going up-river. That it must have risen a bit lower down, perhaps between Grigny and Vernaison, or simply at La Mulatière. It had risen in the darkness and this breath of wind was pushing it very, very gently upstream. On the way it was absorbing the smell of the coal fire which the others had lit to raise the pressure in their boilers. And Christian told himself that without that little puff of wind he could have gone on sleeping another hour or two. But he had an instinct, especially for everything connected with the river.

The remains of anger still stirred deep within him, but as his barges began to come to life, this anger changed to a kind of deep, quiet joy, as hard to rouse as the mud in the bottom of the lagoons. And like the mud, his joy was very much alive. He knew that it had acquired strength from lying so long in his inmost depths. It was going to rise slowly and colour the water of his life for weeks to come.

Now all his barges were beginning to resound dully. The invisible surface of the river, the black night, the stones of the quay, everything rang under the hammer-blows of the boots of his men and the shoes of his horses, who were being moved out to make room for boys bringing in oats and hay. The smell of bedding suddenly gained strength and overcame the stale smell of smoke.

'What can they be up to?' Christian growled. 'Nothing. Nothing at all. They won't be leaving today.'

He thought for a moment. He moved his head, then his thick fingers, counting them off one after the other in the palms of his hands.

For twenty-seven days low water in the Rhône had held them here, to gaze questioningly at the sky. From dawn to dusk the sky changed from mauve to yellow and from yellow to blue, veering to green, then copper, and that was all. Not the shadow of a cloud,

THE MISTS OF DAWN

not a breath of wind other than that dry northerly air which skimmed over the skeleton of the river to pick it clean the more quickly by driving the water southwards. Nothing but this sterile wind which, lower down, must transform itself into a mistral and end by parching the vineyards. Despite the heat, there were days reminiscent of winter, because of the lowness of the river and the solid weight of the sky pressing silence down upon the earth.

They had waited, barges laden, with nothing to occupy the twenty-three members of the crew but the care of the twenty-eight towing horses.

For twenty-seven days they had watched the water flowing, asking themselves repeatedly if there might not come a time when the river would dry up.

It was tragic for river men like Captain Merlin and his crew to see the Rhône so wasted. The old men who came to drag their boredom along the quays could not remember a comparable drought going on into the beginning of October. Some who considered themselves cleverer or better informed than the rest claimed that the whole earth was drying up. They spoke of the fire in the interior getting near the crust. Those who wished to contradict had a good laugh, pointing out that the fire would first have melted the glaciers and swollen the rivers. Others claimed that avalanches of rocks and landslides of mud had caused the Rhône to be diverted at source. All the water was now flowing towards Germany. Or Italy. It was not clear which, any more than it was clear which newspaper had carried the story. But it had certainly been in the papers.

At first, Christian had allowed himself to be caught in the trap. He had tried to argue with the old men. But the old men had heads harder than the stones in the river.

So Christian had said: 'Shit! That's the wisdom of age for you. They've got no more sense than my oldest shoe.'

He ignored their yapping, until one day he boiled over. Out of respect for age, he avoided a direct confrontation, but he got his men back on the barges and ingeniously set to and found them work. His train of seven barges, occupying more than eight hundred feet of quay, had never been in such perfect trim. Every tow-rope had been checked inch by inch, every hull, every gunwale, every deck, inspected plank by plank. All the brasses on the horses' harness shone; and the blacksmiths had a vast stock of shoes and nails ready forged. The cooks were installed in their galley as no one had ever found time to install them before. And Christian himself had worked with Monsieur Tonnerieu, his clerk, checking over all the account-books. Many of the men had also spent their afternoons refurbishing the crosses at the barges' prows.

They had kept occupied during the interminable succession of blazing days, but work had never hindered them from watching the river.

The crews of the steamers, held up even longer because of the deep draught of their fiery monsters, must have been equally enraged. Christian Merlin had tried to find consolation in this, but he knew the steamers' crews were smaller than his own. The companies therefore had fewer expenses to meet than he had. Besides, the companies had more reserves than an artisan whose whole capital was tied up in his seven barges and twenty-eight horses. And the directors of the companies must have been well aware that he was responsible for twenty-three men, most of them with families to support.

He had endured twenty-seven days of anguished waiting, twenty-seven sweltering nights, and now, on the morning of the twenty-eighth day, in this brew of mingled air and water, a fever gripped him as he smelt the good smell of his stables overcoming the stench of boiler fires.

Now everything was alive. Every sound gave him hope. Every lantern gleam eating into the mist warmed his heart. Claude's bare feet rang out on the deck-boards.

'I'm here,' Christian called.

Claude came up. He was out of breath. 'It's risen by more than two feet,' he said.

'You've been quick.'

Christian did not wish to appear hurried or curious at present. He was in process of becoming the Captain once again. The calm man whom nothing astonishes. The steady man who knows how to dominate the moods of river and sky as well as he does the whims of an often wild crew and the crazy actions of his adversaries.

He let his son get his breath back. He resisted the desire to ask questions, and it was Claude who continued:

'It's up by roughly two feet. And I think it's going to rise higher. It smells of earth, but you'd need to see what it looks like. And you can't do that until it's daylight.'

The son paused a moment. He must have trodden on the end of a tow-rope, which rolled and lashed the deck. As his father stayed silent, he said:

'Even two foot six won't amount to much below the confluence.'

'It'll be enough for us. By the time it's daylight we'll be well and truly on our way.'

The wind was hollowing out corridors in the mist, affording occasional glimpses of moving lights, sometimes on the quay, sometimes on the barges. A deeper rent revealed for a moment the entrance to the stables which were on board the barge moored downstream. Three big lanterns appeared, making the animals' sturdy hindquarters gleam. Two carters were hoisting trusses of hay into the mangers. It was a fine, stirring sight. A sight to warm the cockles of the heart and make the blood flow faster.

Christian gave himself time to listen, breathe, and watch the little that could be seen of this activity, then he said with a chuckle:

'We're going to go downstream, lad. The other joker can still boil his kettle, but we'll be starting back upstream before he's even managed to leave Lyons.'

'No, he's lit his fires, he'll start. He's obstinate. He may not get very far, but he'll start . . . I've just come past there, they've even lit up in the shack where they sell passenger tickets.'

Captain Merlin roared with laughter. 'Passengers! Where do they think they're going to find them at this hour?'

'I'm telling you what I saw. They probably won't leave before midday, so there's time for passengers to turn up.'

Christian interrupted his son. 'That's enough talk, lad. Go and join Tirou. Everything to be ready for the journey downstream at first light.'

The son disappeared into the darkness, which seemed to have grown even blacker since the lamps were lit. The glow from the lanterns which the men carried was almost constantly on the move, but between these glimmers nothing existed. And it seemed as if nothing ever could have existed. No more river, now that the sound of men at work had drowned its rippling; no more river banks; no more bridges; no more buildings. Even the prow of the barge was blotted out.

Accustomed from birth to rain, mist, storms, the terrifying rages of the Rhône, Christian had never given these things any more attention than his tasks required. Every glance at the sky, the water, the bank, had its reason. It was an interrogation. Every question asked of the elements provoked a response which required an order to be given or a precise manoeuvre to be executed. It was always necessary to act very fast, to manoeuvre by instinct without taking time to reflect.

The boatmen's only fears were straightforward ones. There was no mystery about them. Fear sprang from what could be seen, touched or felt. It always had a name, a form, a face.

But this morning Captain Merlin had the feeling of menace all around him. He did know what it was. The mist was extremely thick, but he had navigated a hundred times in fog so dense he could not even see the bowl of his pipe.

No, it was not the mist that frightened him. On the contrary, he even wished it might last long enough for him to get ahead of the steamer. Monnier might be a good pilot, but he would not dare risk the *Triomphant* in weather as thick as this. It had already seemed impossible that he could go downstream without running aground, but with the mist as well ...

For a moment Christian rejoiced. He found that the air, though just as thick, was thoroughly good to breathe.

And yet there was something out of the ordinary about this tail-end of the night. Something which came from everywhere and nowhere. Perhaps, quite simply, from his own inmost depths.

Are there really days when everything known since childhood can become charged with sudden mystery?

Christian snorted. He approached the bulwark on the side where the river flowed, and kneeled down on the boards. Leaning forward, his chest pressed against the icy wood at the point where it began to rear up to outline the prow, he stretched his arms down. The water was warm. Much warmer than the mist. Christian took some in his cupped hands and washed his face and body. He rinsed out his mouth, and, as on every morning, he swallowed a mouthful. He always did so, without ever having told anyone and without ever admitting to himself that it was partly out of superstition. He was asking the Rhône to communicate a little of its strength to him. And the river had always responded to his request. This morning he made it with more fervour. For a long moment he left his hands plunged in this substance living as a beast. He caressed this great animal which caressed him in return. It seemed to him that they had known and loved each other too long for the river to betray him.

Christian had ceased to hear the sounds made by his men. He listened only to the song of the water which he was lifting a little by plunging his hand obliquely against the current. The water rose to the hollow of his palm and over his wrist. And the sound which it made there was like a coo of friendship. A clear note above the muted bass choir formed by the eddies of the bridge. Christian was alone with the river. Isolated from everything else by the thickness of the mist and by the night which dragged on. He did not see the water flow, but he felt it. His arms quivered with the friendly struggle that his thick hands waged against the current.

He was alone with the river and happy in this solitude.

It occurred to him that at this hour he was certainly the only man from source to sea to touch it. The only one to communicate with it direct. The only one. And he was going to draw on all the strength of the river.

'I'm not asking you to smash them against a rock. I'm not asking you to drown that bastard Monnier. I'll never ask a thing like that of you. I just want you not to rise. Not to let yourself get too swollen by that whore of a Saône. Two and a half feet, three feet, no more. I can get down, but if they try, they'll run aground.'

In order to say this with more conviction, to feel himself linked more directly with his river, Christian had closed his eyes. When he reopened them, the mist was beginning very faintly to turn white. It was not yet dawn, but the vaguest of milky lights was floating, as if lost in the heart of night.

Christian leaned farther over, one hand clinging to the bulwark; he got as close as he could to look and he ended by seeing what he hoped for.

A tiny, glaucous wink, barely perceptible, from the water which his fingers sought to hold back.

The river had answered him.

Christian stood up slowly. He breathed in. A great calm strength began to flow through him.

Those whose work dragged them from bed well before dawn wondered what such a mist might signify. Those who lived with the river were less astonished. In any case, even if it did not bring rain in the immediate future, this change in the weather could only herald a return to the seasons' natural course.

It was primarily the smell which indicated to the townspeople that the weather was about to change. The narrow streets had begun to stink like wells in which the bodies of animals are rotting. Every crack in the *traboules* was oozing. The spiders' webs spun in the angles of the skylights broke under the weight of droplets. The faintest light evoked a gleam from the night. The cobblestones of the streets and the flagstones of the passages became slippery and prolonged their reflections from one door to the next.

For the carriers it was an anguished awakening. They too sensed the approach of the bad season. So much drought could only bring rains which would drown the roads and make their job more difficult. They too thought of a probable rise in river level and of the resumption of navigation, which would deprive them of a part of their work.

For it was a time of uneasiness. Ever since steam drew carriages along a railway track and propelled iron boats across the water, it seemed that bread might one day cease to be within reach of all. To be assured of a living, it was no longer sufficient to know one's calling and to pursue it. There was a threat which came not from the sky, but from men. And men perceived with astonishment that human folly is more dangerous than that which shakes the elements because it lasts longer.

It was the iron age. Men of the forges and workshops rejoiced that this was so. So did those of the tall furnaces, which all the year round kindled the glow of light at night and spread foul smoke over towns and countryside.

For more than twenty years open ironwork suspension bridges had begun to be slung across rivers great and small. These bridges did not obstruct the river and were less dangerous to navigation than stone ones, whose side arches narrowed the channel, but they threw many ferry-men out of work.

Iron on the river, iron on the roads, iron on the iron rails, soon the masons too would be jobless if some stupid bastard's idea of building metal houses caught on.

Gradually the streets of La Croix-Rousse, the hill where the silk-weavers lived, woke to life. The looms clacked, the shuttles flew, the silk spun its multicoloured patterns by the light of sparse lamps.

On the hill of prayer, which is on the other bank of the Saône, running from the Rue Misère to the top of the slope of Tire-Cul, the priests and nuns filed in silence towards the dimly-lit places where they would say matins.

The darkness of the night confounded ages. The brand-new dyke which protected the left bank against the river's assaults was no more and no less alive than the fishermen's wretched hovels, centuries old and half hidden by brambles. The district of Perrache, which after almost a hundred years was still spreading, thrusting the confluence back towards the south, was shrouded in the same viscous greyness as the houses of Saint-Jean.

It was not yet really dawn, but something invisible, impalpable, indefinable, proclaimed that day was at hand.

Captain Merlin's long deck-tent was lit by three lanterns hung on three stumps of masts supporting the grey awning which was patched in several places. The captain had sent the deck-boy to call his senior crew members together. Those whom he had summoned already knew what Christian was going to tell them. They had realized as soon as the prowman woke them. They did not talk. Seated on trunks, on the three bunks, on coils of rope, they looked gravely at one another. They had had time to sniff the mist, and the smell of smoke in it had informed them that Christian would not wait for visibility to improve before giving the order to depart.

'So,' Christian said, 'we're still waiting for Rapiat.'

'He was roused with the others,' the prowman said.

'He won't come without the spit and polish,' said Auguste Bonnetin.

There were a few timid laughs. The fact that the captain had said Rapiat and not Monsieur Tonnerieu indicated that he was in a good mood. It was an excellent thing, but the uneasiness persisted.

M. Tonnerieu arrived at last. He was a dry, stunted little man who wore black trousers and frock-coat over a white shirt with a big frilled collar. His eyes blinked constantly behind the thick lenses of his eye-glasses, which his nose maintained in position at the cost of a perpetual grimace. He was sixty-seven years old. He was the clerk, which meant that he had the financial and administrative responsibility for the barge-train. He was the one man whom the whole crew addressed formally and always called 'monsieur'. It was the cooks who had nicknamed him Rapiat.

As soon as he came in he removed his eye-glasses and wiped the lenses with a large white handkerchief.

'You will please excuse me,' he said to Christian, 'but those stupid cooks thought it a great joke to hide my glasses.'

General laughter. M. Tonnerieu raised his voice and said in a somewhat grating tone: 'We'll talk about it later, but in your father's day that wouldn't have been cause for amusement.'

The prowman pushed a packing-case behind the clerk, over which the little man spread his handkerchief before perching his sharp bottom upon it.

Silence.

Christian took three paces, stopped, then reached the end of the deck-tent, from which he could see all his men. He had put on a brown shirt and knotted a red silk scarf round his neck. He folded his arms, cleared his throat a couple of times, and began:

'Well, you know that other fool's begun getting steam up. I don't know whether he'll leave. He's daft enough to try it, but with what's come down from the Saône, we've got every chance – '

'Every chance of losing one or two barges and their cargoes,' M. Tonnerieu ground out.

He was the only man who could allow himself to interrupt the captain. His age, and the fact that he had been in the Merlins' service long before Christian was born, gave him certain rights. But he had remained a quill-pusher with limited horizons. His knowledge of the river and of navigation was entirely contained in his account-books and his correspondence. He grimaced as if he were suffering martyrdom every time he saw a barge-hand cut a rope with a blow of his axe, refusing to admit that it was often necessary to do so to save a barge or a team.

Christian let him speak, then went on calmly: 'We have two things in our favour: low water, and mist. At the speed at which they have to move in order to steer, they won't leave before it lifts. I hope it'll last all morning.'

M. Tonnerieu interrupted again. 'Don't you realize that fellow Monnier's set a trap for you? You're falling right into it. He's burned a bit of coal to get you to leave. He knows you. He's said to himself: "Christian's so proud he'll want to go downstream at all costs. And he'll fall foul of the first gravel-bank he encounters." You call yourself smart and you haven't cottoned on to that? Let me tell you that your father would never haven fallen into suoh an obvious trap.'

'If he thought that, it proves that he doesn't know me. Monsieur Tonnerieu, I asked you to come here because it's usual for the clerk to be present when there are important decisions to be made. My father still owns part of the outfit, and it's your business to watch his interests – '

'That's exactly why I don't want you to risk the whole lot – '

'Let me speak!'

Christian was growing impatient. He had just interrupted the old clerk, and that was something he had never done. But he felt time spurring him on. The imperceptible gleam of glaucous light which the river had revealed to him just now was within him. He knew that if the wind freshened at sunrise, the mist would be dispelled at once. He wanted to start before the steamer and he meant to do so.

The old clerk registered the blow. He made an unaccustomed grimace and his eye-glasses fell off. He left them hanging by their silver chain. His delicate hands resting on his thin knees twisted, and his fingers began to tap the black cloth of his ankle-hugging trousers.

'I don't see what I'm doing here,' he wheezed.

He was about to rise, but Christian signalled to him to remain seated. 'I ask you to be here. I have made the decision, but when my father wants the accounts, you'll need to be able to tell him what's in them.'

The clerk restored his eye-glasses to their place, compressed his thin lips and bowed his head.

Christian realized he was not going to say another word. He breathed deeply to regain his composure, then, unfolding his arms and thrusting his thumbs into his belt, he said steadily: 'We've already done the downstream trip in water as low as this. We've done it in mist. But the two combined, that's something else again. You know how it is with the steamer. If we don't show her we can do better than her boilers, she'll destroy us. In five years she's already destroyed forty-three outfits of our size, but she's had the river in her favour, nearly always. Today, it happens to be in ours. I don't know whether the other barge-masters will decide to leave, but I'm going to.'

He said 'I' to indicate that there was nothing to discuss. He paused long enough to look at each of the thirteen boatmen and team-drivers who were gathered there, motionless, their faces turned towards him.

'I've called you together because I've decided to leave at once and every barge will have to manage alone so long as the mist lasts. I'll go first, with Tirou at the prow. The boy will shout any necessary directions to the barge behind, and they'll pass them on to the rest. But you know how it is with mist, especially when the wind makes it patchy. Advance warning can be useful, but every barge will have to have a prowman.'

The men nodded. They looked at one another questioningly, seeking approval. As Christian allowed them time, Joseph Cathomen, the master blacksmith and most senior after M. Tonnerieu, gave it.

'Quite right. It will.'

'I'm going to give you your posts. If anyone doesn't agree, let him say so when his name is called ... Behind me, on the stable barge, Albert Carénal, prowman; Claude, captain.'

The two men designated signified approval with a nod. Christian turned to the others:

'Second lading barge: prowman, Joseph Cathomen, Baptiste Carénal at the tiller. First Seysselander: prowman, Albert Boissonnet, captain, Paul Barillot. Second Seysselander: prowman, Théodore Montfouroux, and captain, Jérôme Thomas. First Savoyarde: Félix Marthou and Auguste Bonnetin. Finally, the second Savoyarde, which is less heavily laden, will have the two runabouts in tow. Antoine Thomas at the prow. Félicien Revolat will captain her.'

He went up to the two men just named. 'I'm putting you last,' he said, 'because if the south wind freshens it'll hold you back since you're higher out of the water. We shan't wait for you. You know the river as well as I do.'

There was a pregnant silence. Christian had the feeling that several of his men wanted to speak. He was on the point of inviting them to do so when he checked himself. To invite discussion meant losing time. His decision was taken, no one had refused his post, all that was left to discuss could only be minor details. Turning to his son, he commanded: 'Go and see if Canut thinks we're going to leave without a mouthful of something.'

The usual 'mouthful' for the boatmen consisted of a salted anchovy and a nip of brandy. Christian knew that it was the best way of indicating that everything was settled.

Nestor Vercheron, known as Canut because he was born at La Croix-Rousse, could not have been far away. Claude returned almost at once with him and the second cook, known as Caillette because he was the son of a charcoal-burner from Condrieu. Caillette was as tall and thin as Canut was short and stout. He was as taciturn as Canut was talkative. The cook was carrying a terrine of anchovies, his assistant a straw-covered flask and a glass.

'So you can't even be on time. No way of waking you up?'

A broad smile split Canut's round, gleaming face. 'We were ready all right, Captain. We were just waiting till the blathering was over. We're discreet, we are, but it's no good the canvas being thick, we heard everything.'

Christian gave the signal to laugh. His thick fingers plunged into the terrine, drew out two anchovies which he held above his open mouth. He munched. They were strong and salty. Coming on top of them, the nip of brandy seemed hardly stronger than a rather dry wine.

The men ate and drank in their turn. When it was over, Christian said to the cooks: 'Give each barge cold food for this morning. And cook for midday. We'll eat on the barges.' He paused a moment, then added, smiling: 'I hope we shan't be far from Condrieu.'

There was a murmur – of satisfaction from those whose wives lived thereabouts; of scepticism, undoubtedly, from the older ones.

After the cooks had left, Captain Merlin said again: 'Tirou will go and allocate the men. Monsieur Rapiat, of course, stays with me.'

Joseph Cathomen, who was getting ready to go out, turned round. 'If you're counting on him to pour you a drink...'

M. Tonnerieu stood up, the better to call them drunkards, but they all began to laugh and no one heard him.

This age of iron was also a time of war. But the risks of war among the Powers that the newspapers talked of, the conflicts which ranged the weavers against the religious congregations who made children work without payment, and what *L'Echo des Ouvriers* had to say about it all, meant nothing to the men of the river and the roads and did not compare with the war against iron. And the worst thing was that there had already been a quarrel between the men of the steam navigation companies and those who talked of building a railway from Lyons to Marseilles as soon as they had finished the line which they planned to extend to Roanne.

More than one hundred and forty transport enterprises still existed in Lyons. More than fifty vessels, three thousand horses, not counting the coach which raised the dust of the road for leagues on leagues.

It was a war on all fronts, with no holds barred. A barge-master had been seen deliberately to drive one of his barges laden with stone against a steamer's bows. The barge and its cargo had been lost, but the steamer was hardly damaged. The train from Saint-Etienne had been derailed three times without anyone being able to discover who had damaged the rails. Barge-hands? Men from the steamers' crews? Carriers? River-dwellers disturbed by the noise and smoke from the railway line? Farmers whose animals were frightened by the monster's passing?

For the barge-crews, of which several outfits went under every year, the most hated activity was that carried on in Lyons by the recruiting sergeants of the steam navigation companies. There were always a few of them hanging about the cafés closest to the eighteen unloading ports which the city boasted. The boatmen despised them. Everyone spoke of them with anger. Some boatmen, strong as oxen, had already calmly beaten up a few of them before making them take a dip. But this did not discourage the others. They knew their trade and they had large sums at their disposal. They knew too that barge-hands were men who found it hard to resist a well-spread table. So they paid for the food and poured out the drink. When the man was well and truly drunk, he was dragged as far as the company's offices, where he signed a contract. After that, they left him to stew. When he awoke, they read the text to him. This did not always pass off smoothly. Violent, proud, devoted to their river and living each day in hatred of that which risked polluting it, some of the men rebelled. The windows of several offices had been seen to shatter and go flying. The oak tables and chairs whirled round within the peeling walls as if a tornado had got into the room. There were some broken arms and quite a few broken noses. If there were other boatmen around, the whole thing degenerated into a pitched battle until the police arrived. It was usually the boatmen who won, for the companies employed bureaucrats rather than men accustomed to using their muscles.

Despite it all, the current flowed on. The current of life is always like a river. Eddies form. They cause one stretch of water to flow backwards, as if it would retrace the way to its source. But the river continues to flow none the less, and ends by carrying everything down to the sea. There were more and more steamers and fewer and fewer barge-trains. The passengers, embarking at Lyons for the downstream journey and at Beaucaire for the upstream, all travelled in the iron vessels. The barges had only those passengers who boarded at ports where the steamers did not call. As for goods, the prices had to be undercut, and there too there was war. A war which ranged the barge-masters against the executives of the big companies. These companies were monsters. Mightier than men. So long as the fight was against men, it was possible to judge more or less how things were going. But it was not so in this case, for these men always said, 'The Company said . . . The Company did . . . The Company has decided . . . I'm only here to carry out orders.'

'The Company' was always on their lips, this Company which seemed to transcend human laws. It was a sort of monster to which heaven had given birth without man having a hand in it.

So the boatmen said: 'What is this Company of yours? It operates on somebody's money, doesn't it? It makes money for somebody, doesn't it?'

'There are too many of them, we don't know them. We're only workers, same as you.'

But they were not the same. They worked in offices, wearing collar and tie. They did not contend with the river but with figures. They played with money which was not even their own.

A barge-master was an artisan. He had five, six, eight, sometimes ten barges. He might own up to forty horses. A barge which cost at least three thousand francs could hardly last longer than six or seven years, even if taken care of. To get a good horse cost in the region of twelve hundred francs. Toiling in mud and water, in heat which raised clouds of mosquitoes from the scrub; spending the winter with hoofs on ice or up to the fetlocks in melted snow, even a strong horse was worn out in three or four years. Renewal of ropes, provisions, lodgings, taxes and river tolls could easily amount to six thousand francs a year; when everything was taken into account, the profits were slim.

Three or four days for the downstream voyage, thirty or forty for the return journey – it was hard labour and a poor return.

Inevitably, there were those who could not keep going. It took no more than the slightest hitch, such as being held up for a month by flood or drought, to ruin a barge-master. In other words, to trample down the fruits of ten generations of labour.

'I sold my barges for next to nothing. I saw them broken up with an axe. The straight planks were used to build garden sheds. With the curved ones, they've made a footbridge over the Rize. When you're fifty, it's enough to break your heart.'

'I wanted to fight. I've lost everything. The bailiff came. They sold the lot. All I've got left is my cross. They didn't dare sell that. It's all I've got left . . . And if my wife is dead before fifty, it's from grief . . . They came to seek out my son. They offered him good money to pilot one of their steam-kettles. "Shit!" he told them. And he spat in their faces. And now he and his three kids are starving. All he's been able to find is a job as superintendent on the bathing-boat. You know, that thing with two decks opposite the college. If you can call it a boat: it's never moved from where it is.'

It was the same story everywhere. From the old men, from the less old, and from those who came down to the quays to gaze at those who still kept going. They were proud and lived on nothing. They kept silent about their hunger for as long as possible, and then one morning they were to be seen lending a hand to stack barrels, or to load crates. And it made them sick to set foot on a barge again, knowing they'd have to get off before it drew away from the quay.

Some went back to hide in their own districts – Serrières or Condrieu – to subsist there on what little they had been able to save from the crash. But those who had lost everything, those who were no longer young enough to begin all over again in another calling, those who were too proud to go cap in hand to men who had envied them in the days when they were the richest and the most vociferous, these went to ground, to end their days wretchedly in the secrecy of the big city.

In Lyons, which is a city built by businessmen, they lived in the shadow of the tall stone houses. The owners of these houses had often negotiated with them for the transport of their goods. But commerce has neither heart nor memory. It devours whatever is before it. It feeds too willingly upon the work of others ever to have regard for their affliction.

So they went to ground there, not too far from the river, in the shadow of the houses where so much wealth slept. And it was their barges which had carried the stones for these houses. They had been entreated to undertake the shipment. They had been paid the top rate. Today nothing was left of that hard-earned money. They had worked for the monster of modern times and the monster had devoured them. They had nothing left but their tired eyes, which gazed at the river flowing past and brimmed with tears.

Day was breaking when they emerged from the deck-tent.

Everything was white. Or rather, as a man moved forward, a white circle several yards in diameter moved with him.

Christian walked slowly from stem to stern of the barge, then, at the same pace, he returned to where his prowman was already standing on the port gunwale against the quay. The two men looked at each other. Tirou winked and smiled. He seemed calm. The rolled-up sleeves of his blue shirt revealed his huge forearms where the tattooed sailors' anchor and cross were distorted, constantly puckered by the rippling of his knotted muscles. His hands grasped a long peeled willow-rod bearing at the tip some red and black painted rings which indicated the water's depth. When they left, he would lean on the rod with all his weight to push the barge's prow off from the quay.

As soon as Captain Merlin reckoned that all his men had had time to reach their posts, he cupped his hands to his mouth and shouted downstream: 'Ready, everyone?'

'Revolat ready!'

'Bonnetin ready!'

Six times the cry was repeated. Each barge-captain replied. The first from far off, then nearer and nearer until his son, who was last, cried: 'Claude ready!'

Unhurriedly Christian moved to the bulwark on the Rhône side. Kneeling down, in the very spot where, a short time ago, he had communed all alone with his river, he dipped his right hand into the current, stood up, and, crossing himself three times, cried:

'To God and the Virgin Mary! To the Rhône! And may Saint Nicholas be with us.'

While he returned to his post at the tiller, the captain of each barge repeated the same prayer.

Back at the prow, he turned towards the quay where the deck-boy, indistinguishable even in silhouette, must be holding the mooring-rope passed through one of the huge iron rings embedded between the stones.

He repeated in a low voice: 'Saint Nicholas, stay with us. Stay with the true boatmen.' Then he shouted: 'Hey, boy! Let go the rope and get aboard!'

He heard Jean-Pierre Carénal's treble voice at the same time as he heard the thump of his soles on the foredeck.

'Boy aboard!'

'Prowman, push out to midstream!'

Christian's voice was sombre. The shout he had directed towards the prow facing upstream pierced the circle of mist which limited the view to the dark green triangle of the deck-tent flat on the deck. The shout did not carry over the water as every cry from every barge-hand did in clear weather. It advanced slowly in the thick air. It carried beyond the deck-tent, then the prow whose carved cross reared up in the dense whiteness. It continued on between the invisible water and the invisible sky. It tangled with the vault formed by the arches of the old bridge of La Guillotière, over which the first wagons were rolling their iron-hooped wheels. But it was stronger than the sound of metal on the cobblestones. Stronger than the clacking of wooden shoes and the cracking of whips. Stronger than the feeble voices of the carriers on land.

Astonished at such volume, Christian listened to his shout rolling on and swelling and rising from his barge, to lie heavy over the sleeping city.

It was rather as if the Rhône itself had uttered a summons to work. There was joy in this solemnity, as there is joy in the pealing of church bells, because their summons seems to come from heaven and rebound upon the earth before going on to lose itself on the wind, which likewise comes from heaven.

Christian shivered. It was not the dawn cold which took him by surprise. He was accustomed to that from time immemorial, for perhaps ten generations of boatmen. No, it was something more secret, something much more removed from earthly things and yet at the same time something much closer to them. It was a strength which rose in him like yeast in the warm depths of dough. In the morning Christian felt suddenly bigger and stronger. He had just mastered the mystery which had so recently unnerved him, the emotion which had gripped him and which he had been unable to define. He was rediscovering himself as the man of the Rhône, the river man that he had always been.

Beneath his feet the boards vibrated imperceptibly. The long boat quivered slightly against the quay. The full strength of the prowman's arms and back had made the willow-rod bend and pushed the barge's prow off from the quay.

Nothing. Christian still saw nothing but the deck-tent, its canvas rippling a little, and a few square yards of deck glistening with water. He saw nothing, but he guessed at the movement of the water caught in the triangle which was opening up between bulwark and quay. The eddies' clear song rose up about him. Everything had to be done by guesswork. Heart thudding, Christian waited a few more seconds. Then, when he felt the full force of the current thrusting on the beam and causing the barge to turn in a half-circle downstream, he leaned slowly forward, arms bent, chest pressed against the icy wood of the great tiller, feet braced against laths nailed to the deck. As he was embarking on his manoeuvre, the deck-boy joined him.

'With me, boy!'

The lad added his young strength to his captain's. The wood creaked a little, but the broad rudder made the river growl. There was a great gurgling. A whole fierce battle between the natural eddies of the Rhône and those created by the displacement of the planks driven by a slow, regular but irresistible force.

'Prow heading downstream . . . That's it!'

Tirou too uttered his cry. He was saying that the current had already allied itself with man's strength. Already the barge had completed its half-circle and was facing downstream in the direction they were to go.

Christian hauled the tiller back to the centre of the barge. He straightened up, still quivering with the effort he had made. The deck-boy also straightened up, and, abandoning the tiller, stood back a couple of paces to allow his captain room to manoeuvre. Christian looked at him. At thirteen, Jean-Pierre Carénal was already as tall as his father, Albert Carénal, the bailey or master of the horse, who was following this morning at the prow of the stable barge where the towing horses, which were his responsibility, were embarked. Jean-Pierre was tall and already sturdy. Next year they would pierce his ears so that he, like all the other Rhône boatmen, could wear the gold rings which were the symbol of their calling.

Already this year, at the fair in Beaucaire, he had spent several hours at the tattooist's. On his left forearm the sailors' anchor was sketched in. Incomplete as yet, it seemed a bit pale, as if it had been executed with poor-quality fluid. But the boy was proud of it; when he folded his arms, he always took care to let his tattoo show.

Like Christian, the boy could not tell how many of his ancestors had been river folk. It went back a long, long way, perhaps to the time when the boatmen were still called *nautae*.

The eyes of boy and master met. There was a brief, silent but deep exchange.

The boy smiled. A great joy beamed out all over his unbearded face. A great joy and a boundless confidence. The master also wore a smile which meant: You see, lad, everything they can retail and invent and fabricate to destroy the wooden fleet is all nonsense. There's the river, and you can't do just as you please with that. There'll be more talk of their boilers and their coal. But this morning the Rhône's on our side. Our side alone. And believe me, if you care to ally yourself with it, you too will be able to earn an honest living from it.

All those who still wanted to earn their living on the river were up already. Cut off from the world by the thick mist, they kept an ear cocked, fearing or hoping for a call which would proclaim the departure of a barge-train.

'I suspected it ... There he goes, off before us!'

'It's madness.'

'He's got more guts.'

'Less sense, I'd say.'

'He's smelt the steamer warming up.'

'Let the steamer go. We've got plenty of time. The Saône's on our side. What's the good of taking risks? Life's risky enough as it is.'

There was a feverishness all along the river – the feverishness which causes some to talk and others to act. A matter of temperament. And also of money. When a man owns nothing but his train of barges and is already in debt, he does not run risks for the sake of an extra day. That can be satisfying only to his pride, not to his pocket.

For the men of the steamers, it was a question of prestige and of the future. Not to allow anything to be done which might give rise to the idea that wood could still overcome iron, that the horse who eats hay might yet prove faster than the one which feeds on coal and boiling water. The fires were stoked up to raise the pressure, and since no one wanted to appear to be leaving solely for the glory of it, men were sent round to rouse the porters of the hotels.

'A steamer's leaving. Tell the travellers that the southbound roads are rutted. And hard. And the dust and so on. We'll be at Beaucaire tomorrow evening. Special price reductions. We'll wait till the mist lifts. Three blasts of the whistle, followed by the bell. And we're off!'

And there was a tip for the porter, to ensure he found the right words to make up the travellers' minds for them.

There was a stirring in the night as the waters of the confluence were stirred. A kind of uncontrolled seething which ran all along the banks, but without too much noise. Alive with questions which were asked without ever being answered. With the throat and chest a little tight.

And still the river flowed on. Once past the confluence, would there be enough water to carry the barges down to those sunlit horizons which had been out of sight for weeks?

The confluence was drowned even deeper in mist than the rest. The Rhône's clear glacier waters and the turbid waters of the Saône married in secret, concealing their embrace behind a thick veil. Even from the bridge, even from the dyke which jutted out from the peninsula, nothing was to be seen. Only heard. The bridge over the Saône whose nine stone piers formed something of a dam made the river sing. The barges moored downstream tugged on their chains. There was the sound of metal scraping on stone, the dull shock of bulwark on bulwark. Below, there was a great mustering of fish, drawn from far and near by the muddy flood. The Saône carried down earth, insects, debris swept from the banks as far back as where the storm had broken. As soon as the sun pierced through, all the fishing-boats would put out: trammels and square nets were ready. In the eddies where the waters mingled they would cast their nets at random; they would trawl in the shallows up to the mouths of the lagoons.

But the great river went its way, keeping the slow, turbid Saône on its right flank a long time before really accepting it, before communicating to it some of its own strength and cleansing it. Having suddenly doubled in volume, it felt more powerful, more invincible, more Rhône than ever.

It entered into that valley of which it was master. There it had its freedom. Its own world all to itself. Men whom it had to carry, but whom it liked because they never tired of flattering its pride as a great river. Of repeating to anyone who would listen that it was the finest, the strongest, and also the swiftest. Men who fought for it. Men who had invented resounding words for speaking of it, words which only its boatmen and the dwellers on its banks understood.

Ever since the time of Charlemagne and Lothair, when it had formed the frontier between the Kingdom of the Franks and the Holy Roman Empire, the boatmen had called its right bank Reiaume and its left bank Emperi. And when they shouted orders, they shouted:

'Push towards the Empie!'

'Pull for the Ryaume!'

Everything connected with a barge-train, otherwise known as a rig, had a name peculiar to the river. When they spoke of the river itself, the boatmen also used expressions which distinguished it from other rivers. And when the prowmen, wielding their boat-hooks or sounding-rods, called out the depth at the barge's prow, they did so in spans, the measure of an open hand.

So they went their way, uttering their cries, wary alike of shoals and whirlpools, and of the sandbanks brought down and deposited at the mouths of tributaries.

So the boatmen went their way, alert to the river's caprices, but taking care never to accuse it of treachery, since each of them secretly venerated it as a god.

They had not learnt their river's history from books. But they said proudly that its name came from far back in time, from an old Celtic word, *rhôdan*, a word which meant to turn swiftly, strongly. And it was true: the Rhône flowed and turned so strongly that only those who knew it for a god might hope for anything from it.

As soon as his barge was well and truly in the grip of the current, Christian became Captain Merlin once more. The captain, a solitary figurehead, buffeted by cares as the current buffets a swimmer. Despite the fact that visibility was still limited to the white circle which did not extend beyond the bulwarks, he sensed his train of barges had taken the current behind him. The cries of the prowmen and the helmsmen reached him one by one, right down to the last, very faint, scarcely carried on this over-thick air which seemed to amplify only his own voice.

When the last of his barges put out from the quay, his own was already passing the steamer. Christian saw the black mass on his right, riding high in the water and shaken by the pounding of the machinery. For several minutes the stench of coal was so strong that he held his breath.

The monster lay a few yards off, passing at the speed of the current as if it were sailing upstream. The prowman could have touched it easily with his sounding-rod.

The steamer looked as if it were passing alongside them, but it was moored and it was in fact they who were going downstream with the flow of the Rhône, noiselessly, propelled only by the river's vast friendly strength. Deep within him, Christian felt his fear clinging to life. For the moment it lay still, but it was not sleeping. Numbed, as if caught in the cold of the morning, it would not fail to reawaken as soon as the sun and wind cleansed the valley. For the steamer would leave. Christian had no doubt of that. Would she get far? In such shallow water, would she be able to make a half-circle to turn her pointed, metal-clad bow to the south? Could that heap of scrap iron plough into a gravel bank and remain undamaged? Would the paddle-wheels find sufficient water to churn up to drive the vessel forward and allow her crew to manoeuvre?

All these questions beset Captain Merlin. He gave his full attention to his course, but the questions crowded into his mind, one nudging the other as an overloaded barge nudges a lighter one held back by the south wind.

At the prow, still invisible as though he were walking ahead of the boat, Tirou relayed ever-changing information at the top of his voice; it floated on the mist from one minute to the next.

'Four fingers' depth!'

Which meant that there was barely the width of four fingers between the river bed and the barge's keel.

'One span!'

There was slightly more water, but only just enough to prevent grounding.

The deck-boy, standing beside the captain, facing aft to where the others were following in the mist, repeated the cry, which was taken up by the prowman of the second barge after he himself had checked with his sounding-rod, since only a yard or two to right or left might see a variation in depth. So from stem to stern and from stern to stem the cries were taken up by these strong, sometimes hoarse voices, which were the only link between the boats riding the current.

In theory, since the master-barge was the heaviest, the others ought to be able to follow wherever it led. But it was only possible to guess at where the first barge was heading, although everyone was on the alert, eyes aching from peering through the mist.

It was not even possible to be sure where the banks were. It was a case of trusting to the river, which always tends to bear whatever it is carrying towards the mainstream of its current. But after so many days when no boat had been able to make the journey, sandbanks might have changed their position, creating unlooked-for eddies which risked turning a boat broadside on and driving it against an embankment.

At long intervals the prowman's cry altered. When the depth was called, he added: 'Push to the Ryaume!' Or else: 'Push to the Empie!'

Then Christian leaned on the wooden tiller which vibrated with the current. He felt the quiver, which is the sign that the river is very much alive, reverberating through his arms, his shoulders, the muscles of his chest. Via the rudder, he was directly linked with his river. He leaned on the tiller to alter the boat's course. For every effort of his, the Rhône responded with one of its own.

The boy passed on the call, and all the rest did likewise behind them. And all the barge captains in turn felt the river's beneficent strength flow through their limbs.

Then Christian felt that men and Rhône were like a single animal, all its nerves and muscles animated by the sole desire to attain their goal.

The smell warned Christian of the approach of La Mulatière, where the Saône flows into the Rhône. A smell of water impregnated the air, which was even thicker here than upstream. A smell of mud reached him even before he distinguished the sound like a dam which the tributary made in passing under the bridge.

'Watch out on the Ryaume!' he shouted to his prowman.

But Tirou was aware of it too.

'Right you are!' he yelled. Then, almost at once, and speaking very fast, he added: 'Full depth! Watch out for eddies!'

'Full depth' meant that the sounding-rod was no longer touching bottom and it was possible to navigate freely. As for the big eddies – virtually whirlpools – Christian was ready for them. He knew well that when the Saône carries more water than the Rhône, everything is different at the confluence. He sensed the presence of the muddy waters of the tributary, churned up by the piers of the bridge. He could hear its ill-omened gurgle on their right. He did not like the Saône because it was slow and easy, and because it was on these waters that the first steam vessels had been able to navigate. He did not like it, but today it was going to bring them sufficient water for them to go downstream without too many risks. The one thing that mattered was that it should not supply enough water for that filthy *Triomphant* to be able to navigate as well.

Tirou's cry of 'Full depth' surprised Christian somewhat; his mind immediately began to race. It was not possible for the Saône to have brought down sufficient water to raise the level so high. Therefore the river bed must have been scoured out at this point while the boats were held up. If that were so, then a bank must also have formed. It could equally well be to the right or left, or even downstream. Christian was opening his mouth to shout a warning to his prowman when the prowman himself cried:

'Shallows ahead! Hard to the Ryaume! Quick – quick!'

A wave of strength surged over Christian. Raging, bracing his muscles, back arched, hands clenched on the wooden tiller, he pushed with all his might as he yelled: 'Shallows ahead! Hard to the Ryaume!'

He looked round as he shouted, then, swivelling back to the deck-boy, he cried: 'Pull, lad! Pull towards you!'

The boy had understood. Without wasting time in getting round the tiller to stand beside his captain, he grasped the wood and pulled with all his might. The rudder tore at the water. Beneath them it sounded like a waterfall, more distinct than that of the bridge which was now louder than ever.

Opposite each other, Christian straining forward and the boy arching backward with the effort, the two men worked eye to eye but without really seeing each other. For an instant the river was as strong as they were. The barge's whole frame shuddered. Its trembling made them realize that the prowman was helping them all he could by leaning on his sounding-rod to brake their progress. Then, slowly at first, then faster and faster, the tiller turned on its pivot. The boy, half lying beneath it, withdrew. The heels of his boots made the strips of lath crack. The captain clung on, his feet firmly planted at an oblique angle. As the tiller was going to swing right to the bulwark as a result of their efforts, Christian gasped hoarsely: 'Jump towards me!'

Lithe and supple, the boy was off like a shot. Using both hands as a springboard, he vaulted over the tiller and his feet clattered on the deck which rang like a great cask. Without losing a second, he began pushing to help Christian maintain the rudder in position as it threshed the river.

'Shallows past!' the prowman shouted. 'Full speed ahead!'

The two men hauled back on the tiller.

There was no question of informing the others of the second phase of the operation. Once warning had been given of the gravel-bank, each had to judge for himself. It all happened within the space of a few yards, and the detour to be made required such precision that the time spent in transmitting orders might jeopardize everything.

Ears pricked, face deeply lined, Christian gazed at the deck-boy who was getting his breath back. Beads of sweat stood out on the boy's forehead.

Christian too was hot. Hot with the effort of hard work, hot with the fear he had felt, hot with the thought that the others behind him still risked running aground.

One by one the prowmen's cries came through: 'Shallows past! Full speed ahead!'

The mist muffled and distorted voices, but Captain Merlin had only to count the calls to know that finally his seven barges had triumphed over danger.

Again he felt the warmth rise in him. A warmth of joy, a warmth also of hope at the thought that perhaps the steamer would not get beyond this first obstacle.

At the tip of the dykes were laundry-boats and boat-mills. Real wooden houses with tiled roofs. Night and day the current turned their great paddle-wheels, and the millers continued to listen to the river even while they slept.

At first light the mules' hoofs rang out on the little wooden bridges which connected the boat to the bank.

'Hey, miller! Two sacks to be delivered. Got room for them?'

'Yes, I've got room for them, Ferdinand. And the Rhône's risen during the night. That'll make the wheel go round.'

At the laundry downstream the washerwomen chattered. From time to time one of them called out: 'Don't shake your flour bags into the Rhône. You're making our laundry like dough.'

The men laughed.

'That lot have got as much cheek as the boatmen.'

They were calling through the mist, unable to see one another.

'You wait! On the way up the boatmen'll lay your mill flat with their tow-ropes.'

'I'd like to see 'em try!'

'Don't be so cocky. You know they're the strongest.'

'Not for long. Coal will finish 'em.'

'It'll finish you too!'

'And it'll make your washing dirty!'

There were often quarrels between the millers and the boatmen. When the tow-path ran behind a mill, it was quite a dangerous business to swing the tow-ropes over the roof. But the steamers did far greater damage. At La Tour de Millery two mills had foundered, swamped by the huge waves which the monsters raised. The millers had had to moor more slackly, or find another place. Despite these precautions, it was not unusual for a paddle-blade to pass over the edge and soak several hundredweights of flour.

There was no question of compensation. Who was there to complain to? What proof was there? What law?

For centuries the bargemen had made the banks tremble. Horses, shouts, axe-blows, they spared nothing and respected only the river. But all that they did was in the order of things. Everything fell within the larger compass of the river. With the paddle-steamers it was a different matter.

The boats were so big and so fast that when they passed the river was half emptied by virtue of all the water which their enormous paddle-wheels churned backwards. Banks and dykes, suddenly laid bare, offered up their secrets to anyone's inspection. The thousands of creatures which lived in the mosses, under roots and gravel banks, between the rocks, were terrified. Fish were stranded on the sand. And once the steamer had passed, the water was in turmoil for a good quarter of an hour afterwards. Everything was jostled, shaken, soaked, churned up and spoilt. The mud from the quiet reaches rose to the surface and spread towards midstream in long brownish trails. The oil from the connecting-rods, the smoke and cinders, all helped to poison beasts and men. For the past two years, very few beavers had been seen on the islands. Several poplars had fallen, undermined by this ebb and flow which were no part of the river's nature.

The mist did not last as long as Christian had hoped. Navigating in this fashion, they passed La Mulatière and Oullins, where once again they had to manoeuvre very fast to negotiate a sandbank which had formed at the mouth of the Yseron. Then, as they entered the straight stretch which begins above Irigny and ends at the first islands of Vernaison, there was a gust of warm air straight from the south. A large tunnel hollowed out the mist, which all at once acquired colour. Straight ahead, the white became whiter, so filled with light that it was almost painful to look at. To each side, greys and blues hastily sketched in the outlines of trees with long vertical and oblique strokes. Patches of rust formed on the greys and blues. It was a universe not yet clearly defined. A world which did not look like a world where men might live, but like a bath of mingled colour washes, as if the wind had suddenly plucked hand-fuls of different hued dust from earth and sky to play with in the hollow of the valley.

The river had not yet recovered its identity. It limited itself to piercing through its white coverlet here and there with a dazzling ray of light or a long blade of darkness.

On the barge, the supple waves of mist swirled like clouds. They blotted out the deck-tent, then parted as suddenly to reveal it. Occasionally the prowman's gestures pierced the swirl. A shaft of light enveloped him, his tall shadow defined against it. His arms rose and fell, ceaselessly manipulating the long rod which con-tinued to spell out the barge's course on the bottom.

'One span! . . . Three fingers' depth! . . . Push to the Empie! . . . Push to the Ryaume! . . . Shallows ahead! . . . Debris on the Ryaume!'

The cries staked out their journey. Outside Oullins the washer-women had replied, shouting: 'Beware of coal!'

Captain Merlin had growled an oath, but in the background he had recognized the loud voice of Paul Barillot bawling: 'You old bags still washing? All very well for you. The rest of us gave it up long ago!'

And the sally had released a long laugh all along the river.

Above Sellette, while they were passing the island of La Grande Chèvre on their left, Christian raised his metal loud-hailer to his lips and yelled: 'Ferry-boat ahoy! Seven barges going through. Captain Merlin.'

From far off came the answer: 'Ahoy! Go ahead, Christian. And watch out round Tabare. It's bad there. Scoured out deep on the Empie. You're the first to go down since the drought. I'm not surprised it's you. But be careful, the river's altered.'

'Thanks, Grandpa Barillot. Things all right with you?'

'All right for one pushing eighty.'

'You keep it up.'

'Go on, lad . . . Saint Nicholas is with you.'

All the boatmen knew Old Barillot, who, like the majority of ferry-men, was a former barge-hand. As the barges passed, the conversation continued, each in turn taking it up to reply to this voice coming out of the mist. The old man must be on his ferry-boat, of which the barge crews could see only the cable like a black line in the sky above the Rhône and passing very fast above their heads.

They were nearing the island of Tabare when there was a second gust of wind, stronger than the first. Suddenly everything was aglow. The gilded river steamed like greasy soup. Its vapour of light rose towards the sun. Everything was light. Even the shadows of the big aspens, even the tufted undersides of the scrub already bronzed by autumn. Every leaf was a droplet of light. The whole valley wept tears of sunlight which dripped on to the banks and the stagnant water of the lagoons. Against the embankments on the left, the current's scum piled up; it was like that lacework of fire which the bellows raises in the blacksmith's forge. Long mauve scarves trailed among the islands, catching on the gnarled trunks of dwarf willows, tearing on the golden masts of poplars stripped by the drought before autumn had fairly arrived.

Turning round, Captain Merlin saw the full length of his seven barges, which were following in line as if linked by a perfectly taut cable.

A great joy swept over him. All at once, he was like the valley, where light, still damp with the last of night, unfurled from one side to the other. Each prowman's every gesture as he manipulated his rod was a salutation addressed to the sun, every cry giving the depth a summons to joy.

It was clear! Everything was clear!

'Shallows on the Ryaume, push to the Empie! Push, push, push!'

Even Tirou's trumpeted warning rang out like a joyful laugh.

'Shallows on the Ryaume!' the deck-boy repeated.

'Push with me, boy!' Christian yelled.

And the boy pushed. And his whole face laughed in the sunlight.

Scarcely had they altered the barge's course and guided the prow towards the left bank from which the light was coming, than the prowman shouted: 'Shallows on the Empie! Push to the Ryaume! Push, push, push!'

'God in heaven!'

An oath. A jerk sufficient to dislocate vertebrae. A gasp which rose from the depths of the chest. Other cries and oaths behind. A running over the bulwarks, a straining on the sounding-rods, weight and nerves applied to the tiller, whose wood creaked as if it would break. The wood was caught between the river's terrible strength and the strength of men who move faster than the current.

Everything happened at once beneath the rain of light.

The south wind gusted in the sun and, gathering strength, swelled out in the valley's great bed. On waking, it stretched and stirred, turned over and over. It pressed back the remaining rags of mist against the banks, it shook the poplars which shed water-drops and leaves in great whirls of russet and crystal.

It was not anger on the wind's part, it was joy. Having stretched, it bounded from bed and now was trampling the uneasy shadow.

And it talked. It talked before starting to sing. It got drunk on scattered sunlight. It moved northwards, gathering up armfuls of leaves. Startled villages clattered all their shutters, pressing their first smoke-wreaths against the hillsides.

Tabare, La Table Ronde, Le Four à Chaux – so many islands to be skirted opposite Vernaison. It passed so quickly, was so dotted with gravel-banks constantly displaced that the men had scarcely time to notice the village on their right.

Now that the light had come, Christian fixed his eyes on his prowman, whose red hair and beard were a glowing ember in this vast hearth of dawn. From the amplitude of his gestures, he could practically guess the water's depth, and Tirou's cry was often no more than confirmation of what he had seen at the same time as the prowman.

Between them ran the full length of the barge, some fifty feet. Starting at the stern, the captain let his gaze skim over the canvas deck-tent, linger in passing on the pile of crates and bales, see without registering the galley, which was a small wooden structure where the cooks and the clerk worked; finally, beyond the stout foremast round which were coiled the ropes and cables for the upstream journey, on the prow which lifted its snout a little, was the prowman capering about like a demon.

From Vernaison to Givors it was a succession of shallows, with barely three feet of water. For years the valley's barge-masters had been agitating to have them dredged. Now, those who had been able to hold out against the steamer's competition no longer agitated. Deep down, they hoped that the river bed would never be deepened because it would benefit the steamers too much. By virtue of their calling, by virtue of their toil and skill, by virtue of allying themselves with the river, whether on the upstream or downstream journeys, they got through, whatever the cost. They had realized that everything that might be undertaken by the authorities would serve only to hasten their end. Here, for example, the tow-path was so bad, the floods had attacked it at so many points when it was exposed to the current, that it might be described as virtually non-existent. On the way up the horses often had to skirt the edges of the islands, through the jungle of scrub where the ropes got caught round tree-stumps. The bailey and his drivers went ahead armed with axes to clear a way for their horses. In other places the beasts were obliged to cross side reaches where the dykes were crumbling. They struggled for hours to gain a few yards, up to their chests in water, their hoofs seeking purchase on the shifting sandy bottom or on the mossy rocks as slippery as ice.

But no barge-hand ever reckoned up his trouble. The worst of evils came not from the river, but from man and his machines.

As far down as Givors, all the little ports had died since that accursed day when the railway linking Saint-Etienne and Lyons had begun to smoke out the valley.

Captain Merlin, more obstinate, more unco-operative than the other barge-masters, had always refused to join forces with this monster. He knew that one day attempts would be made to extend the twin steel serpents to the sea. So, to emphasize that he detested and despised it, he refused to load at Givors the coal which the wagons brought from the Loire mines. Other captains did so. He sailed proudly by in midstream, without a glance at this port whose foundries spat black. He had freight enough for his seven barges.

Beyond Givors the river was deflected eastwards by the hills of Ban. There too the route was not easy. The waters divided at the islands of Loire, and it was necessary to pass on the Empie because the other branch wound too much.

'Three fingers' depth!' cried the prowman.

And Christian felt his hands tremble with the rolling of the shingle. The rudder had raked the bottom.

'God above! If that filthy paddle-boat gets through here, it'll be because she's got the devil on her side!'

They progressed moderately. The river was never finished with making and remaking its bed and it was probed by eye as much as by rod. But the water, already ruffled by the south wind, was hammered by sunlight which here shone slantwise into the valley and was getting hotter and hotter. It was impossible to guess at anything. Only objects which really stood out were visible. Rocks, tree-trunks half buried in sand, ends of broken dykes, the whole skeleton was visible on the surface.

Nerves were tense. With a normal depth, the barges which followed ought to have been able to navigate without a prowman now that the mist had lifted. But today it was necessary to navigate to the nearest inch, and each was obliged to pick his way yard by yard through the river's shallow water.

Christian turned round. On the stable barge which was following him, his son was at the prow. Albert Carénal was at the tiller; he gave him a friendly salute, flourishing his big black felt hat. Carénal must be tired and they had made use of an easy stretch to change places. The two other men aboard stayed near them: a driver beside Claude, a barge-hand with Carénal. Obstinate as always, Christian had wanted to have on his barge only the usual complement. And neither Rapiat nor the cooks in the galley were likely to lend him a hand. He was suddenly ashamed that his son should be more humane than he was. As they had just left L'Isle Richard on their right and entered a stretch where calmer water indicated the bottle-neck at the narrows of Estressin, he summoned the deck-boy.

'Take the tiller, lad, and keep an eye on me. I'll give you a signal. But you ought not to have to move it much in the time it takes me to go for'ard.'

Without hurrying, but at a good pace which rang out clearly on the planking of the bulwarks, he went for'ard. The barge was travelling at the speed of the current and the river seemed stationary. But Christian was moving faster than the river. The water was calm and a little clouded by that contribution of mud which the Saône had received from the storms.

'One span!'

Tirou had given this reassuring cry four times already. It did not mean full freedom to navigate, but the water was sufficiently deep for them to proceed without worrying.

'Give me the sounding-rod, Tirou, and go and take the tiller.'

'I'm not tired.'

'I know. But I need to loosen up my shoulders a bit. Come on, hand over.'

The prowman plunged the wooden rod into the current once more, then, instead of withdrawing it, he let it pass along the bulwark, and Christian grasped it and held it up, crying: 'One span depth!'

The prowman moved away, rubbing his forearm over his sweaty forehead.

'Have a glass of wine and send the boy down to me with the flask.'

Christian turned to his task. He manipulated his rod with sweeping gestures. As he pulled it out, his right hand ran down the willow's supple length to where the wood was wet. It was good to have this direct contact with the river.

His gaze flitted from one bank to the other; he skimmed the

surface of the water like a kingfisher; he was questing, seeking. He was proceeding in this fashion when he plunged forward suddenly in the same instant as the rod. When the water is not very deep, when a gravel bank is very close, the bottom alone reveals in passing the speed of the river and of the boat it bears.

Downstream, in the sunlight which gnawed at the mountain and nibbled the bell-tower, Vienne appeared. They were going to head straight for the town, then, when they were practically rubbing against the bank, they would steer for the Ryaume in order to pass under the big ironwork bridge which linked Vienne to Sainte-Colombe. Only then would they begin their manoeuvres to come alongside.

In the wooden huts built on the islands, the fishermen were preparing their nets. They had sniffed the mist and felt the slight rise in water-level. The fish were going to sweep over the gravel banks, into the stagnant side reaches, and ransack the land which had not seen water for weeks. To make the most of it, it would be necessary to act quickly before the first steamers got through. That terrible tribe shook the banks to such an extent that there was no fishing for more than an hour after each had passed.

At La Tour de Millery the dawn rang with the accustomed sounds of dull blows and the screech of rending wood. Rusted nails squealed like animals as pincers wrenched them out of planks. Two men were at work demolishing the landing-stage. The port had been dead since 1827 when the railway arrived. For thirteen years the landing-stage had been left in position. Men had hoped for the impossible, for a miracle, but it was steam that was the miracle. There was a railway station, but not a single barge now put in to the silted-up port. So the council had decided to demolish the landing-stage.

At Givors, the two teams of unloaders were at work: black for coal, red for iron ore. Great mounds were piled up at the port. The low water had not halted the train, only the boats. So the coal piled up on the quays. And the unloaders continued to bring it on their bowed backs, emptying the black, powdery baskets from shoulder height, spitting thickly into the dust. They watched the sky whiten. Soon it would be as hot here as it was in front of the great furnaces where they went sometimes for night work.

Seated in the depths of their ferry-boats, the ferry-men breathed more easily now that the sun had broken through. Their gaze went towards the opposite bank, the farthest point in their ceaseless to-and-fro. After so many years of freedom on the river, they were ending their days in these boats attached to a wire, like dogs who are permitted only to cross the farmyard. They shuttled from one bank to the other, answering the summonses of those who wanted to cross, suspicious of boats whether travelling upstream or downstream, and they too hated the steam monsters. They were the prisoners of a cable, but very glad to be so and glad that not too many bridges were being constructed. Glad to be there because, in spite of all the damage inflicted upon it, the Rhône was still the Rhône.

Constricted downstream by the foothills of the mountains of Saint-Romain-en-Gal which thrust back towards the east the last spurs of the valley of Levaux, the river gradually lost its momentum. It began to dawdle and the banks slid by less fast.

Still taking soundings, Captain Merlin began to put pressure on his rod before withdrawing it. It was no use. It would have needed ten times as much to make the heavy barge advance more rapidly than the river. The two were a single entity. One went where the other had resolved to take it, and that was quite understood by the barge crews. They had always made their downstream journey with the Rhône, without trying to cheat, without wanting to demonstrate that they were smarter than the river. It was a law of nature which only the fools on the steamers might call in question. Captain Merlin was well aware of it, but that morning his eagerness to arrive drove him to make gestures which he did not properly control. And then, he felt such a vast reserve of energy within him that he needed to waste a little of it purely for pleasure and because his body had suffered too much from enforced idleness.

The barge was advancing into the light. The wind was still driving trails of mist before it, but it was as if a great calm lay over this quieter water. The cross fixed to the prow showed up darker than the still distant mass of mountains, which seemed to crush the sparkling mirror of the Rhône.

Silence. If you turned your head, the wind barely sang in your ears. A disturbing silence that was suddenly split asunder.

Christian started violently. He spun round.

His eyes were still dazzled with sunlight as he peered upstream where the greyness seemed lacklustre. He could barely see beyond the last barge of the convoy. But what he could not yet see was all too apparent to the boatmen astern. They waved their arms. They yelled at the tops of their voices. The prowmen leaned on their rods to push their barges towards the bank. The other men had seized poles and were pushing too.

The steam monster gave another whistle which filled the valley. The first thing to appear in the clearing sky above the mist was her smoke. Heavy, black, thick, impervious to light, it had difficulty in rising. It lay like a huge, writhing, repulsive worm, swollen with evil. It was the forerunner, and then, immediately following, came the red and black heap of scrap iron which bit into the river. The waters parted. A mound of foam rose in puffs which whipped against the banks. In the centre was the stinking brute. The brute which spat ever blacker and repeated her whistle-blast, which released a puff of white swallowed up at once by the smoke.

'God's curse!'

Christian roared his rage. He let himself go and gave one shout of anger, then, compressing his lips, bracing his muscles, he threw all his strength into the struggle with the river. The deck-boy had seized a rod and battled beside him. Tirou leaned on the tiller. The cooks came bursting out of their galley and seized boat-hooks.

Already the steamer was level with the barges astern. From the sound of the engines Christian realized that the man in command had reduced speed, but the monster still came on at a fearful rate.

The barge-hands raised their fists and spat out insults which the other crew did not hear.

But, God above, how could human beings live in that infernal racket, amid that roar and clatter and squeak of machinery, that displacement of water by the paddle-wheels?

'Scum! Traitors!'

It was Tirou who shouted. Canut gestured obscenely towards the steamer and roared at the top of his voice: 'Devil take your kettle!'

Captain Merlin, very dignified, remained silent. He did not even raise his head to look at the monster, which he wished to ignore. Nevertheless, his gaze darted like an arrow from beneath the pulled-down brim of his hat which left his lowered face in shadow. The stinking brute was going by a few yards from him. She was black and red, and the only clean thing about her was her gleaming brass. On the foredeck, the passengers crowded for a look at the barge crew. They laughed. They jostled. They had the gall to jeer at honest men's toil.

Captain Merlin bit back his rage. There was the bitterness of bile in his throat. O God, to get his hands on one of them and give him a taste of the river!

After hollowing out the river as if to empty it of its water, the steel bow raised a wave that set the barges rocking and the boatmen could barely keep them in line. The foam whipped along the bulwarks and spread over the decks.

Christian trembled all over. His hands clenched on the sounding-rod were ready to burst with the strength of his grip. But he would say nothing. Nothing. He would not even answer the sailors on the steamer who were laughing with the passengers and calling the barge crew laggards.

Christian wanted to muzzle his hatred. But though he managed to hold back the insults which burned in his throat, he could not prevent a prayer from rising within him:

'Saint Nicholas, I don't wish harm to any of those damnfool passengers, nor to the sailors who have betrayed their calling and their river. I don't wish harm to anyone, but let that iron hull that fouls your river strike a rock . . . Let that filth that fouls your river ground on sand to scour it clean. Let all these scrap-iron vessels founder and all the companies go bankrupt. Saint Nicholas, let the true boatmen still be able to earn a living by their labours, those who honour you and honour your river.'

The monster passed.

Slowly, the water which had been disturbed began to flow again as a river should. The eddies swirled, hesitated, reformed. The current, held back and thrust upstream, rediscovered its true direction.

Now the Rhône again accepted the silent barges and began once more to bear them to the south.

No more insults, no more shouting, nothing. Nothing but the depth which the prowmen again began to call.

The steamer also had a man at the prow. But the man did not call out because of the infernal din. He had an assistant beside him who looked at the rod and indicated the depth of water to the helmsman and the course to follow by means of signs. And these men were all betrayers of their calling.

Captain Merlin watched the big iron boat ride high in the water as she drew away, her paddle-wheels making her three times the size of his barge.

What sort of freak was a boat with wheels?

He watched her draw away in midstream, ploughing the water and throwing up two mighty furrows which the banks thrust back, groaning.

The monster soon disappeared behind the rocky foot of the mountains of Saint-Romain-en-Gal, but her pall of smoke still floated above the river. For a moment it blotted out the sky. It turned the dazzling sun to a red ball, like that which plunges earthwards on drear winter evenings.

Gradually the sun broke free. It regained its brilliance. The wind made haste to scatter the spew of coal, but something lingered. Something which ended by becoming invisible, but which darkened the morning and tarnished the metallic gleam of the Rhône.

When the steamer captains entered those stretches where the river was compressed by a mountain gorge and flowed less swiftly and varied less in depth, they went full steam ahead. With deeper water and fewer obstacles, they could speed to their hearts' content. Everything vibrated and clanged, and the heap of scrap iron seemed ready to fall apart at every turn of the paddle-wheels. The funnels spat more blackly. If there was a bridge and the funnel had to be lowered by hauling on the shrouds, the steamer was suddenly in thick cloud. At water-level it was impossible to breathe. Passengers, sailors, helmsmen, all held their noses and shut their eyes until the tall red and black pipe was back in position.

All the river folk hurled insults and threw stones which never reached the vessel. There had been only a few minor accidents due to rocks thrown from bridges by carters whose horses had bolted.

When a steamer overtook or crossed a barge-train, some captains slowed down. In contrast, others gave orders for the steamer to go even faster, laughing at the barge crew's insults and retaliating with gestures of hate.

Every time a steamer went through, whether downstream or up, the river was disturbed. For a long time afterwards it was contorted. It was not accustomed either to the disturbance or to the filth. And that kept hope alive in the hearts of the barge-masters. So long as they felt the river and river folk were on their side, they would go on fighting. For the river folk too were suffering from the advent of these great vessels. Gradually the little ports were dying. The waterside inns and hostelries, which had made a living from the barge crews and their passengers, closed their doors.

In 1783, when the Marquis de Jouffroy d'Abbans had launched his first steamboat on the Saône, many had made the trip to enjoy the machine. To them, the madman nicknamed Jouffroy Steam-Pump was just a showman exhibiting freaks. Fifty-seven years had passed since then. The old men had often described that day. They had laughed immoderately as they drank the wine of Côte-Rôtie. Those concerned with the steamer had encountered many set-backs, but by dint of hard work and so much money that men wondered if they were minting it themselves, they had perfected their machines.

So long as they had kept to the Saône, the barge crews and river dwellers had gone on laughing. The accidents which befell the first steamers and made them reluctant to risk it on the bigger river had made them shrug their shoulders.

Did these rich fellows think money could buy anything? It could buy many things, certainly, but mastery of a river was not yet one of them. For years the true boatmen were solidly united. And then gradually, just when the old men were retiring to the banks to await the end sitting in the sun and recounting their misfortunes, a few seconds-in-command who knew very well that they would never own a barge-train had let themselves be tempted by money. They had acted as pilots for the men of the steamers, who had ended by teaching them to handle their machines. It was only this treachery on the part of a few that had allowed the river to be spoilt and fouled. It defended itself as well as it could with outbursts of temper and drought, bringing down tons of gravel and huge trees which it placed across its course; but the others had such resources that a boat was quickly repaired or replaced.

So ever since that day in 1829 when the *Pionnier* had gone upstream from Arles to Lyons with more than a ton of freight, a shadow had hung over the valley. Already people began to recall nostalgically the time when more than two thousand boats plied the river and maintained a whole population of barge-hands and river folk. Today, there were no more than twenty barge-trains to keep the small ports going. They loaded and unloaded all the way along on the downstream and upstream trips, putting in at every quay where the steamers could not risk it.

More than ever, the people of the small ports made a fuss of the barge crews. They got to know one another, asked for news, talked of those who were navigating for another captain.

From time to time faces lengthened. Old So-and-so was dead. Such-and-such a lad of good sailing stock had given it all up to sell himself to steam. That was the most distressing news of all for a barge-hand to hear.

After the steamer had passed, the sun's return failed to bring back joy. Christian had watched the big black boat disappear at the apex of its triangle of foam. He had cursed a hundred times those who built her and those who served on her; nevertheless, seeing that great heap of iron moving without mishap among the gravel banks, he had been unable to refrain from muttering: 'That bastard Monnier can navigate all right. He knows the river as well as I do. And to think I taught him all he knows.'

A gleam of pride tinged his anger and bitterness. All the deck-boys whom he had trained now knew how to plot their course on this watery highway. All had become either head prowmen or seconds-in-command. Two of them had even set up their own rigs and sailed independently. But others, like Gérard Monnier, whom he had always considered a good lad, had put their knowledge at the service of the steam navigation companies.

Right down to Vienne they were in muddy, choppy water. As soon as the barge, piloted by Tirou, had doubled Saint Romain's point, Christian glanced at the straight line stretching away to the south-west and forming a long ribbon right to the hills of Ampuis.

The steamer had already disappeared, but her smoke still hung over the left bank which was sheltered from the wind. It floated among the scrub like an unhealthy miasma.

'One day,' Christian growled, 'the wine of Condrieu will reek of coal, and the cheese will be uneatable because the goats have browsed on poisoned grass.' He plunged his sounding-rod in twice and withdrew it; then went on: 'That's how it'll be one day, unless the steamers' crews are poisoned by their machines.'

After the bend the current strengthened and took hold of them again. The barges' speed increased. The shallower water required redoubled care. At the same time as he took soundings, Christian had to keep an eye on the approach to the bridge, whose left pier was a danger for anyone having to come alongside.

His keen gaze went from the rings on the sounding-rod to this block of masonry whose embankment set the river churning.

He turned round long enough to shout to Tirou: 'One span . . . Hard to the Ryaume! Push, push, push!'

Helped by the deck-boy, the prowman bent over the tiller. The barge quivered. Sliced by the prow which reared up as the current caught it broadside, the river began to slap against the bulwarks. Christian held back the prow. Lying broadside on, the barge ended with its stem towards the whirlpool formed by the bridge pier it had just passed.

Even broadside on, it continued to move forward. Its prow grazed the stone quay and its rudder scraped the gravel of the bank formed downstream from the right pier.

The barge had turned. It was the longest of the seven, so the others would manage the manoeuvre. Christian was confident of that. He knew his men. This thought comforted him, for it would be a long time before a steamer could succeed in executing such a manoeuvre.

While he was engaged on it, the captain had glanced towards the port to which he could now allow his barge to drift. Along the quay, well downstream, a train of five barges like his own was moored. Horses were grazing in the meadow near by. Already four barge hands were running upstream. The first, Joannès Etiévent, was the captain of these five barges. As he ran he shouted: 'Hey, Christian! Throw over your rope!'

The deck-boy had caught on and was already holding the rope, whirling its weighted end round above his head before sending it towards the quay.

A few yards downstream from the bridge the end of a dyke deflected the current towards midstream, creating a quiet reach where the slack water was fairly deep. Carried round by the eddy, prow pointing upstream, it was easy for the barge to come alongside.

Before jumping down on to the quay, Captain Merlin supervised the arrival of his barges which came in one by one to range themselves downstream from his own. Men's cries, shouted orders, ropes whipping the air, iron rings resounding on the stones of the quay, all gave momentary life to the port.

Not enough, however, to blot out the monster's passing.

No sooner was Christian on the quay than Captain Etiévent was wringing his hand and crying: 'Did you see that filth going downstream?'

'I saw her. And I was lucky enough to be in a pretty good spot, otherwise she'd have run me into the bank.'

'Here, she passed barely a yard from my last barge. I've got some bales of cotton which are soaked through. I've sent for a constable to lodge a complaint. My client'll sue . . . And if he doesn't, I will. It may take every penny I've got, but by God, they're not getting away with that!'

Etiévent became increasingly excited as he talked. Tall, broad, rough-hewn, his face all bones and tendons, he was gesticulating, his face contorted with rage.

For Christian, who had known him ever since he could remember, it was good to see him like this, filled with hatred and resolved to battle to the end.

There were a few of this breed, and the steam vessels would have to reckon with them.

All along the quay, the men of the two barge-trains were talking in threes and fours. Everywhere voices were rising. Anger set arms waving and tongues wagging.

For an instant Captain Merlin let himself imagine a steamer putting in here carrying all the captains of the companies and all the traitors to the barges. He pictured the battle. He could already see the duckings his lads and Etiévent's would deal out to this select company.

But it was a dream, and dreaming has never been a boatman's daily fare.

Etiévent was certainly not dreaming. When the worst of his anger had passed, he said simply: 'At the rate she was going, I'd be very surprised if she made Beaucaire without leaving a few of her plates on the bottom.'

Christian merely said: 'Filthy swine,' and boarded his barge again.

Etiévent followed him. They took a few steps towards the stern, then Christian asked: 'You on your way upstream?'

'Yes. Held up here for more than three weeks.'

'Same as me in Lyons.'

'Same as everyone everywhere . . . This morning when I saw the slight rise in the river and its colour, I reckoned that came from the

68

Saône. I thought about leaving, but I merely risk being held up tomorrow a bit farther upstream. It'll take me at least six days to get up to Lyons. If the south wind lasts three days the glaciers'll send down water, and then I'll risk it.'

Having reached the tiller, Captain Merlin put his loud-hailer to his lips and shouted: 'That's enough jaw! Back aboard for sorting out the freight.'

The men obeyed, boarding the barges. Those from Etiévent's crew followed to lend a hand.

As Christian put down his loud-hailer, Etiévent said calmly, but with an undertone of sadness that surprised his friend: 'You can break it to them that they'll have to do the unloading themselves, but we'll give you a hand.'

'What about the unloaders?'

Etiévent sighed. His broad shoulders hunched, his hands clenched, and the muscles of his tanned face began to quiver. 'Gone to the silk factories,' he growled. 'Or else to the railway. Quite a few had gone away, and when the drought put a stop to river traffic, you see, the others cleared out too.'

It was Christian's turn to sigh. 'You've got to see it their way. They've got a living to earn.'

'Yes, I understand. You know me well enough to realize that I've always understood men. But I was there when the last lot left. I talked to them. They said to me: "You're done for too. A few years from now and there won't be anything but the steamers. The little ports have had it." That's what they said to me. If my three lads hadn't held me back I'd have knocked two or three of 'em into the Rhône just to teach 'em, but as it is . . .' He broke off, leaving the sentence unfinished.

Christian was going to pick up his loud-hailer to give his men the order to unload the freight themselves and take on board whatever was to be loaded, but he saw that his boatmen and drivers, aided by Etiévent's crew, were already shifting crates and barrels.

He also saw M. Tonnerieu going from one barge to another, his papers in his hand, checking and counting the goods unloaded.

'Don't worry,' Etiévent said, 'my men will have put them in the picture.'

They turned towards the midships of the barge to join in the activity.

'You won't have a lot to load, you know,' Etiévent explained. 'Some goods have gone by road during the hold-up. They've had to.'

He struck a pose. Christian realized he had something more to say. He looked him straight in the eye and asked: 'What other good news have you got for me?'

'My poor old friend ... I don't know what we're coming to.'

There was a pause. Even the shouts and the noise the men were making, even the rumbling of the carts over the bridge whose planks resounded, seemed to be stilled.

'What is it?' Christian asked again.

'The companies have paid carriers to cart freight up to Lyons where the steamers can take it on board. It's costing them a pretty packet, but – ' he lowered his voice as though exhausted – 'but they'll do anything to break us.'

Christian was thunderstruck. The news he had just heard, the sight of this strong, vital man who seemed reduced to a cipher, all combined to quench the hope he had been nursing within him by repeating to himself that the river would never accept steam.

'My God!' he gasped. 'My God, that's all we needed!'

Etiévent's horny hand, clumsy and unused to gestures of affection, rested on his arm. It gripped as if it were grasping a sounding-rod to push a heavily laden barge off from the quay. Its quivering communicated itself to Christian's arm also.

Etiévent's voice also shook as it issued from between his clenched teeth and uttered words into which he sought to put all his conviction:

'But we'll fight, Christian. You and I, we'll fight to the finish. You and I and a few of the younger ones ... such as your lad and mine.'

It was not only the small ports of no significance that were dying bit by bit. The steamers could not put in to Vienne on the down-stream journey. When they did so on the way up, it was because night or the state of the river compelled them to. But neither goods nor passengers were embarked or disembarked. And what benefit could that bring to port or town? None. Only three or four sailors, black as sweeps, who peacocked in the cafés.

They had something to be proud of all right.

As they passed, the old men spat on the ground in disgust, but some of the girls made up to them. For them, that filth must have an aura of adventure. It was a novelty, an unknown. The future, as some dared to call it.

A mass of metal which spends the night alongside a quay brings nothing except oil slick on the water and smoke even in the ware-houses.

A barge-team, with its men and horses, means warmth and life even when asleep. A boiler goes cold as soon as its fire is out. There is no more life. The metal is dead, colder and more inert than the stone of the quays. These steam monsters were so heavy that, once moored, they were as unmoving as a stone bridge pier. And they were actually called boats! Said to be one with the river when they hadn't even the character to tug on their chains to ask to put out to midstream.

At night, a train of good barges is like a long animal stretched out full length along the quay. A lightly-sleeping animal, ready to wake at the water's least movement. An animal still haunted in sleep by the day's weariness, and stirring in its slumber because it is filled with the thought of moving on.

The captains felt in a strong position with their crews, whom they had trained for river life. It was good to see them unloading huge casks, carboys of acid holding thirty litres and destined for the dyers, crates of gear for the looms, bales of silk. It was child's play for their iron-hard muscles and their lithe backs like those of animals accustomed to all dangers. These fellows were the true men of the Rhône. Their hands were not covered in black oil, nor their lungs choked with coal smoke. With them, it was still possible to formulate new projects. On them depended the future of the barge traffic which refused to go under.

The two crews together were just finishing loading the goods entrusted to them for the downstream journey when the harbour master arrived. He was an old man, desiccated and somewhat stooped. He had sailed in his youth, but an accident which had left him with a weak back had obliged him to go ashore. Since he could read and reckon, he had worked as a clerk in the warehouses. Because he was honest and had acquired a certain authority with age, for the last ten years or more he had been responsible for the port of Vienne.

He looked about him for a moment among the groups, then, catching sight of the two captains, he made straight for them, lengthening his stride and flailing the air with his long arms. The two captains looked at each other, torn between uneasiness and a desire to laugh. The harbour master was normally calm and seldom hurried.

'Must be a fire somewhere for the old boy to gallop like that,' Joannès remarked.

'And it makes him look downright ridiculous, with that great carcase of his.'

The two captains went forward to meet the old man.

'Hallo there, Monsieur Tavernel,' Joannès called. 'Have you got the Devil himself at your heels?'

Several men had come up. There was joking and laughter. But the old man was not listening. He had removed the well-chewed stem of a short black pipe from beneath the yellow moustache which hid his lips, and was regaining his breath. When he raised his hand to indicate that he was able to speak, everyone fell silent.

'Don't talk to me of the Devil,' Old Tavernel panted. 'Perhaps that's who he is.'

There were a few chuckles in the growing circle of men, but the harbour master's stricken face did not encourage mirth.

'At all events he looks like him,' he went on. 'Bless my soul . . . There's a man in the office come straight here from Ampuis . . .

He's from the *Triomphant* . . . He borrowed a horse and he's come to seek help. Their damnable machine's run aground . . . just above Tupin island.'

Only the two captains who were standing near the old man could catch the last words.

A shout went up from the circle of boatmen. Broad-brimmed felt hats were tossed into the air. The men fell upon one another, clapped each other on the back, howled with joy. Canut, who had just emerged from his galley, began to dance in the middle of the circle, brandishing a huge ladle dripping with hot fat.

Old Tavernel began gesticulating again, demanding silence. When he was unsuccessful, he shouted under Christian's nose: 'Will you make these loud-mouths shut up?'

Christian put his finger to his lips and whistled. The tumult died down. There was still some laughter and questioning, a stamping of boots and clogs on the cobblestones, then the circle gathered closely round the harbour master and the two captains became attentive once more.

'God damn it,' the old man grumbled, 'someone comes to ask your help and that's all the answer you can give.'

'Help?'

'Shit, let them sink.'

It was no longer laughter but a growl of hatred that rose from the group. A threat directed towards the old man who straightened his bowed back and eyed them grimly.

'I'm against them too. You know that. Their filth's ruining me as it is you. But the steamer's leaking by the bows and there are twenty-three passengers on board.'

There was a heavy silence. The old man glanced swiftly from Christian to Joannès. It was Joannès who answered.

'What are the banks there for?'

'They've started, but they've only got one trumpery little cockle-shell. And they're at a spot where you know damn well it isn't easy.'

Christian could picture the spot perfectly. He could imagine the steamer and what had happened to her only too well.

'I'm on my way up,' Joannès growled. 'My barges are fully laden. I can't do anything.'

'You could detach a runabout and six oarsmen . . . That isn't loaded. And it's fast.'

The two captains looked at each other, then Joannès asked again: 'What exactly do they want?'

'Help in taking off their passengers – ' The old man broke off. He looked uneasily round the circle before returning to the two captains. He went on in a less assured voice: 'And at least thirty horses to try and shift their fire-eater.'

There was another outburst. Laughter and jeers mingled. Cries of rage and victory.

'Our horses to tow their filthy machine! I'd like to see it.'

Christian, taken aback at first by the news, had regained control of himself. The clamour his men were making did not prevent his brain from ticking over. He whistled again, and when silence was re-established, he explained in his powerful but composed captain's voice: 'Joannès and I will each take one of our runabouts. We'll take two men from each barge-train and go down and deal with the passengers.' He paused long enough to single out the red beard of his prowman. 'Tirou, you'll take my place. Claude and two men with you. When you come up with the steamer, try and stop not too far downstream. The other barges will go on to Condrieu. We'll join up with you there. Start eating without us. The cooks will move to Claude's stable barge at once and Baptiste Carénal will captain her.'

The men hesitated. There were a few murmurs.

'Well, haven't you understood?' Christian shouted. 'Do you think I'm going to miss this? Hell, I've waited for it far too long. Go on, to the Rhône, and may Saint Nicholas be with us.'

The men scattered, laughing and commenting on Captain Merlin's decision.

Christian was about to jump into the runabout when he thought better of it. He ran along the quay and caught up with Carénal.

'Albert,' he said, 'when you tie up at Condrieu it wouldn't surprise me if men from the steamer didn't approach you again for horses –'

'It wouldn't surprise me either.'

Albert Carénal had interrupted him almost roughly. A nervous tic twitched his right eyelid. He sought for words for a moment, then, as Christian was about to speak, he forestalled him to add: 'But what does surprise me is that you should think me capable of –'

It was Christian's turn to interrupt. 'Albert, I don't think you capable of anything bad. You know that perfectly well. I merely wanted to tell you that if they come you are to say I'd rather slaughter my horses than see them tow their filthy ship.'

Carénal chuckled. Shrugging his shoulders, he drew his whip from his belt and cracked the lash above his head as he said: 'I won't waste that many words on 'em. I'll let them hear that music round their ears and I'll just tell 'em that we all piss on 'em – even the horses.'

The runabouts were flat-bottomed boats some twenty-five feet in length which could accommodate up to six pairs of oars. They were used for crossing the river in order to run a cable between the banks. This was used in the manoeuvre known as *culissage*, which consisted in transporting the horses from one side to the other when the state of the tow-path required it.

This morning two oarsmen only had taken their places in each runabout, one captained by Christian Merlin, the other by his friend Etiévent.

The men pulled hard on the oars, the leather of the rowlocks squeaked despite the tallow, and the water sang in the wake. The captains steered with the aid of a long oar whose iron tip allowed them to push on the shoals to help the oarsmen.

'It's a long time since I came downstream so fast,' Christian shouted.

The boats were travelling abreast, handled by men of equal strength and experience.

'If anyone had told me that last night!'

'Or me!'

They were talking at the tops of their voices for the pleasure of crying their joy aloud to all the valley.

'But this morning I had an idea she wouldn't make it.'

'I told you: she's going to leave a plate on the bottom.'

'So long as she blocks the route for the rest of 'em.'

'And stays there till her bottom drops off.'

'We can always get through.'

The sun was brighter. The valley was overflowing with light. The hills of Ampuis, with their drystone walls, their vines and apricots, were yellow, red, white. On land and water the only colours were those which sang for joy. The wind too was singing in the willows and the aspens. It skimmed the river, going against the current and raising thousands of flakes of silver without chipping them off.

When the runabouts rounded the bend which begins above Ampuis, it was a different picture altogether. Farther down, blocking the whole valley, a huge black cloud climbed to the right and wallowed on the flank of the hills, restricting the view to the first strips of sand about the islands.

'Filth!' Christian exclaimed.

The two captains looked at each other, hesitated on the verge of anger for a moment, then burst out laughing simultaneously. Intrigued, the rowers stopped pulling. They paused long enough to turn on their benches and they too burst out laughing.

'She isn't half burning some coal this time, trying to get herself out of that.'

'Let her keep at it. If she goes on like that till my horses come to the rescue, she'll exhaust the mines at Saint-Etienne.'

The steamer was lying slightly athwart. Her bows had been stove in by a gravel bank which must have extended towards midstream a good hundred yards above the island. It was a stretch where the swift current ruffled the surface, so that neither prowman nor helmsman, dazzled by sun and reflections, had been able to see it coming. By the time the sounder had recorded the bank, it must have been too late for so fast and heavy a vessel to be able to avoid it.

As they drew nearer, the smell of coal caught in their throats. They coughed much more than was necessary, cursed, swore, but went on laughing.

The noise also came to meet them. A pounding of connecting-rods shook the metal. The roar of cascading water, shouts, cries, blows of a sledge-hammer. All hell was installed in the heart of the valley.

The smoke was dense, but the wind lifted it quickly enough for visibility on the runabout itself to be perfect. Only wreck and men were in twilight. A moving twilight like that trailed over the earth by the first clouds of a summer storm.

Nevertheless, as soon as they were within hailing distance, Captain Merlin began to shout: 'Steamboat ahoy! Can you hear me?'

'We can hear you.'

'If you want help, stop your machinery!'

Three small fishing-boats were already ranged along the bulwarks. Men and women were clambering down into them, aided by the fishermen and the crew of the steamer. The cockleshells bobbed wildly, shaken by the huge waves churned up by the paddle-wheels. There was barely room for three passengers in each.

'Stop that!' bellowed Joannès.

'They can't stop it,' one of the fishermen shouted. 'Caught like that with their bows crushed in the gravel, if they don't spin their blasted machine backwards, the current'll turn them broadside on and they risk capsizing.'

Christian had brought his runabout forward of the great wheels beside the fishing-boats. The water seethed. It was necessary to keep a sharp look-out for eddies and for the paddle-blades, but it would have been dangerous to halt upstream, for if a clumsy passenger fell into the water while boarding, the giant wheels would crush him at once. Above them, the steamer's whistle gave a long blast.

It was the first time Christian had come near enough to a mechanical vessel to touch it with his hand. It occurred to him that he risked fouling himself as never before in his life, but he was carried away with joy. He was happy that his first contact with the monster should show her immobile, wounded, snorting with helpless rage and spitting like a wildcat in a trap.

The sledge-hammer blows on the ironwork were coming from forward. The mechanics must be trying to patch the rent made in the plates by a rock hidden in the gravel. On the foredeck two sweating men were working a pump from which muddy water poured into the river in waves.

Along the bulwarks everything was black. Men and objects.

'Well, you sweeps,' Christian cried, 'you're sending us some passengers.'

A fat man whom Christian had already seen coming out of the company's offices leaned towards him and demanded: 'Are the horses coming?'

'The horses are going straight on to Beaucaire, my good sir. They're slow; they've got no time to lose.'

'You've no right to refuse help –'

The man said no more. A boatman from Etiévent's barge had seized a large, long-handled baler and had just dashed a bucketful of water full in the man's face.

'How's that for help?'

'Hide your belly, fatso, and let us get on with our work.'

'Come along, ladies, come along. The sluggards are going to take you to the bank.'

Women and children wept, others cried out, all were passed from the hands of the steamer's crew into those of the crew of the barge fleet.

'Don't be scared,' Joannès called, 'we won't drown you. We know how to navigate too.'

'And we won't get you dirty,' Christian carried on. 'We may be slow, but we're clean slow.'

For the time being, the passengers were quiet.

Hampered by their clothes, filthy, encumbered with hand baggage, soaked with sweat and spattered with the foam which the paddle-wheels determinedly threw up, they had no sooner set foot in the runabouts than they were crouching in the bottom, clutching the thwarts or the bulwarks. The boatmen standing on the poop, heedless of the movement, continued their work without pausing in the jokes and laughter.

'Now then, ma, mind you don't get dirty!'

'This runabout is built to take four horses and six men; it'll hold two dozen chimney-sweeps.'

'Our runabouts are going to stink of coal and our horses will refuse to board them.'

The laughter was larded with insults directed at the men on the steamer, who were careful not to reply. They were not in a strong position at present. They no longer bragged.

Standing on the prows of their runabouts, the two captains maintained them in position. When all the passengers were aboard, a woman asked: 'What about our luggage?'

'If you've got any hams in it, they're going to be well smoked.'

'Don't worry, we'll get it, but we're going to have you high and dry first, and get you out of that smoke.'

The captains pushed out to midstream, and, letting themselves be carried by the current, they sailed until they were out of range of the eddies and waves whipped up by the monster's frantic efforts.

'Where shall we land them?' Joannès asked.

Up to then, Christian had been thinking in terms of taking the unfortunate passengers down to Condrieu, the nearest inhabited area downstream, but he had a sudden brainwave which delighted him. Giving Joannès a conspiratorial sign, he made straight for the tip of Tupin island.

'We'll put them ashore there,' he cried, 'and afterwards we'll see. The sun's just at the point when my stomach begins to want food.'

The boatmen began to laugh, while their passengers watched the approach of the shingle beach surmounted by thick scrub, which must have looked to them like the least hospitable of desert islands.

In between villages the banks were wild. They were the haunt of poachers, pirates, all who had something to hide, be it only themselves. It was necessary to know the scrub. It was easy to get lost in it. It was not so vast as a big forest; walking straight ahead, one quickly reached either the river or more civilized parts, but how did one walk straight ahead? It was a jungle. Everything twined, tangled, struggled for a bit of light. Pollard willows, aspens, briars, reeds, bindweed, wild plum, hawthorn and blackthorn. In places there were even vines run wild which climbed high up the poplars. Was it proof that these islands had once been cultivated? Or had the river carried down a seed or a plant torn away farther upstream? The thrushes knew where these vines were to be found. In autumn the red of their leaves showed up among the gold of the poplars.

These islands were wild. A whole tribe stole away there, fled there, lay low there. There were secret duels and clandestine assignations. A world of many facets. Overcrowded, never still. Under the huge roots, the floods had helped the rats to dig their runs. The otter came there when the river level rose. The adder slid more silently than a trickle of water. And then there were the hollows in the mud, the sand which looked perfectly dry, only to cave in when trodden on.

There were tracks, but they crossed and recrossed, twisted, petered out and began again, divided only to end abruptly and turn back on themselves.

And anyone who found the way out on the landward side had still to find a ford which would enable him to cross the river's lesser arm. An arm which was often divided up, meandering, irregular, grassy-bottomed. An arm where drought formed a crust on the surface, leaving the underside viscous, sticky and swarming with leeches and larvae. On this constantly shifting terrain the river had mapped out patterns of flow which it altered from season to season. It lingered there. It explored the undergrowth. It paused beneath the thick vaults of overhanging branches where thousands of mosquitoes and midges hummed.

For anyone unfamiliar with it, it was a jungle which proclaimed that the Rhône was something more than a river flowing seawards, and was not on the verge of being tamed by men.

The raised prows of the two runabouts grated on the gravel banks of the island. Everywhere the beach shelved too gently to allow them to come alongside and the passengers had to wade knee-deep to reach the shore.

Some went into the water with their shoes on; others took them off and carried them. They lurched and staggered, groping for the uneven bottom before putting their feet down. The women shrieked; the men said nothing out of dignity, but they grimaced.

'A little footbath does no harm,' Joannès told them. 'And you're lucky it's a pebble beach. It isn't easy on the feet, but there's no risk of sinking in.'

He took off his own boots for the pleasure of it and jumped into the water. Accustomed to going barefoot, he ran over the pebbles as if he were on a polished floor. He splashed the women, who cried out, gathering up their skirts.

A man wearing a decoration and carrying a fat red leather brief-case said to Christian: 'Aren't you ashamed to inflict such treatment on ladies?'

'Shame or not, it's the regulation.'

'What regulation?'

'I don't have the right to carry passengers who haven't paid their fares.'

'But we will pay whatever is necessary.'

The man's anger made his neck swell. He was small and plump, and his belly was spanned by a huge gold chain hung with diamond ornaments.

'It doesn't work like that. If you're willing to pay, we can take you where you want to go, but not on the runabouts. On the barges. And on condition that you embark at a port, after paying your dues to the harbour master.'

The fat man's double chin shook with rage. Looking down on him from his six foot three, Christian chuckled. Pointing to the chain and the ornaments, he could not resist saying: 'You're ready to pay to avoid getting your feet wet, but at this moment you'd pay a damn sight more to be stronger than I am.'

The fat man's face went even redder. For a moment he seemed about to burst.

'We're sluggards,' Christian went on, 'but we're not yet reduced to poverty. We don't depend on a couple of dozen passengers to make a living. In the old days we could have taken you anywhere free of charge. We've all done it, and done it more than once. All that mattered was that you wanted to go and that the Rhône behaved itself. Now there's a regulation. I didn't want it, nor did the other bargemen, it's the steamer boys. If you want to lose your temper with them...'

Christian's calmness had its effect. Swallowing his anger, the fat man stepped over the bulwark without removing his elegant boots or even rolling up his grey trousers. Without saying a word, hugging his briefcase to his chest, he waded slowly ashore.

There was no one left in Christian's boat except an old woman dressed in black who was sitting on a seat in the stern and leaning against another younger woman who held in her arms an infant a few months old. When Christian turned towards them, the younger woman stood up without saying a word and walked towards the prow to disembark. When she came level with Christian she eyed him coldly, but without hate.

'I'm going to take the baby to the bank. I'll come straight back for my mother.'

Christian lowered his gaze. He gritted his teeth, for something had just knotted itself in his chest. Sullenly, almost brutally, he caught the woman by the arm at the very moment when she was hitching up her skirts to step over the bulwark.

'Go and sit down,' he growled. 'We'll put you ashore at Condrieu.'

The woman straightened up. The baby opened big black eyes. Its lips were thrust out as if for the nipple, and it was blowing bubbles of saliva.

'I thought there was a regulation...'

'Go and sit down,' Christian repeated. 'And don't bother about the rest.'

The young woman still hesitated. Her gaze had not softened and Christian thought she was despising him.

'Come and sit down,' the older woman said. 'Since Monsieur is kind enough to take us . . . Come along, now . . . It's very good of you, sir. Thank you.'

The old woman's voice was gentle, but it seemed to Christian that she was making an effort to master herself. She must have had to pocket a good deal of pride to get out that thank-you. He would have liked to know who she was, whether she or her daughter had cried 'Sluggards' at the moment when the steamer overtook them. He would have liked to know if they were rich.

The young woman returned to the seat in the stern. Christian looked towards the island. The passengers stood on the shore, a pitiful group, and he had to harden himself in order not to call out to them to get back in the boats. He knew the islands well, and he knew they would have to pick their way through a positive jungle of dwarf willows, reeds and brambles before they came to the river's lesser arm which they would have to cross by a muddy-bottomed ford. They had a good two hours' walk ahead of them before they reached Condrieu.

'There must be a path across the island,' Christian called. 'Take that. Beyond it, you come to the road. We'll put your baggage off at Condrieu.'

Having said that, Christian turned back to the river. He could not bear the sight of these people any longer, nor the sound of their distress. If he stayed there another few minutes, he wouldn't be able to hold out. He would shout to them to come back. And what would that make him? A weakling? An idiot who didn't know his own mind? What would the crew of the steamer think of him? That he was acting thus from greed, to persuade the travellers to continue their trip with him? Wouldn't they also think that his behaviour was prompted by fear? Fear of the morrow's poverty which for so long had hung threateningly over those barge-hands who set their face against progress?

Undoubtedly he had good reason for going against the promptings of the good fellow Christian who laboured under the pride of Captain Merlin.

Still splashing gleefully, Joannès Etiévent returned to his runabout. Was Joannès asking himself so many questions? Did the same struggle between Joannès and Captain Etiévent rage in him? What would he say if he saw Christian weaken?

Beneath the black cloud still forming an enormous mushroom and blown towards the vineyards by the wind, the river was dark. But upstream and downstream it shone in the sunlight. Christian saw his barge-train rounding the bend. The prowmen still handled their sounding-rods with sweeping movements. It would take about ten minutes for the first barge to reach the point where the steamer was smoking away. Christian glanced quickly towards the beach. Some passengers had already disappeared down the shady vault of the path. A woman was just setting off, dragging a large basket and followed by two little girls of about ten. At the water's edge men and women were sitting or crouching to put on their shoes again or struggling to wash their faces a little.

'Oh God,' Christian groaned, 'I may be a bastard, but all the same we've got to teach those who laugh at us an occasional lesson.'

He had spoken to himself.

Behind him, his two men had taken up their positions on the thwarts again and were waiting his orders. He still hesitated, then, turning to the other runabout where Joannès was just finishing pulling on his boots, he asked: 'Joannès, are you going back up straight away?'

'No, I'm only going as far as the tip of the first island. Once there, I'm going to tie up in the shade. I'd like to see how that bastard's going to get his filthy stew-pot out of this.'

'In that case, if he gets horses for towing, try and find out who they belong to.'

'Trust me. Anyone who'll do that can be sure I won't fail to have a little surprise in store for him.'

The bargemen laughed, but their laughter no longer gave Christian the happiness he had felt on the way down from Vienne. Something was urging him to get away as fast as possible from this shore where the last of the passengers were preparing to set out along the path.

'That's good!' he exclaimed. 'I don't want to lose any time. I'll make for Condrieu to have them prepare what I'm to take on board. We'll eat before going on. When my lad passes, tell him to let the barge-train go on down to join me and to stop here himself to take on the baggage.'

He pushed on his long oar. The shingle hissed beneath the metal and the runabout's prow drew away from the bank and headed for the mainstream. The rowers were already pulling on their oars. Christian could leave them to manœuvre on their own, nothing was really urgent. But before laying down his oar and taking up position on the thwart in the bows, beside the anchor, he shouted again to Joannès: 'The baggage on'y, mind! Tell him straight out: no merchandise.'

'Trust me. And may Saint Nicholas drive you downstream and tow you upstream as vigorously as I'm cursing the crew of the steamer.'

Raising their hats, they gave each other a friendly salute, then Christian sank heavily on to the thwart. Something indefinable was weighing on his neck and tightening his throat.

PART TWO

The Noonday Sun

At Condrieu the Rhône is just six miles long. Except that it flows, it could be taken for a lake. But flow it does. It emerges from beneath the hills of Chonas and Saint-Prim, to disappear again beneath Saint-Michel. It has a brief existence. It performs an almighty conjuring trick and disappears. At least, that is the impression given by its great Z-bend, with one angle upstream and the other downstream. To get a better view, it is necessary to climb the hillside a bit, among the stony fields and the vines planted between small retaining stone walls. There are places where the whole hillside is terraced. Like a Roman theatre with graduated seats for spectators to watch the river flow.

But the vinegrowers have no time to stand and stare. The river is there only to bear the wine away. It is there for boats, for boatmen, fishermen.

And also as a source of anxiety.

Not the worry of floods. It was quite usual for the river to spread over the low-lying land every time it swelled with rage. It did damage, but it also brought down silt.

The anxiety was connected with the river all right, but there was good reason for it.

Some men had already left the district. Others were preparing to do so. Others, who wanted to hang on, had to change their occupation, sell a fine house in order to live in a couple of rooms. To lodge there with their family and their sorrow. Proud men who now hid themselves as if they had committed a crime or contracted a loathsome disease.

Those who remembered the cholera said the valley smelt the same as before the epidemic. They said 'the same' because there were certain words they dared not use. And when they said 'smell', they were not talking of an odour, but of something which could not be seen, touched or defined. An uneasiness. A sort of mystery which snuffed out joy.

People got on one another's nerves. One minute they were mak-

ing themselves depressed, the next they were trying to be strong
and silent.

'We've seen others. Haven't we been deafened with talk about
tow-boats? And what's become of them? Nothing. So much scrap
iron! And their chain rusting on the river bed.'

'It's a long time since the river piled gravel on the chain they'd
run along the bottom so that their tow-boats could hook on to the
links on the upstream journey.'

'You must admit it was like nothing on earth – a boat on the end
of a chain.'

'And what do you think their paddle-boats are like?'

'All the same, they're beginning to go pretty well. And regularly.
And always fully booked.'

'If you think the river can be mastered ...'

'Are you by any chance reckoning that progress can be halted?'

They had not even tried to halt this progress which was causing
them so much anxiety. They endured it. And because it was not
possible to spend one's whole life plunged in gloom without
running the risk of doing something stupid, they clung to everything that went on just as before. So when a barge-train stopped on
its way up or downstream, there was always a celebration. Only
six or eight years ago the traffic was such that the port was often
too small. Stable barges, savoyards, barges of all kinds lay alongside
the quay three or even four abreast. When it was time to leave,
everyone hauled on the ropes to move those barges which were
hindering their departure. The women lent a hand; so did the
children, more hindrance than help, but they were allowed to
swarm round because it was good for the youngsters to get
acquainted with a river worker's toil.

It was a good life. The inns always full. The rope-makers never
able to twist enough cable for those blasted boatmen who needed
such miles of it.

At the port and in the narrow streets there was a kind of perpetual swarming of life, as well as on the highway where the carts
hustled to provision or unload the barges. The merchandise came
from all quarters and was bound for all the points of the compass.

Towards the Alps via Les Roches, and towards the mountains of Central France.

The river aroused fear when it was swollen and came growling at the threshold, and now it was the low water that men cursed. It was no longer the river which aroused fear, but what it carried, when she passed spewing blackness. Each time a barge tied up there was the fear of hearing the captain announce that he was making his last trip downstream. That he had already sold his outfit at Beaucaire. Barges, horses and everything on board. Already files of barge-hands had travelled slowly upstream along the river bank.

And whenever the line neared a village, a man would break away from it. 'I'm from here,' he'd announce. 'I'm stopping off.'

The others didn't even ask him how he was going to stay alive and feed his family. No one knew. No one would have known how to reply. Find something to do which was not too far removed from the river . . . But something which, so far as possible, had nothing to do with steam.

It was past noon when Captain Merlin's runabout passed the embankment around the first island upstream from the port. And at once Captain Merlin realized that news of the accident to the *Triomphant* had preceded him. The whole of Condrieu had turned out, and no doubt a good many people from surrounding villages as well. There were as many people as for a fine Saint Nicholas's Day or a big jousting feast. They waited crowded on the quay and on the river banks, perched on the low walls in front of the houses, sitting or standing in the fishing-boats and on the passenger landing-stages. When the runabout appeared a great shout went up, only to die away as it came towards him, like a wave travelling against the current. Even though it was impossible to hear from the boat, Captain Merlin knew that the people were questioning one another in low voices. They had seen the two women and the child in the bottom of the runabout. And their attention was fixed on these three far more than on Christian and his two men.

The boatmen had stopped rowing, and the runabout, moving

forward under the impetus, was approaching the port. Christian stood up and plunged his master blade in to reduce the trajectory and come alongside the upstream landing-stage. He manœuvred by instinct, continuing to scan the faces of all these people who had shouted so loudly and now were silent. Disconcerted at first, Christian thought: It's just as if I'd promised them a cargo of gold and was bringing them pebbles.

He was coming in to the landing-stage when he recognized Adrien Baron, one of the fishermen who had been standing by the stricken steamer when the runabouts arrived. Christian realized very quickly what had happened. Adrien had taken only two people in his little boat. When Christian had decided to put the passengers ashore on the island, Adrien had laughed, like the boatmen. He had set down his two passengers, and then, without waiting for the runabouts, he had rowed as fast as he could to bring the news to the port.

That was undoubtedly what had happened. He heard Adrien recounting the story, saying: 'Christian played the damnedest trick on 'em. Put 'em all ashore on the island. Even the fine ladies with their skirts.'

And all these people had been rejoicing quite as much over the trick played on the passengers as over the accident to the fiery monster.

While the runabout was coming downstream, Christian had tried on several occasions to take a look at the women, but each time the hard, proud, slightly mocking gaze of the younger woman had compelled him to lower his eyes. He felt a fierce, heavy anger against himself. He did not really regret having repaid the passengers for the insults heaped on him when the still proud steamer overtook his barge. No, he did not regret it, but he was a bit ashamed that he had not been able to think of anything else to do.

Christian had just laid down his oar and grasped the mooring-chain. On the landing-stage the people parted to allow him to jump ashore. Christian jumped, attached the chain to the grating in the landing-stage hatch, and straightened up, telling his men: 'Get the women out.'

When he turned round, Adrien too had just set foot on the landing-stage. He looked fixedly towards the runabout, then said with an infuriating little laugh: 'So that one was too pretty. You didn't want to let her get her feet messed up in the scrub.'

He had barely finished his sentence when Christian's great fist connected with his jaw. His head jerked to the left and the rest of him followed. His right arm sought for something to cling to. Off balance, he was about to fall against the barge's bulwark, but some men rushed forward. Four hands seized him. Half stupefied, he gasped: 'Bastard!'

And a trickle of blood ran down from his mouth. A murmur started up in the front ranks and ran through the crowd. Those who hadn't seen anything asked questions. The others answered without turning round, anxious not to miss anything of what was going to happen.

Christian heard several voices addressing him.

'Are you out of your mind, Christian?'

'What's up?'

'He didn't insult you, did he?'

He did not even try to find out who was talking to him. Teeth clenched, staring straight ahead, he walked towards the crowd which parted before him.

You behaved very badly to those people you put ashore on the island. You get here, and that wretched Adrien who's not over-bright and who'd thought to please you by summoning the whole village makes a trifling remark to you and you teach him a lesson. You practically knock him out, yet you know very well he's not as strong as you are. His health isn't good. His father was a friend of yours; you went to school together; he died of a fever a couple of years back. You're angry with yourself so you vent your anger on that poor devil. And it isn't the first time you've taken it out on others when you've been angry with yourself.

He was telling himself this as he continued to lengthen his stride, thinking:

Christian, at Lyons last month you dismissed two of your men for fighting without good cause. And what have you just done? Go

back to the landing-stage. Go and ask Adrien Baron's pardon . . .
You ought to have helped those two women out of the boat yourself. Aren't all those people going to laugh at them?

He had walked through the ranks of onlookers without a word
to anyone, without even recognizing a single face. He reached the
corner, turned into the street that led from the harbour, and
quickened his pace. The sun struck slantingly between the grey
stone walls and the house-fronts with their half-closed shutters.

It was midday, yet the houses were empty. Everyone was down at
the port because the arrival of a barge-train had been announced.
For weeks nothing had gone up- or down-stream, so it was very
natural that the first-comers should be fêted even more than usual.
Christian knew all that. And he knew too that his attitude risked
spoiling the happiness of a whole village. Spoiling his men's meal
and the all-too-brief moment of relaxation they could allow themselves in port.

He was going to spoil everything by his anger; he was going to
rob himself of happiness, he knew, yet he continued to walk
unseeing, teeth and fists clenched, through this village which lay
supine under the sun.

In the villages the boatmen had been masters for centuries. They
lived in the best houses. They took on their crews when and where
they chose. They provided work. They provided bread. They were
respected. Admired. They were the richest, the strongest, the best
able to read, write and reckon.

They themselves did not know for how many generations they
had been barge-masters. It went back far beyond the earliest registers. The registers were carefully preserved. Everything was noted
in them. Every consignment loaded, the name of the consignee,
the recipient, and the amount due for carriage. The handwriting
varied from volume to volume because the clerks who kept the
accounts were not eternal, but the captain's name at the top of the
page was always the same. His first name was not recorded, so that,
looking at these entries, one had the impression that Merlin, or
Cuminal, or Bonnet, or Marthouret, or Barillot had gone on living

for centuries. They were the most envied and respected in the valley, because they made it live and also because everyone knew that to have got where they were, they had had to battle ceaselessly with the river, lose everything and start again from scratch several times. Ruined by the Rhône when a flood destroyed a train of barges and drowned the horses, they asked help from the Rhône to begin afresh. They were too proud for self-pity. When ruined, they began again with one or two barges. They had a name for them which was known from Lyons to Beaucaire. They had confidence. They had courage and a knowledge of the river which drew more on racial instinct than on lore which could be handed down.

Their calling was mastery. Knowing how to be superior. Stronger physically than others, more intelligent, richer too, because it was the barge-master with the best outfit who did best. To dominate other captains, dominate their own crews, above all, to know how to dominate the river.

Such a calling needed strength, but it also needed pride. A high and mighty pride.

The door was wide open to the street. Christian entered the big, rather gloomy room. He took three steps forward and stopped in front of the long table whose vast oak surface shone. Everything was neat, and clean, the benches shining also, the armchair in the background, the hearth where two logs were burning under a small iron stew-pot. There was the smell of burning wood, and the smell of soup with vegetables and bacon. A little steam was escaping between the lid and the rim of the stew-pot. It mingled with the grey woodsmoke and went almost straight up, drawn by the chimney's regular draught. On the dresser were four red-glazed earthenware pots, each with a white spot on its round belly which was the reflection of the rectangle of light which the open door cast on the pine floor.

It was almost cool.

Christian hesitated a moment. That quick march through the sunlit streets had made him hot. Something else had made him hot too. He crossed the room and opened the cupboard, lit only by the two heart shapes cut out of the wood of the doors. From the ceiling with its great incurved beams he took down a pewter jug which he filled from the barrel.

At once the cupboard was filled with the scent of new wine. Christian carried the jug to the kitchen table, took a glass from the bottom of the dresser whose door had always squeaked, filled it brim full, and drained it at a gulp, standing jug in hand. Directly he had finished, he filled the glass again, put it on the table and sat astride the bench. A little hunched, one elbow on the table, he gazed towards the door.

The raw light entered into him. It burnt him a little, but he went on sitting there, eyes half closed, incapable of movement.

He had walked very fast, as though there were someone waiting for him here to deal urgently with a matter of transport, and now he felt drained.

Without hurrying, he drank his second glass in three gulps.

He had fled the port, where his barge-train was due to arrive. It was not unusual. Such an easy mooring was child's play for his son and his men. A barge-master sometimes had business to transact which obliged him to entrust command of a manœuvre to his head prowman and his second-in-command.

'No one will be surprised.'

Christian jumped. He had spoken aloud, and in the silence of the room his voice rang oddly. He raised his head, removed his hat which he placed on the bench in front of him, and wiped his forearm over his sweaty brow. A cloud of flies rose and fell between the door and the table. From time to time one fly broke away, perched on the table, walked, stopped, shook its wings, then flew off in the direction of the green globe of the big copper suspension lamp which hung down at the height of a man in the middle of the table.

In the silence there was a scratching of claws against the shutter, which banged lightly against the wall. The cat had jumped down from the loft. Christian knew even before he saw her come in. The black-and-white creature crossed the threshold, rubbing her flank

against the door-jamb. She took a few very slow steps forward,
sniffing the air and looking to right and left with her wide eyes
which shone green in the half-light. Then, at a trot, she came
straight to Christian and jumped on to the bench between him and
his hat. Her belly was distended. Christian ran his hand over her
back and flanks, warm from the sun, then felt her belly.

'You little whore, you're pregnant again. And you went to the
loft to seek out a corner where you could have 'em, eh? You've no
sooner had one lot than you're at it again, aren't you? You whore
... you little whore.'

The cat had rested her front paws on Christian's thigh and thrust
her ever-twitching pink nose towards his face. She was purring, and
Christian's voice talking to her gently was like a big purr of
friendship.

'We'll have to drown your kits again ... And you'll yowl all over
the place for a day or two. Make a bit too much fuss about it, don't
you, eh? Don't you?'

He spoke gently and it did him good. His anger was still there,
he knew, but he forced himself to concentrate all his attention on
the cat, repeating softly his affectionate reproaches.

He stayed there, not touching his glass, not raising his head, until
the moment when the sound of wooden-soled shoes approached,
ringing out in the dry street. As soon as he heard it, Christian
recognized it. He knew at once what he had been waiting for. What
he most hoped for and feared.

His father's footstep was still distant. It sounded natural, no more
hurried than usual. Christian drained his glass, got up, and stood
an instant undecided, stationed beside the bench where the cat was
washing herself, one front leg in the air, the other resting on the
wood beside the hat.

Christian breathed deeply. His glance went from the bench to the
table, from the table to the hearth, and there stopped. On the
border of smoke-blackened stone a barge cross stood. A cross
carved by his grandfather. In a low voice, Christian muttered
quickly:

'Lord Jesus, who resisted hatred, don't let that evil temper which lurks in me and which I don't always have the strength to control, come over me again.'

There were crosses on the barges and in every house where a barge family lived. Every deck-boy, team-driver, blacksmith, barge-hand and captain carved at least one in his lifetime, which he brought on board or left to protect his family. These were little crosses that could easily be placed inside a big lantern. They were less elaborate than the large ones, but to be true barge crosses they had to bear at least the Holy Face crowned with thorns and placed where the two arms crossed, the Sacred Heart, the scarlet robe, the hammer and nails, the sponge, the lance, the dove, the cock crowing day-break, and a pair of oars. One or two of the small crosses, carved by men who were particularly skilful, bore as much as the big ones. That is, they bore in addition the gaming dice, the purse with the thirty pieces of silver, keys, barge lanterns, a little keg or a straw-covered flask, the sun and moon, the chalice, a ciborium with consecrated Hosts, the hand, sword and scourge, the ladder, the skull and crossbones, the vernicle. The most patient sometimes carved the characters of the Passion at the foot.

There were certain items which had to go on, and then, once tradition had been observed, everyone worked according to his taste, character, ingenuity and talent. The blacksmiths added a horseshoe and nails, the carpenters a square or an adze.

The big crosses, sometimes more than three feet high, were not made by just anyone. They were designed to be erected on the prow of the master barge, and they were carved by the barge-masters. When a barge-master sold his barge or demolished it, he took his cross on board his new one. When an old man handed over a barge-train to his son, he also handed over his barge cross. And when the son had carved his captain's cross, his father's was retired in its turn. It was nailed up on the wall of the house, in the shelter of the eaves, or on the living-room wall.

The curés blessed the crosses, but this was of no great significance, since there was the river which was one vast living stoup of holy water. A good handful of river water was sprinkled over the cross as soon as the red, blue, white and gold paint on it was dry. And in the eyes of all true boatmen, that was the most effective blessing.

It was not the sign of any particular piety, for the river men were very much like all others: some of them were believers, others believed only in themselves. But they all had a healthy respect for the river. The most devout addressed themselves to Jesus, the Virgin and Saint Nicholas when they prayed, but over and above these it was the river which they recognized. For them, the river was the most awesome and the most generous, for their ruin or riches depended on its moods.

But the crosses which were so lovingly preserved in families were there mainly to show that they were barge families. They liked to have them on show, and if they derived a little glory from them, it never occurred to anyone that this might be the sin of pride. They had paid enough for all they possessed in sweat and toil, anguish and suffering, to feel that they had a right to pride without the fear that it would cause one of the wounds of him whose image was carved on the cross to bleed again. Such a thought never entered their heads. And because, without being particularly devout, they were in the habit of asking the Virgin or Saint Nicholas aloud every morning to give them a satisfactory day, they prayed willingly when they felt themselves to be in difficulties.

When his father came in, Christian was standing by the table, facing the door.

'Hallo, Father,' he said.

The old man came as far as the end of the table and took off his hat, which he placed on the bench where his son's was already lying. The cat stopped washing herself, twitched her nose in the direction of the table, hesitated an instant, then jumped down from the bench and sauntered out.

Christian saw it all without really taking it in. Silence hung heavy. Warmth from the street came in.

Old Merlin was the same build as his son. The years had not bowed him, but they had dried him. His velvet waistcoat was much too big for his body, which was all bones and tendons. His sunburnt neck issued from the over-large collar of his white shirt like a worn tow-rope stiffened by rain. But the rope was alive. An inner strength animated it. Its muscles brought those of the face into play, and his beard, still black, in which a few white hairs glinted, seemed to be inhabited by an ill wind. He looked Christian in the eye and his gaze did not falter.

Christian realized that his father was grappling with a rage that must have been burning him up all the way back to the house.

At last the old man breathed more evenly. His beard still bristled and his lips trembled a little, revealing his three remaining stumps of teeth.

'Is it customary for a captain to quit the port before his rig arrives, unless he has urgent business to transact?'

His voice scarcely shook. It was strong, hard, but his anger was well in hand.

'I wanted to see you,' Christian said.

'You want to see me and you walk right past me without so much as a glance.'

'I didn't see you in all that crowd.'

'You didn't see anyone. I know. But everyone saw you. And you weren't a pretty sight.'

The father had raised his voice. He fell silent, and Christian sensed that he was still struggling with his emotions. He was relieved to see him lower his gaze at last as far as the table. Picking up his son's glass, the old man filled it, took a couple of swigs, pushed out the bench and sank down upon it.

'Sit down,' he said. 'No sense getting carried away.'

Before complying, Christian went to fetch another glass. When he returned to the table, his father had taken out a thick, short pipe and a pig's bladder containing his tobacco. His left hand cradled the bowl, and his thin, spatulate right forefinger was tamping down the tobacco. His hands were shaking slightly. When he had lit his pipe and taken three puffs at it, he pushed the pouch towards Christian, who felt for his own pipe. While he was feeding in the tobacco, the old man chuckled.

'Your hands are shaking too,' he observed, 'but in your case it

isn't from age. It's because you're in a temper. And because I know
you so well, I can tell you it's yourself you're furious with.'

'Listen, Father –'

'No, let me speak. You're in a temper. And I know you so well
because I used to be exactly the same. Thanks to my age, I'm done
with all that. Otherwise, when I came in here I'd have knocked you
down just as you knocked down that poor devil Adrien. He
couldn't do anything because you were stronger than he was. You
wouldn't have been able to do anything because I'm your father.'

'But look here, Father –'

Christian tried to interrupt the old man, yet if the old man had
let him speak he would probably not have made sense.

'I know you so well that I'm going to tell you what you're
thinking at this moment. You're thinking: I cleared out because all
those people were making me feel uncomfortable. I preferred to
clear out after what I'd done. But I've chalked up one more success.
The others respect me. They'd have looked at me askance, but
they'd have left me in peace. The old man's another matter. He'll
go on about it for a good hour . . . That's what you're thinking.
Here and now. Filling your pipe and glancing at me like a sly dog.
That's what you're thinking! I know. And I know you won't dare
pretend otherwise. Well? Am I right?'

As the father continued speaking, his voice had changed. From
barely controlled anger he had turned to mockery, and by the end
he gave the impression of a man who would enjoy a good laugh.

Christian looked up. Their eyes met, and across the table where
the light shone through the wine shaken in the glasses, there was
something akin to an embrace. At the same time, they both burst
out laughing.

The old man coughed, and leaned to the left to spit a long jet of
saliva into the hearth; it hissed on the glowing coals. Then, wiping
the back of his hand across his mouth, he said: 'God, it's curious
how things work out. I was angry on the way up from the port. I
forced myself to walk when what I wanted to do was run. I walked.
And all the way I kept saying to myself: That snivelling Christian,
I'm going to belt him one, a real good 'un, one he won't forget.

Never mind him being forty-five, he's going to listen to me. All the way here I kept telling myself that. And I got here. And there you were, like a fool. And I saw your empty glass and I said to myself: He's like you, anger makes his throat dry. And I still wanted to belt you one. And I looked at you. And I said to myself again: Félix, at his age you were the same. Today you're seventy-two, but at forty-five you'd have acted just the same as he has.'

The old man stopped talking. He took a swig. Christian, watching him, suddenly began to laugh.

'What's the matter?' the old man demanded.

'I was thinking of what else I had to tell you.'

'Ah!'

Christian explained how he had reached his decision to leave Lyons. He mentioned M. Tonnerieu and his warning.

'You did well to leave,' the old man said. 'It's not exactly what you'd call full flood but you've got down to here; you'll manage the rest of the journey downstream. Only I don't see what you find to laugh at in all this.'

Yet Christian began laughing again even as he explained.

'Yes, there is. After what you've just said to me. I can't help laughing. For more than forty years I've heard you tell me: "Whenever you're in difficulties, lad, you've only got to say to yourself, 'What would the old man have done in my place?' And then do it. And it'll always be all right."'

'You rogue, do you want to end up as cunning as I am?'

'No fear! And I'm not saying I asked myself that question before I hit Adrien, but it would have been all the same if I had.'

The father had another little laugh which broke off short. His face became grave. The lines which laughter had etched on his forehead and round his dark eyes deepened still further. He took three short pulls at his pipe, then, leaning towards his son, he said in a voice which no longer shook with anger but quavered a little:

'You're lucky you can still ask yourself such a question, lucky you're still afloat. But look, lad, I too ask myself a few questions. Not the same ones. And I never know if the river is going to give me an answer. Sometimes I'm even afraid it might.'

In front of the door the wind set a bit of sand as fine as dust racing over the flagstones. The sand sparkled, but the wind did not sing. Between the two men, the light stretched out across the table, where the glasses had left damp rings.

The father turned his head. As he looked towards the street his face caught the light, and Christian saw that his gaze was moister than usual. The cat returned to sit on the doorstep. The old man smiled and said: 'When I came in, she went out. I thought: she scents a storm, she prefers to make herself scarce. And you must surely have thought the same.'

'Perhaps, but she knows the storm isn't going to break at present.'

'It would be stupid to row between ourselves over things that aren't worth it.'

Christian realized that his father had something important to say to him, but he dared not ask what it was.

The old man waited a moment longer, gazing blindly into the light, then, turning back to his son, he made up his mind.

'I never thought steamers would come to anything. Not with the river as it is. There are too many accidents. But they're going to change the river.'

'Change the river? They'll need to be strong.'

'They are.'

'Not that strong.'

'They're stronger than you think. Or rather, yes. We do think. But up to now we've deceived ourselves so as not to recognize it.'

'But change the river...'

Without raising his voice, the old man interrupted. 'Look here,' he said. 'And then, like me, you'll be forced to understand.'

Picking up his glass, he poured a little wine on to the table. He dipped his forefinger in it and then drew a curve on the wood, followed by another in the opposite direction. His raised hand returned to the pool of wine and his forefinger dipped in afresh to trace a line parallel to the first one. Still without saying a word, he drew short lines running at an angle between the two curves. Christian watched. He had realized that the two lines represented the banks of the river, but beyond that he did not see what his father was getting at.

The old man took time to relight his pipe, then, indicating the little lines, he explained: 'These are stone dykes. They run out from the bank at the point of maximum curve. They're at an angle to the direction of the current. The current sweeps down and is checked by them and swung against the opposite bank, on the inner side of the curve where there's nothing but a rocky embankment to prevent erosion. So far, so good. Then the current swings towards the next curve, is checked by the other lot of dykes, and it's the same story over again. And within the straight lines there are dykes on both banks.'

Christian began to understand. He too knew the force of the current. His throat contracted as the old man's explanation went on. Nevertheless, he demanded: 'And what then?'

'Then? Well, they're going to do that from Lyons down to Beaucaire. And the Rhône will hollow out its own channel . . . all by itself, by the force of the current. No more need for dredging. But with the dykes and the embankments it'll be necessary to sail in midstream all the time. And where are your horses going to go? And what about your tow-ropes? And what's going to happen to the towpath in the midst of all that?'

His voice, which had been growing shrill, cracked. He could only growl: 'Ruined. It'll all be ruined.'

Christian stiffened. He cleared his throat and snapped: 'But what's all this nonsense about?'

'Not nonsense. A project.'

The old man had difficulty in speaking. However, after he had drunk a last half-glass of wine, he explained that men had come to the river banks. He had got them talking and had seen their plans.

'But it'll never happen,' Christian growled.

'It won't happen overnight. I shan't see it, that's for sure, but you . . . I'm very much afraid your son will never be captain of a rig.'

For a long moment the two men stayed silent, their eyes fixed on the table where the wine marks were gradually drying. The gleam was going, but once they were dry the lines would show up dully on the polished wood. From time to time Félix sighed, grunted, cleared his throat, shifted on the bench a little without taking his elbows off the table.

Christian sat motionless. He was not really thinking. He was staring at the wood. He kept telling himself that they were going to try and kill his river, and that was all. A great emptiness was spreading within him. Without moving his head, he raised his eyes at intervals to his father's face. The old man's lips moved, but did not open. His beard moved. His throat moved. All his wrinkles continued to live, but his hard eyes were fixed.

After a long, long moment the old man got up to knock out his pipe on the head of an andiron. He lifted the lid of the stew-pot and the room was filled with a strong smell of soup.

'Your sister put it on to cook for midday, but she's sure to want to stay down by the Rhône to make the most of Claude's company.'

He came back to stand in front of Christian. He stood very straight, legs apart, as once on his master barge. He swung three times from one foot to the other, then, straining his voice to make it sound untroubled, he exclaimed: 'I'll be damned if I'm going to eat soup that hasn't even finished cooking all by myself here, like a savage. Your Canut must have made a stew. He'll give me a bit of that.'

He paused, then, when his son did not budge, he went on, trying this time to recapture the tones of anger: 'Shit! The Rhône's still the Rhône. The port hasn't seen an outfit for weeks, and now that one's put in for once, we're not going to let it spoil our pleasure just because it's captained by a rogue. Here's the whole place wild with joy. Everyone's saying, "The good life's starting up again." And on top of a rig going downstream, a steamer's run aground. And the whole town wants to celebrate that. So what? Are we going to miss out on the fun just because one fool's knocked another fool down? Not on your life! We don't get the chance that often. If your poor mother was here and if your wife hadn't died of the August fever, you'd have seen the pair of them hitching up their skirts to run down to the port. And if we two hang about here, we're not going to get down there until those guzzlers have cleaned out Canut's stew-pot.'

Christian had risen slowly to his feet. The old man went on talking, endlessly repeating himself. He evidently needed to talk in order to appear detached, to appear like someone with no thought for the morrow, whose only desire is to spend an hour today in eating, drinking and making merry.

When they were out in the street, each having picked up his hat and relit his pipe, the old man still went on talking.

Gradually he worked round again to what was weighing so heavily upon the future, but – perhaps because they were walking in the sunlight, perhaps because of the clear sound of their wooden soles ringing out on the cobblestones between the burning walls – he spoke impersonally, without allowing anguish to show through.

'You're going to think, listening to me,' he concluded, 'that the old man doesn't give a damn. He knows he's got enough to last his lifetime and that he won't see what's coming. Well, you're wrong. I worry about the young folks more than you can imagine. And I ask myself a question. I say to myself: All right, they're going to fight back. Quite right. Is it? Are you sure? Those of your age, yes, of course. You'll go on to the end. But your Claude, for instance, and the others of his age. Wouldn't the wisest thing be for them to try to get out while they're still adaptable enough to turn to something else?'

Christian stopped in his tracks. The old man went on a couple of paces, then stopped too and turned towards him. They eyed each other for a moment, and Christian asked: 'Steam?'

The word cracked out like a whiplash. All the old man's wrinkles hesitated between rage and laughter, but laughter won.

'If my name were Adrien,' he said, 'I should get another on the chin.'

Christian walked on. He didn't really want to laugh. He wanted a clear-cut answer. His father must have understood, for his face turned serious again. He shook his head. His thin shoulders shrugged abruptly, then he turned round to resume his walk, saying:

'Steam really sets your head spinning. Things can't go round any faster in the steamer's boilers than they do in your thick skull. God in Heaven, anyone would think there are only two things on earth: your rig and steam.'

'On earth, no. But on the river there are only those two. And Claude's like us. He's a river man.'

'So were others. They've pulled out. I don't say they're happy, but they make a living.'

The old man said the last words very low, as if to himself. After which, he gestured with his hand to indicate that he knew nothing more about it.

And they continued their walk through the deserted streets in silence, towards the murmur which rose up from the port like a surge of happy life.

As soon as he emerged on the esplanade, bordered on one side by plane-trees and on the other by the port, Christian realized that knocking the fisherman down had not cast a shadow for long over the reunion of his men and their families. Everything was *en fête*. At trestle-tables hastily erected under the trees, on benches, on the ground, under the awnings of the barges, there was eating, drinking, laughter. As always, the food brought by the boatmen's wives and friends had been added to the meal prepared by the two cooks on board. Everything was shared, and everyone helped himself, listening or talking with his mouth full as he gobbled. There was a great deal to say and not much time to say it in.

The first to see Christian hailed his arrival, and his progress through the noise of the happy crowd was marked by a long backwash of murmuring. In spite of himself, Christian slowed down, half hiding behind his father. At once, a picture came back to him. He was a small boy again. His father was away on the river, and it was his mother who was walking beside him, taking him back to school where, only that morning, he had been punished.

When they reached the first groups, the old man raised his head, pushed his hat back, and cried: 'Well, you pack of starving jackals, have you left a bit for the old man?'

There were shouts, laughter, every table clamoured for Félix. He took a few steps forward, then asked: 'Where's Adrien Baron?'

A score of voices answered: 'Over there.'

'Under the last plane-tree.'

'His wife had cooked a couple of pike. He gave them to the people who were in your son's runabout.'

'And his wife brought some milk for the child.'

'And some pears.'

'And they're eating at the same table.'

Old Félix said: 'Good. Just now he said a damnfool thing to a fool. That can only lead to further folly.'

The people around him began to laugh, and the joke went from one group to another, raising a gale of laughter every time it was repeated.

When the joke got as far as the last plane-tree, Christian saw Adrien get up and come weaving towards them through the crowd. He went to meet him. Adrien was smiling, thrusting back with the flat of his hand those who accosted him as he passed.

When the two men came face to face, the clamour redoubled.

'Have a joust, take up your stances.'

'No, a swimming match.'

'Bite him, Adrien!'

'Into the Rhône with him, Christian!'

The two men clasped hands for a long moment, then, seizing Adrien under the armpits, Christian lifted him as if he were a child to embrace him, saying: 'I was overwrought, don't hold it against me.'

'I said something stupid,' Adrien replied. 'You were right to knock me down.'

Applause spread like a brush-fire in August. One or two voices shouted:

'Mind you don't put him in the family way!'

'When's the wedding?'

And there was more laughter, which old Félix quelled with a

gesture. When there was silence, the old man raised his voice as when he used to give orders to his barge-train, and shouted: 'It's not a laughing-matter. We need two or three big wagons harnessed to go and meet the stranded passengers. It'll take them a good hour to get here on foot, and Christian tells me he can't wait that long to take on those who want to continue the downstream journey with him.'

There was a murmuring, sporadic hand-clapping, and Christian sensed that many people were discussing his father's idea. Personally, he felt soothed. His father had not told him of his intention, he had not even asked him what he was reckoning to do, but he had undoubtedly guessed what was going through his mind. He said: 'Thanks, Father. I'll go with the wagons.'

'Of course you'll go. And go first.'

Half a dozen men had got up and come towards them. Christian surveyed them. He singled out three of them with his forefinger and said: 'I'll take Norbert, Etienne and Henri. They live nearest, so it'll save time.'

The old man had just sat down near his grandson, and already he was being served with a heaped plate of sailors' stew which gave out a strong smell of oil and garlic beneath the plane-trees. Before joining the three men who were going off with their mouths full, Christian leaned over a table, filled a glass and drained it at a gulp, tore off in his huge hand a good quarter of a loaf, and placed a whole pork pâté on top of it, together with some goatsmilk cheese.

'It's always the same story,' he said. 'With wild beasts like these, you can't count on anything being left over.'

Condrieu had always been the centre of barge traffic. Without anything being known of its origins, it was said to be the cradle of the race and no one disputed it. Many in this village thought the river belonged to them.

Shipwrights, horse-breeders, blacksmiths, inn-keepers, fishermen, all made their living by the river. Sometimes they died by it. Apart from shipwrecks, accidents, drowning, there was also August fever, malaria, Malta fever, and all those diseases caused by water and lumped under the general heading 'fever'. It was not the lovely, limpid waters of the Rhône which bore disease germs, but everything which defiled its banks. The lagoons and the secret recesses of the scrubland harboured clouds of midges and mosquitoes, which transmitted disease. The inhabitants had asked for drainage, but their health had a low place on the list of governmental responsibilities. Consequently, every time the season favoured the development of vermin, the river folk saw their weakest members carried off by epidemics. And perhaps this helped to strengthen the breed, for only those who were stronger than the fevers survived.

It must be said that the boatmen were seldom affected. It may have been the river, as they claimed, which preserved them, but it may also have been because they never drank a drop of water.

In the evenings, or on sultry, overcast days, these men could sail stripped to the waist, their bodies covered in mosquitoes, without suffering in the least. It was one of the things they were proud of. For their horses were less robust than they were, since it often happened that a barge-train lost half its animals in the course of a few weeks, simply through the effect of these fevers.

There was talk of starting the long-desired drainage scheme. But now the river folk no longer wanted it, for it would be part and parcel of works whose main purpose was to aid steam navigation.

They preferred to do battle with the river and the fevers, rather than allow themselves to be swallowed up by the faceless monster of the big companies.

The wagons had met the long straggle of shipwrecked passengers on the high road, some two miles from the village. They were tired and dusty, sweating, their feet twisting on stones and on the rock-hard ruts; there was no need to tell them to clamber aboard. Only the fat man who had insulted Christian was missing, and the others explained that he had gone off in the direction of Ampuis, where he was hoping to find a carriage. He had also announced his intention of stopping at the gendarmerie to make a charge against Christian. One of the passengers who was a lawyer said that the charge certainly could not be substantiated, and Christian answered: 'Substantiated or not, I've got that bladder of lard where it hurts!'

When the wagons reached the port, Canut, Caillette, Christian's sister and some of the local women had set a table where the passengers could eat. The men were finishing loading the merchandise to be shipped, which had been waiting weeks for the first rig to pass. To avoid losing time, the harbour master and M. Tonnerieu went from one to another while the people were eating, taking down the names of those who wanted to go on downstream and collecting the price of the passage. Everyone wanted to come aboard. Every single one.

Old Félix also went from one to another. He had drunk more than usual and was loquacious in consequence. With sparkling eye, jutting beard, his black felt hat pushed to the back of his head to reveal hair almost as dark as his beard, he was in full spate, recalling that for more than ten years he had been the best jouster in the whole valley. The strangers studied this man from an unknown world, and the locals who had heard him tell the same story a hundred times listened without missing one word of his discourse.

When everything was loaded and registered, when there were only the passengers to be embarked, the old man stopped chattering. He put his hat back in its proper place and relit his pipe. Drawing Christian right to the edge of the river, upstream from the master barge, he rubbed his beard several times before resolving to talk. Christian, who had scarcely taken his eyes off him since the wagons returned, was delighted to see him in such fine form. Now, standing before that face which had again turned grave, almost sombre, he felt a return of the distress which had been quenched in him by the happiness of the feast.

The old man spat on the quay several times before saying: 'You're the first to make it downstream. That pleases me, you know. I've put Rapiat in his place. He's getting old. He forgets what we risked when I was captain.'

'He's safeguarding your interests. I understand it.'

'Let him safeguard them with clients and competitors, that's all he's asked to do.'

Félix fell silent. His pipe was out. He sucked nervously three times, but did not light up again. Pointing the end of the chewed and brownish horn stem towards the river, he went on:

'So long as that doesn't betray us, we shall hold on. But only if we avoid getting embroiled in this silly struggle against steam. The companies will never be interested in the smaller ports. We'll have to be content with them.'

Christian told him what had happened at Vienne, and the old man seemed put out.

'Of course,' he said, 'of course the old days have gone for good ... But listen to me ...'

He hesitated. Since he had left the shelter of the trees where happiness sang in the luminous dance of stippled shadow and sunlight, he seemed to have aged ten years. Something from which he could not free himself was weighing him down. He ran his eye over the barge-train, which was making ready to depart amid a hubbub of goodbyes, endless commissions, promises.

'You'll bring me back an earthenware pot for the bacon?'
'All right.'
'You'll remember?'
'I've made a knot in my whiplash.'
'Make another for the olives.'
'All right.'
'And don't get drunk anywhere where there are whores about.'
It was a joke.
'Oh, Germaine, he got drunk enough in Lyons.'
'With whores all in silk, too.'
'There are seventy-five whorehouses in Lyons, did you know?'

Christian heard it all with half an ear. His gaze went from the barges, which he was watching more from habit than from necessity, to his father's anxious face looking towards the opposite bank.

'I'll have to go, Father.'

The old man seemed to return from somewhere a long way off. He gave a quick glance towards the barges, then he said unhurriedly: 'I've taught you everything I know of the river and of our calling. But you can't always pass on to someone else what

you've learned of life. Age teaches us a few things. I'm going to tell
you something: you get carried away too easily, and it worries me.
You remember that madman Daniel Roméral who drove his barge
against the paddle-wheel of a steamer?'

'Father, you know very well that –'

'Let me speak. I was here this morning when the fishermen came
with news of the accident. I'd seen the tiny rise in water level. I was
pretty sure you'd be coming downstream. All of a sudden, I was
afraid.'

Christian wanted to reassure his father, to tell him that he would
never do anything so foolish, but the words would not come. They
looked at each other intensely. Perhaps the old man read the
promise in his son's eye, for he nodded his head and smiled. In a
voice which barely carried beyond his moustache, as though
despite himself he had admitted an action of which he was ashamed,
he went on very quickly: 'In the mornings I always come and wait
here for the sun to rise. I can't face the day without knowing how
the river's going to be. And then . . . then . . . I've always swallowed
a mouthful of river water. It's not enough for me to look at it, I've
got to taste it. It may seem stupid to you, but I think a lot of boatmen do it, in order to acquire a little of its strength. I no longer
need much strength, but I go on doing it.'

Christian wanted to interrupt his father to admit that he did the
same thing himself, but he dared not. The old man was still talking
very fast. Saying his piece.

'One misty morning last spring, I drank. You couldn't see more
than a foot or two. A steamer going up river must have been caught
by nightfall and moored upstream. I didn't know it, but I realized
it at once. The water tasted of oil and coal. It was only that day that I
understood that the river had – well, that it wasn't solely ours. You
understand what I mean?'

The old man's voice broke. His eyes had moistened. He turned
towards the barges and began to cough. Christian no longer saw his
face, but he realized his father was wiping away a tear.

'Well, now,' the old man said, 'it's time to go on board.'

He turned round. His face was already composed again. He

stuffed his pipe into his pocket. His gestures were nervy, jerky. His tall, dried-up body leaned forward slightly, his arms hesitated an instant, then, coming up suddenly, they gripped Christian by the shoulders. The swift embrace was almost brutal. Christian had barely time to feel his father's beard against his own when the old man's horny hands were resting on his arms to push him away.

'Well, now get along . . . get along.'

With long strides, without turning round, Christian reached his post at the tiller of the master barge.

He began to shout much louder than was necessary to summon those who were lingering over their farewells. He was very hot, and his hands were shaking a little.

It must have been more than thirty years since his father had last kissed him.

PART THREE

The Farthest Point Downstream

It was a harsh autumn, ever drier, starker, serer the farther south one went.

The south wind which had arisen scoured a sky unclouded by day or night. It snatched great whirls of leaves from the trees and from the ground; they rose high in the air before scattering on the water. Mingled with them at times was the glittering sand from the banks; it fell faster than the leaves, like fine hail burning with sun. Whirlwinds of dust rose from the arid hillsides, the white squares where the stone was quarried which the barges carried down to the masons' yard at Valence; the dust powdered the vines, the fields, and the flat roofs of the villages, pink and blue in the distance.

The mornings were mistless, and the days sank to sleep in evenings whose orange glow bore down on the sharply silhouetted mountains. To west and north, the sky was violet.

In such weather, with day trickling into the valley long before dawn and the river retaining the evening light long after the land had drowned its contours in shadow, the working days were as prolonged as in the longest days of June.

But there was little life on the river; its water, still low, was not receiving anything from the tributaries. Even the Isère, which normally brings to the Rhône at least a quarter of what it has already rolled down as far as a point upstream from Valence – even the Isère was no more than a thread of sky between banks of sand and pebbles.

The news of the *Triomphant*'s running aground had travelled faster than the Rhône. It ran along the banks from village to village, leaping the river every time a man went over a bridge, every time a ferry or fishing-boat crossed. Keeping pace with it went all the details of the rescue, somewhat embellished. There was talk of wounded, of boatmen jumping into the water to save the passengers. It was astonishing that news could travel so fast and acquire such substance when the newspapers had not even carried it as yet.

The women crossed themselves as they prayed there might not be any dead; the men concurred; but everyone was delighted that a rig could go downstream, whereas a steamer ploughed head on into the sand.

Made cautious by this, the company men kept the other steamers in port.

For the true boatmen, it was a victory which the whole valley celebrated in great draughts of new wine. Sorrow never takes root in a valley where the south wind blows. Not content with welcoming the news, the people had made a big thing of it, out of wishful thinking.

From the river banks to the narrow streets farthest from the port, from the arcades of the Place Vieille to Vignasse, the news of the arrival of a barge-train had roused the inhabitants from their torpor. For the people of Beaucaire went to sleep for ten months of the year, and woke only as July approached in order to get ready for the fair, which would enable them to earn in a few weeks ten times a workman's annual wage. They rented out to merchants their rooms, kitchens, cellars, mews, doorsteps, window-sills, trestle-tables, benches, chairs, planks, bits of canvas. It all brought in money.

July filled the port with boats from all quarters, laden with merchandise for sale and to be sold off cheap. By sea from the Orient, by way of the canals and rivers from the North.

The fair had been the only means of making a living in Beaucaire for as long as anyone could remember.

For the rest of the time, the only people to work were those connected with the port and the Customs, because the river traffic was continuous. Sea-going vessels came upstream to this point, where trans-shipments were effected. In other words, it was still taxes, dues and percentages which filled the town's coffers.

For some years the people of Beaucaire had felt that steam, whether on the railways or on the river, was threatening their fair.

The hard-working barge crews, almost all natives of clean places like Condrieu, Serrières, Vernaison or Givors, did not much like this dirty town, but it was their farthest point downstream and the spot where they picked up freight for the return journey.

The people of Beaucaire were well aware of the low esteem in which they were held by the river folk, but since they lived by their work, they felt a not disinterested gratitude. The fear they felt of seeing their own privileges disappear nerved them to appear friendly to the boatmen. And it was a simple matter for these southerners with their ready speech and easy gestures to swamp overworked, more taciturn men beneath a flood of compliments.

The impending arrival of a rig after so many weeks of slumber for their supply port made it well worth going down to the river bank with a few lanterns. Generous by nature, and well knowing that there is no real celebration without food, drink and music, they had laid the tables, cooked ratatouille, got the grill ready, set up a platform for dancing, and put the wine to cool.

So much light and noise had attracted the people of Tarascon, who had only to cross the bridge to reach the feast. The people of Vallabrègues, who had seen the rig on its way down, came too. And they came from even farther afield, so great was the jubilation at seeing the valley returning to life at last.

Night was already in the sky and on the river when the barge captained by Christian Merlin passed through the narrows below the castle and came in sight of Beaucaire.

It was a night spattered with stars which bathed the valley in a light without shadows. The river glittered, sequinned with points of gold which it strove to carry with it towards the sea, but they escaped from the current to cling to the wave at the eddy's edge and remain there where heaven had scattered them.

As soon as they rounded the bend of the river, the prowman cried: 'Beaucaire in sight.'

His cry was carried on from barge to barge, down to the seventh and last savoyarde. Then Tirou and the other prowmen began sounding the river once more.

'One span ... Three fingers' depth!'

Their arms were heavy with weariness, their voices hoarse, but the port lay ahead and that heartened them.

The lighted windows of the houses and the lanterns on the quays came closer, dulling the light of the stars. On board the master barge, the passengers, already stiff from sleep, got up to look.

'Well,' cried Christian, 'didn't I tell you we'd be there this evening?'

They had made the downstream journey in three days. Three days begun before dawn and extended late into the evening, but devoid of the least incident.

Several times they had felt the barge's keel rumble over pebbles or scrape on sand, but the prowmen were watchful. There may have been only one finger's depth, but it was there none the less. Each time, Captain Merlin had mumbled very fast, without even opening his lips: 'Saint Nicholas, be with us . . . Saint Nicholas, protect the true boatmen who respect your river.'

And each time, drawing his strength from the vast love he felt for the river men, the boatmen's Great Captain had lifted the heavy barge a fraction.

They had passed unhindered through the narrows of Donzère and Crussol and all the most unexpected shallows. Often during the first day the passengers had come up to Christian, their faces strained with anxiety. They scarcely dared enquire: 'Do you think there's any risk?'

'Risk of what?' the Captain asked. 'If it's grounding you're worrying about, you can get off. The steamer coming along behind will pick you up.'

He spoke lightly, and very soon the passengers' anxiety turned to admiration. Good humour reigned on board, and these people, accustomed to the fetid air of towns, had rapidly acquired good appetites. The cooking of Canut and Caillette was to their taste, and even the most delicate ladies had begun to appreciate fish stew, anchovy salad, meat with garlic, goatsmilk cheese, and even a greasy soup at the end of the meal. The wines of Le Vionnier and the Côtes Rôties, Aramon and a nip of spirits played no small part in the breath of gaiety which travelled constantly from one barge to the next.

To save time, they had stopped only in the evenings, and no one had found the work heavy nor the journey long.

Yet it was only their pride that hurried them forward. It was no mean feat to be the first to make Beaucaire after so long a period of total lay-off for barge traffic; to be the first even though they came from as far off as Lyons. They all knew it, and they all awaited with impatience the welcome which the town would give them.

And that welcome was on a par with their exploit.

They were still far from the quays when the echo of the first cheers reached them. The wind carried them in gusts which rolled over the river against the current. They were like another river flowing upstream, a river which passed over you, flowing bank high as far as the crest of the mountains farthest distant from the river banks. It was like a river warm with friendship and joy.

As the first wave passed, Christian felt a shiver down his back, to which his sweat-soaked shirt was clinging.

Tirou, who had heard, could not prevent himself from calling out: 'Hey! Captain Merlin! They've all turned out as if for the first arrival at the fair.'

'I heard, Tirou. They've all turned out. And look at the fires!'

Three fires had just been lit on the esplanade behind the port. Three fires whose flames rose clearly, bending with each breath of wind, stretching and rearing as if for a dance of joy. Already, silhouetted against the glow, black figures were visible. The lanterns were going from right to left, the flames leapt up now here, now there, to be quenched almost immediately. All the life of the town seemed to be concentrated on this right bank of the river where they were going to tie up.

On the left bank, Tarascon too was lit up, but only by the open windows of the houses. And it was only necessary to look at the bridge, where lanterns crossed ceaselessly, to realize that the people from the Empie side had hurried or were hurrying to the Ryaume. At times the bridge was like a long caterpillar of fire barring the river, in which its reflection danced. There were also lights on the tip of the island in midstream, but care had been taken not to light a fire there. That would have been tantamount to insulting Captain Merlin by warning him: 'Look out, there's an island in the middle of the Rhône; we're reminding you in case you don't know just where it is any longer.'

Overhead the night was darker, the stars sparkled less brightly. They had accompanied the boatmen to this point, had studded with nails of moving gold the whirlpools and shoals along their route, but now that hundreds of men, women and children were carrying their shimmering lamps to the riverside, the stars allowed themselves a brief respite.

'Prow to the Ryaume, stern to the Empie!'

Above the cries from bank and bridge, Captain Merlin's voice filled the night. His order rang out over the water and winged towards the town. This first shout was more to silence the crowd than to order the barges to heave to. Everyone knew it. And even the strangers to the town who had come only out of curiosity must have felt it, for silence was quickly obtained.

And it was a night so perfect for their arrival that even the wind dropped for a moment. The flames from the fires rose straighter towards the sky, the reflections of the lamps in the river quivered less.

'Prow to the Ryaume, stern to the Empie!'

Rounded, strong, serious in the night, Christian's voice rose at the same time as it advanced towards the banks, travelling upstream and even downstream, where the wind stopped it only much lower down.

One after the other, swinging broadside on to turn their lanterned prows to the current, the seven barges approached the bank. Without a bump, without the smallest deviation, they lined up downstream from Captain Merlin's barge, which had been the first to tie up at the quay.

The watchful crowd stood silent, leaving to the boatmen's mighty voices the whole vast void of the night.

As soon as the seven barges were moored, a cornet, a trombone, a flute and two tambourines which were assembled on the quay in the front row of spectators, broke into the music of a local dance. It was not the sort of music which meant much to the boatmen, but it was pleasant to hear, all the same. There were so many people to greet their arrival that Christian had to stiffen himself to hold back a tear of emotion. It was true that he had succeeded in making the downstream trip when no one else had dared risk it, but it had not seemed to him that he was doing anything more than the job he had been doing for so many years. That evening, once the first emotion had passed, he growled: 'They're southerners. They're piling it on, as usual.'

And he was not the only one to think so. While the passengers were disembarking, Canut, who was lending a hand with the unloading of their luggage, came up to him. His pleasant round face was split in a huge grin. 'In ten years' time,' he said, 'when they describe our journey, the way they're going on they'll be telling how we arrived on foot, in water up to our knees, carrying horses and barges on our backs – the barges with the bodies of the people killed in the *Triomphant*!'

As they went ashore, the passengers came to thank Captain Merlin, who said to them: 'You've paid, you don't owe me any thanks. But I hope you're going to spend the evening with us . . .'

And they all accepted with a pleasure that was obviously unfeigned.

When the passengers' luggage was on the quay, being disputed between the porters and the servants from the inn, three agents arrived to unload urgent packages. They were agents of the steamship company. They were not wearing caps with the company's initials, but Christian knew them.

'Not tonight,' he shouted to his son, who was about to hand over the packages.

'But, Father, they're urgent goods. When I took them on board, I promised to deliver them as soon as we arrived.'

Without being able to define what he felt, Christian had a sensation of unease. Was it fatigue? Was it the sight of these three men who had also betrayed their river and gone over to the steamer? Was it something in his son's glance that disturbed him?

Christian repeated, in a tone that brooked no argument: 'Not tonight. If we'd done the trip in normal time, the goods would have arrived tomorrow afternoon. They'll be delivered tomorrow morning.'

Claude turned to the agents with a helpless gesture, and the three men made off.

'What's the meaning of that?' Christian enquired. 'They don't want to get them on the road tonight, surely? Do they think someone's going to come and steal them off my barge?'

Claude hung his head, then, looking embarrassed, he stepped on to the quay, where he mingled with the crowd of spectators. Caught up in turn by the celebration, Christian forgot his son's distress. The harbour master and a few boatmen friends carried him off to a table where the meal was being served. Men shook his hand as he passed, brown girls with wild black eyes embraced him. The music of the flutes was drowned by the shouts, laughter, cries of joy of those who were reunited.

'It's worse than it is at the fair.'

'How many weeks were you stuck in Lyons?'

'How many were you stuck here?'

'Is the water really going to rise for good?'

'With this wind, the Rhône's going to fill up.'

'Couldn't that whore of a Saône have given a bit more? It only needs a drop and we could go upstream.'

'Some people have taken their goods away from us and given them to the carriers.'

'The roads won't hold out.'

'Between Vienne and Lyons they're all rutted. Might as well go over open country. As soon as there's a drop of rain, the carts are going to sink in.'

'So long as there isn't too much water.'

'Another three days of this wind and we'll be going upstream.'

Everyone was talking at once. Everyone was asking questions, and then more questions, without waiting for the answers. Already the wine was flowing in the glasses, making the reflections of the lanterns and torches dance ruddily. Even those who weren't sharing the meal served to the boatmen were there, clustered round the tables which were lit as brightly as by a blazing July sun. Thousands of moths and mosquitoes swarmed round, going from one lamp to the next. Some of them fell in the glasses and on the plates; the largest were fished out with the point of a knife and squashed on the table, but a great many were swallowed down with everything else.

'It's all grist to the mill,' people said, laughing.

'They only eat fish. And that doesn't kill 'em. And you like eating fish too.'

They laughed at that as they laughed at everything. Happiness chased away black thoughts and weariness.

When the meal was over and pipes lit, the older men continued to talk while the younger ones led the girls towards the platform where the tambourines and flutes were installed. The first arrivals were already starting to dance when there was a movement among the groups who were still standing about between the tables and the quay. Christian turned round. Men were running towards the river. He stood up. It was his barge they were all looking at.

The hubbub was still too great for him to be able to guess the cause. He elbowed his way forward.

When he reached the edge of the quay, three men were picking up a fourth, who had blood pouring from his nose. Another man began to run along the barge's bulwark, making his way towards the poop, from which he leapt like a cat on to the quay. From behind the piled-up freight a cry went up: 'Stop him, for God's sake!'

Christian recognized his blacksmith's voice, breathless and somewhat hoarse.

Trapped by the crowd, whom he would have had to trample underfoot to follow the quay, he took up Joseph's cry: 'Stop him, for God's sake!'

It must have been done already, for at the far end of the quay there was shouting and scuffling. Without lingering to see more,

Christian snatched a lantern from the hand of a bystander and leapt aboard his barge. Running along the bulwark, jumping over crates, he reached the blacksmith just as he emerged from behind the piled-up freight, wiping his brow on his forearm and saying: 'My God, but he's a tough 'un! But he got his come-uppance all right.'

The blacksmith's great fist was red with blood.

Christian shone the beam of his lantern on to the deck. Between two big bales wrapped in green canvas and a long crate of light-coloured wood, a man was lying. His split lip was streaming blood and showed the white of his teeth. Blood was also running over his right eye and down his cheek.

'God above!' Christian said. 'You certainly hit him.'

'And I hope I left a mark on the first one I hit as well.'

'You marked him all right.'

'One of 'em got away.'

'I think they've caught him on the quay.'

'Do you recognize that one there?'

The blacksmith was out of breath. He spat, breathed deeply and sighed. 'I could surely be his grandfather ... But, God in heaven, I may be sixty-three but I'm not done for yet. And when I was holding that little shit down, he tried to kick my privates. I should think I had to knock him out!'

Christian, who was leaning over the man, lightly turned his head to one side to bring the less damaged side of his face into the light. When he recognized one of the agents of the steamship company, he straightened up and said between clenched teeth: 'What's been going on here?'

Other men had swarmed on to the barge.

'You'd better send the spectators packing,' the blacksmith said calmly.

Christian turned round; lifting his lantern level with their faces, he ordered: 'All those who aren't members of my crew, back on the quay! Come on, lads, clear the onlookers.'

Thrust back by the boatmen, the spectators regained the quay. Doubtless thinking it was a drunken quarrel, they went off laughing and joking, eager to get back to their wine or their dancing partners.

In the ordinary course of events the crews never stayed on their barges. They had nothing to fear from the inhabitants of the ports, tradesmen or artisans who worked with them.

The river world was rather like something sacred. Even a man who would not have thought twice about stealing apricots from an orchard, emptying a pike trap, and snicking the wooden bolt of a rabbit-hutch, would take care not to steal from a barge.

If he were caught by the gendarmes or a peasant, he might spend a few days in prison; but if he were caught by the boatmen, he would end up in hospital for sure. Their strength was well known. They had an accretion of legends to their credit, in which they felled at a blow bulls who were running amok on their barges; hauled two or three times and pulled out a horse stuck in the mud; returned fully laden barges to the water . . . Of course it had all been greatly exaggerated and embellished, but there was an element of truth in it. That was well known. And anyone who still doubted it had only to look at these bearded giants to feel any desire to pick a quarrel swiftly evaporate.

One year when there had been a battle between two crews, the gendarmes had sought to intervene. Herd instinct had promptly led the river men to rediscover their solidarity, and the constabulary had been well and truly trounced. Since the incident took place at night, it had proved impossible to discover those responsible. The river folk had formed a solid front with the barge crews. No witnesses, no pursuits. And to think a whole posse of gendarmes had acquired broken teeth and black eyes simply by falling off their horses! Thereafter they took care not to intervene.

Besides, the barge crews had no need of their services. At Beaucaire, the only time the barges had to be seriously guarded was during the July fair. For merchants from all over Europe and even from the coasts of Africa gathered for it, and thieves followed in their wake. Thousands of pickpockets and pilferers of all kinds and from all countries met there every year, operating alone or in organized bands. When newcomers ventured on to a barge which seemed to be deserted, they learnt their lesson before they had taken twenty steps.

The boatmen stripped them, then, holding them by the ankles, they ducked their heads in the river, letting them come up from time to time until they were heard to cry mercy. When it was over, if the man knew how to swim, he could still take a header to try and recover his garments which had been scattered broadcast on the river. But those who risked it at night were few and far between. So all they could do was to keep to the shadows, their bodies devoured by mosquitoes, until they found something with which to clothe themselves. It was one of the boatmen's amusements during the fair, and the robber could count himself lucky that they did not paint a huge THIEF plumb in the middle of his back.

Joseph Cathomen had dragged the still unconscious agent under the deck-tent. When Christian bent down to help him, he had said, pushing him aside with his hand: 'Let me alone, man. This is one delivery I really can manage.'

Grasping the man's wide belt in one hand and the front of his canvas jacket in the other, he had raised him at arm's length as if he were a feather bolster. Short, broad, thick-set, he scarcely had to bend his knees to raise his arms straight above his head. Lying face downwards on the blacksmith's fists which were like two huge sledgehammers on the handles of his hairy arms, the man had his head, arms and legs hanging down and swaying from left to right.

A few shouts went up from the quay. 'Into the Rhône with him!' 'Throw the shit in the cesspool!'

Now the man was sitting on the deck, leaning against the second mast of the deck-tent, which was lit by three big prow lanterns. A bucket of water had half brought him round. He was beginning to open the one eye he could still see out of, when the bailey and the prowman pushed aside the canvas flap and thrust the other two agents in front of them. The one whom Joseph had managed to reach was stripped to the waist and held his rolled-up shirt to his nose. The greyish canvas was all spotted with red. The other, who had been caught on the quay as he leaped down from the barge, was scarcely marked. He was a tall, dark fellow with a dry brown skin and a bold glance. As soon as he was under the deck-tent he turned to Christian and cried: 'Let me go and take these two with me. It's ridiculous, we'd just come to check our consignment. We're not thieves.' Joseph started forward, angry, ready to strike again. 'Now then, you bastard, you recognize me, do you?'

Despite himself, the other made a movement to protect his face.

'Leave him, Joseph,' Christian commanded.

The blacksmith regretfully stepped back.

'We'll get to the bottom of this,' Captain Merlin went on, 'but to start with, it's for you to tell us what happened.'

Joseph had got his breath back. He took his pipe from his pocket and, showing it to the others, he gave a great roar of laughter as he explained: 'Tell you what happened? Well, you see, I'd lost my pipe – the other one, the one with the clay bowl with a heart engraved in front. Not the latest model, but I'm fond of it. I found it had gone just as we finished eating. I filled this one, but it bothered me. I said to myself: I must have lost it on the deck of Christian's barge when I went to help with the baggage. I was sure I had it up till then . . . It bothered me. I said to myself: If anyone steps on it, it's done for. I came back here –'

Joseph was interrupted. M. Tonnerieu had just come in. Alarmed, his glance darting from one to another, he demanded: 'What's the matter? What's going on? Someone told me there was fighting on the barge.'

Seeing the two wounded men, he started. 'But what's the matter with them? . . . Here's a fine thing. And who are these people?'

The little man's attitude was laughable, but Christian controlled himself. He longed to ask the old clerk if he had happened to see the local monster, the Tarasque, but he wanted to get the thing over. Something told him that this was not a simple case of theft. He merely said in a calm voice: 'Sit down. You're going to hear all about it.'

The clerk perched his skinny buttocks on the edge of a

bunk while Joseph went on: 'Well, as I was telling you, it bothered me –'

'What bothered you?' M. Tonnerieu demanded.

'My pipe, man! If you keep stopping me, I can't tell you.'

'Go on, Joseph,' Christian said, giving the clerk a hard look.

'Well,' Joseph went on, 'I got here. I was about to go on board when what should I see but that fellow ducking down behind a crate. As there wasn't much to be seen, I said to myself: It's one of the crew who's drunk and gone to sleep it off. I came on board. The bastard must have thought I hadn't seen him. I was still bent on looking for my pipe, but nevertheless I went towards the crate to see who it was. I was just going to go behind the crate when this one started up like a snake when you tread on its tail; he gave a whistle and swung his fist at me with all his might.'

At this point Joseph stopped to look at the man with the flattened nose. He laughed, and, striking his hard barrel chest with the flat of his hand, he shrugged his shoulders.

'Just let him touch me, the shit! You know, it had as much effect on me as if he'd looked at me. No more than that. He touched me and took to his heels. I still hadn't recognized him, but I thought to myself: You're up to no good. And that's when I hit him. It knocked him on to the quay. But it's not my fault if vandals like him can't float. So then –'

This time it was Christian who interrupted to summarize, indicating with his chin the other two agents: 'That one got away, but you cornered the third. And of course you had no idea what they wanted?'

The blacksmith scratched his bald head, on which sweat glistened. 'Well,' he said, 'they surely didn't come to swab the deck.'

'I tell you we wanted to check our consignment. That's all. And the Company will lodge a complaint –'

'That'll do!' roared Christian. 'Since you're so eager to talk, talk. But the truth, mind! Otherwise . . . look at your colleagues. Joseph isn't tired and neither am I.'

There was a weighty silence, broken only by the men's breathing and, muffled by the thickness of the canvas, the distant sound of the feast.

Since the dark man stood motionless, eyes downcast and forehead obstinate, Christian advanced slowly. The man sought to retreat, but his back bumped into a section of the mast supporting the deck-tent. The lantern hanging there swayed. There was a light metallic clink. The flame guttered. The men's shadows danced on the canvas walls.

With a quick, precise movement, Christian seized the lapels of the agent's jacket in his left hand. The man gripped the Captain's bony wrist in both his. They were just about the same height, and Christian thought very quickly: Lucky he's not a weakling. I wouldn't dare.

All the strength of his body was concentrated in his left arm. His hand bore down slowly, slowly, the stiff material twisting a little. His gaze never left the man's face; the man, rediscovering his pride in combat, stared back at him. Imperceptibly, the man's face tightened. The veins in his temples stood out. His jaw muscles quivered under the taut skin. For a few seconds the two forces cancelled each other out and remained thus, tense and immobile.

Silence. The others watched, feeling that the least word or gesture would be too much. They too were tense and holding their breath.

Now Christian Merlin's slow, irresistible strength was at its height. The man's legs began to tremble, then, gradually, his knees bent, his waist jack-knifed, his shoulders bowed a little. He continued to resist for as long as it took to count three, then, as if broken, he let himself go, his knees striking the deck, which resounded hollowly. His head was thrown back, his eyes never left Christian's.

'Talk!' Christian commanded in a voice that whistled. 'Talk, or I'll hit you.'

His right hand came up, ready to strike with the side of the hand, like an axe.

'Talk!' he said again. 'What was it you were after?'

He used the singular *tu*, because the others no longer counted.

There was only this man betrayed by physical weakness but still glaring at him like a wild beast.

The man seemed to hesitate. His lips parted, his gaze left Christian's almost reluctantly, to turn in the direction of the canvas flap at the entrance, where the prowman had stationed himself.

Christian realized that he would not be able to keep control of his itching hand much longer.

'You're going to talk!' he shouted.

He was still in control of his temper, but he could not hold back that cry.

'It's not worth it,' the man said. 'If you want to know, ask your son and your head prowman. They're in on it too.'

This time the wind was blowing steadily.

It was coming from the south-west, and though it was still barren, men knew that it would quickly tire of racing fruitlessly across so wide a sky. They knew it, and they forgot the miseries of drought. Even in those places where the barge-train had not stopped on its way downstream, it had brought a whiff of joy. The boatmen's cries had penetrated deep into the valley, zig-zagging from one bank to the other, and the night was still vibrant with them.

In all the houses of the riverside villages there had been talk of this rig. The talk had taken place on doorsteps after night-fall, when the inhabitants gathered there to chat in the darkness because of the moths and mosquitoes which the wind had driven indoors.

It was a warm wind which had risen far off. It had winged its way across the burning lands of those countries talked of at the fairs by brown-skinned men clad from head to foot in white. It had raced over vast tracts of sand burnt up by the sun, but after that it had crossed the sea. And it had become charged with water. Three, six, nine days at most and the clouds would be here. The statement was on everyone's lips. The wind was recognized as a wind of hope.

It roused men from their lethargy. It had an effect on their nerves. Those who were not goaded into working were impelled to talk.

At Beaucaire it infiltrated everywhere. It scraped the roofs, howled in the lofts, swore in Provençal as it squeezed through attic windows too narrow for it. In the streets where the slops were emptied, it trailed along the ground; but it swept away the worst of the smells without in any way losing its own. It was a strong, salty wind, with a mixture of iodine and resin, a wind in which the scent of the marshes of the Camargue mingled with that of the honeyed mountain paths of Spain.

It was a strong, nourishing wind, but also a disturbing one. Running at the heels of autumn to meet the winter coming from the north and east, it confused the migrating birds. The arrowheads of duck and geese hesitated in the wild sky. What point in heading south if the south were coming to them? But instinct triumphed. For this wind was blowing at the level of men, and perhaps they were the cause of its wildness. Men do not act like reasonable animals. They have modified nature too much for instinct still to operate. So the migrating flocks rose higher, higher until they were no longer visible from the earth. They rose until they flew above the region of the wind and once again headed for the south.

Christian was alone beneath the long deck-tent still lit by the three lanterns. Outside the noise had noticeably diminished, but it still drowned the river's song.

As soon as the agent had mentioned Claude and the prowman, Christian had pictured again his son's embarrassed look at the time of disembarking. His right hand had fallen back against his thigh, his left had released the man's jacket.

Christian had turned towards his prowman. Still stationed at the entrance to the tent, Tirou looked at him with his frank, wide eyes in which points of gold glinted. Christian had known his prowman long enough not to need to ask questions. Tirou's expression said very clearly: It's true. We'll explain. You can let them go. He said it, and at the same time betrayed a deep distress.

Tirou had moved away from the entrance, lifting the canvas flap.

Christian had looked at the three agents and indicated the way out. The tall, dark one had got his two wounded colleagues out, then, before leaving the deck-tent, he turned round. His eye unrelenting, he said to Christian: 'I shan't hold it against you. In your position I'd have done the same.'

He had run his hand over the front of his jacket where the material was still crumpled, then he took time to smooth down his black, gleaming hair before leaving.

Christian had looked at his prowman again, then at the others, before saying in a dull, tired voice: 'Tirou, if you know where Claude is, will you go and fetch him. Some men keep an eye on the cargo. The rest of you can go.'

'Just as well, since we're not to be told anything,' the clerk grated.

'Tomorrow, Monsieur Tonnerieu, tomorrow.'

They had all gone out, Joseph Cathomen the last. Christian had rested a hand on his shoulder, saying: 'Thanks, Joseph. Thanks, friend.'

The blacksmith, who undoubtedly had an idea of what was afoot, had murmured: 'Poor old Christian.'

And Christian had remained alone beneath the long deck-tent. He had walked from one stumpy mast to the other, then he had sunk down heavily on a trunk, bowed with a fatigue which he suddenly felt weighing on his shoulders and invading his limbs.

For three long days he had toiled on the river with his men, his nerves strained constantly, his gaze riveted to that moving water which bore the barges but might at any moment destroy them. A downstream journey had seldom demanded such concentrated attention from the men.

They had successfully negotiated all the most dangerous stretches, had cleared the Table du Roi with two fingers' depth to spare, and passed at least a handsbreadth from the pier of Pont-Saint-Esprit, only to change direction directly afterwards in the full force of the current and skirt the sandbank immediately downstream. The train of seven barges had executed the manoeuvre quite perfectly. On the quays the old men must have been shaking their heads and saying, 'That Christian's quite a captain!' They had done all this with effort, but also with joy: they were alone on the river, absolute masters of its flood.

A great joy and a great pride.

They had achieved so much, been fêted everywhere, and now he was alone, a prey to fears, overwhelmed by fatigue as never before.

The minutes slid by. Empty. Absolutely empty.

Christian had only one idea in his heavy head: that what had happened was something to do with steam. He sensed it. It couldn't be otherwise. But what was it? The question was in him, boring into him, but his brain could produce no response, clouded as it was with sleep, against which he must battle.

He got up, walked to the entrance to the deck-tent, and lifted the canvas flap. The night was heavy with warm wind – a wind still racing over the river, ruffling the still reaches, passing flat and un-apparent over the tensed muscles of the swiftest currents. At the ends of the dykes the eddies swirled, attempted to put out to mid-stream, then, beaten back suddenly towards the bank, dissolved in the calm waters, where their decreasing movement gently lifted the reflection of the stars. The clear sky howled.

Upstream, the river banks merged with the more distant hills in one dark mass. The milky light made distances deceptive. The base of the sky seemed to bear down evenly on top of the earth. A neat joint, as if traced by an engraving tool at the edge of two pieces of metal, one polished and studded, the other darker, uniform and matt. Beneath was the reflection, with the same precise limit, but lively, living, enamelled in places, and transparent over the darkest depths of all.

Mystery.

What lay beneath this water? What lay in the depths of a human heart? Is it ever possible to know a river? Do not men keep deep within them a secret part which is always dark to other men?

Christian turned to face the bank. The wind swayed the last lanterns still hanging on the lowest branches of the plane-trees. There was no one left at the tables still piled with remnants of the feast. Ten or eleven dogs were prowling about between the benches, crunching bones. One small black and white one, his plumed tail curled over, was up on a table, licking a plate. Farther off, the orchestra was still playing, but with the stronger wind its tinny music reached the river only spasmodically. Some thirty people were dancing. Everywhere drunks were sleeping it off in the grass.

The wind blustered in the branches of the plane-trees. Dry leaves floated into the lantern light, falling on tables and in the sparse, trampled grass, sometimes rolling a long way before taking off, only to fall again.

It was all there, near and far intermingled, slightly nauseating.

The people of Beaucaire had prepared this feast for Christian and his crew. Now the celebration was drawing to a close. It was in process of dying, and the esplanade was gradually becoming the domain of the wind. And the wind, hurrying in the direction of the mountains of the north and east, barely lingered, snatching a few leaves which it cast aside at once to continue its journey up-stream.

When Claude Merlin returned with the prowman, Christian had gone back beneath the deck-tent. Seated on his trunk, elbows on his knees, hands clasped, head aching, he was waiting.

Wooden soles scraped on the stone of the quay, then on the deck of the barge. There was a very brief silence, and the tent-flap was gently raised. Head bowed, eyes fixed on a knot in the deck from which three cracks rayed out starlike, Christian did not move. He let the two men enter. The movement of the canvas had made the lantern flames waver. Silence returned. The light steadied.

Slowly raising his head, Christian looked at his son, then at his prowman. As neither of them seemed resolved to speak, Christian said: 'Well? It seems you have something to tell me?'

It was hardly a question. The voice was measured, calm, composed.

The other two exchanged a look, asking each other who should be spokesman. Christian thought they had had time to settle that before coming in. He said: 'I'm tired. We're all tired. It would be better to say what you have to say at once. And it might be just as well to sit down.'

He knew himself. He knew what difficulty he had in keeping his temper during an argument, and because he preferred to remain seated, he wanted the others to be seated too.

Claude and the prowman took their places side by side on the edge of a bunk. They looked like two schoolboys awaiting a telling-off. Christian asked himself: If my father were here, what would he do? He would say to me: Christian, don't get carried away. Whatever they may tell you, you'll be stronger if you keep calm than if you lose your temper.

In the same composed voice, he repeated: 'Well?'

His son shrugged his shoulders. He drew a deep breath as if he were about to dive into the river.

'Perhaps we've done something stupid,' he began, 'but all the same...'

He stopped, looked at the prowman, then back to his father, who said again: 'Well?'

'Father, if you know, it's pointless to make me tell you about it.'

'If I know? It isn't necessary to be a magician to know you've been up to something with the crew of the steamer. I realized that right away. But as for what you've been up to – that's a different matter.'

'Up to something ... up to something. No, we haven't been up to anything,' Claude said. 'You had told us to take urgent goods, and we took them.'

Christian knew his son too well not to guess how upset he was at talking. Tirou must also be embarrassed, but he was even more upset by this interminable delay than by a blunt admission; he shrugged his shoulders, shifted his legs, rubbed his huge hands together, and came to a decision.

'All right, all right, we didn't think carefully enough about it. But we're bastards, just the same. We ought to have refused that crate. They didn't try to put anything over on us. They told us what was in it.'

He stopped and looked at Claude, before repeating: 'That's right, so we might as well admit it. They told us what was in that crate.'

'That's right,' Claude agreed.

And they both looked down at the deck between their black leather boots with wooden soles.

Christian allowed a few seconds to elapse, then demanded impatiently: 'What crate?'

His voice had not yet reached the pitch of anger, but it had risen and rang out beneath the deck-tent.

Almost simultaneously, the two men raised their heads. It was Claude who spoke, admitting: 'The steamer that's held up here – the *Rhodan* – she isn't just held up. A part's defective. A connecting-rod, it's called. So a crate was being sent down with a replacement in it.'

The end of the sentence was almost inaudible. Claude's face was miserable. His chin was quivering. Christian thought he was going to burst into tears, and he dreaded it. He asked very quickly: 'Who else knew?'

'No one.'

'What about Rapiat?'

'No. He entered it in the register as "Crate containing metal part".'

'Who's the consignee?'

'Monsieur Beuker.'

'The address?'

'To be collected at the port of Beaucaire.'

The questions and answers had gone smoothly. Christian was regaining his control. Claude seemed to have himself in hand. There was a very brief pause.

Christian cleared his throat, and asked: 'Of course he's an employee of the Company. Or perhaps non-existent, with a name like that. But you knew the agents would be here when we tied up?'

'Yes,' Claude said, without lowering his gaze.

Without allowing his son time to reflect, and speaking this time to him alone, Christian shot out: 'This isn't the first time you've had dealings with men from the companies.'

Claude's face flushed. Christian had spoken with a ring of certainty, yet nothing had ever given him cause to think that his son might have had truck with the men from the steamer. The idea of saying so had come to him all of a sudden, he had come out with it on the spur of the moment, and Claude's dumb answer, that blush which was an admission, caught him unprepared.

Claude gave a glance towards the prowman which was a plea for help. Seeing it, Christian chuckled to remind his son of the cry which the evil-tongued claimed was the only life-belt ever thrown by a boatman to a man struggling in the river: 'Pray to Saint Nicholas, but keep swimming!'

It was the prowman, however, who answered. 'That's right. For more than a year they've been asking us, but we've always refused.'

'What exactly have they offered you?'

'A command.'

Christian whistled briefly and asked his son: 'You too?'

'They said to me, "We need men like you and your father. And you could..."'

This time Christian had to make a considerable effort to remain seated. His hands, resting on the edges of the trunk, had begun to shake. His voice also shook as he interrupted his son: 'And you could earn big money! I know. That's what they said to you. And didn't you answer that if they needed men like me to keep their Company going, they could kiss it goodbye? Men like me will never consent to sully their hands with coal and blacken their consciences with their filthy lucre that's going to ruin the whole valley.'

As he spoke, Christian had risen to his feet unconsciously and approached his son and the prowman. Planted between them and the lantern in the middle, he drowned them in his shadow. Fists clenched, he let his anger rip.

'The whole valley will be ruined if steam wins. You know that as well as I do. But the difference is that I'd rather be ruined with it than dip anything more than the tip of my little finger into their foul goings-on . . . Damn progress, if it's going to finish off thousands of poor devils who never asked a thing of anybody. Today, honest toil like ours doesn't count for anything any more. The only thing that counts is cash. Nothing but cash! Well, so far as I'm concerned, I – I shit on their cash.'

Now anger was carrying him away. Every word issued from the depths of his being as if from a land of fire. He was no longer shouting, he was spitting out his words. Any words. Those which came uppermost. Those which were the scum from a simmering rage too long suppressed.

Short of epithets, unable to find further insults, for all that he had so often brooded on thousands and thousands of much stronger words to hurl at the hated world of steam, he fell silent.

The other two had not budged. Heads down, shoulders bowed, they waited for the storm to pass.

If Father were here, what would he do? Christian asked himself. Nothing. Because there's nothing to do except go under.

He was sickened. Fearful lest his anger should make him go too far, he merely said in a voice already slightly calmer: 'Filthy muck!'

Then in three strides he was at the flap of the deck-tent. He lifted the canvas and went out. Before letting it fall again, he turned round to add: 'Get to bed. We'll settle this in the morning.'

It was a night in which the life of the sky was more in evidence than the life of the earth. So long as the feast had cast its spell of music, light and sound, men collectively had gone on believing that they were the valley's sole life. And then, the lights and music dowsed, each going his separate way, they had all felt the sky's presence pressing down upon them.

River, trees, meadows, fields, bridges, barges, houses, nothing slept as on other nights. Everywhere there were uneasy dreams, long moans and sighs. It was one of those nights when the wild sky and the earth make love. Violent, fierce love, suggestive of conflict. There was not a star that did not tremble, not a square inch of stagnant water that remained asleep.

It was a much more lively night than the days which had just dragged over the earth in motionless, heavy heat. The heat was still there, but it had begun to run with the wind. It chased out the little coolness which the least naked trees had managed to conserve in the depths of their great trembling bodies.

Tomorrow there would be no more cool shade.

It was a night which ruffled men as it ruffled the river. It carried a foretaste of rain and hope, but it was too turbulent for the hope to be devoid of impatience.

Fortunately, the wine consumed made sleep possible. Wine cast a kind of mist over men which the wind would not dispel. A warm, sonorous mist, with more colour than the river mist which would not rise so long as the wind kept up. And the mist of wine made the sky totter. In this night of wild wind the whole valley reeled from side to side, as though river and earth had also partaken of the wine poured out at the feast.

As soon as he had left the deck-tent, Christian felt his anger changing into a deep sadness. What was happening within him was like what happens when a stream begins to freeze. The water flows. Its flow is like its bubbling, boiling course. It seems as if nothing will ever be able to halt it, and then, bit by bit, the cold flowing down from the sky links up with the cold of the banks. Like stars, it crystallizes. The banks bristle with thousands of pinpoints. The water shrivels, but there is nothing to be done. The frost is stronger than all.

Calm and silence.

Only streams of icy air continue to slide above streams frozen stiff with ice.

It was the same with Christian. The stream of anger had frozen over. He felt himself cold and hard beneath the buffeting of the warm wind.

Once down on the quay, he walked along the bank until he came to grass. There, in the darkness of a clump of dwarf willows, he lay down on his back. The sky and stars were in his eyes; so too was the path of the wind, betrayed by the dance of half-stripped willow wands.

He breathed in great gulps. He wanted to laugh when he said to himself: Christian, it's crazy to go seeking calm in the wind's wildness. Yet calmness came to him from what he breathed in through his open mouth and flaring, quivering nostrils.

He turned on his side and raised himself on his elbow to look at the river. As the night wore on, the light in the sky intensified. Now all the lights of men were out. Opposite, Tarascon was no more than a dark, inert mass lying level with the gleaming river.

What am I going to do? Christian asked himself. I haven't punished them. Father would tell me I'd done well. But what now?

Now that his anger had cooled, he felt weariness gradually weighing down his limbs.

Christian did not want to return to the deck-tent, where Claude and the prowman were. Nor did he want to run the risk of being found where he was in the morning. He stood up slowly. Already his lower back had begun to go numb and a dull ache climbed up his spine, while another, sharper one ran down his legs. He returned to the barge, which he boarded after taking off his boots. Soundlessly, he slipped in among the huge packages, groping and peering.

'Looking for somewhere to sleep? Come here, there's room for two.'

Christian recognized the blacksmith's voice. He moved forward and found Joseph Cathomen lying on a folded awning which he had placed between the long crate of light-coloured wood and the bales of silk, in the very spot where he had done battle.

'There's room here, lad,' Joseph repeated.

'What are you doing there?' said Christian.

Joseph began to laugh. 'What are you?' he said.

Christian sat down beside him. The freight cast a shadow, but the crate of new wood was still very visible, lighter than all the rest. Joseph struck the wood with the flat of his hand and went on: 'There it is, you see, their blasted crate of shit. They're not going to need that tonight, that's for sure, but they said to themselves, You never know, Christian might take a look before handing it over. I looked through the slats with the lantern; you can easily see what it is.'

'And you think they might try to come back for it?'

'You never know.'

Christian waited a moment. The wind was blowing at the height of the piled-up freight. From time to time it allowed a puff to trail behind which came down to where the two men were sitting.

'After all,' Christian observed, 'now that I know, what the hell can it matter?'

'Oh hell! I'm not with you over this. So far as my views are concerned, well, I'm not the captain, am I? But in your place I should say: The crate is for the *Rhodan*; if the captain of the *Rhodan* likes to come for it, I'll hand it over.'

The man commanding the steamer was named Jules Vaudin. For several years he had been in Christian's service. He was intelligent, a good sailor, by no means a bad sort, but one evening when he had had a drop too much he had met in a café in Lyons a little tart whom he had ended by marrying. From that day, Vaudin had changed. He was no longer the same man. He had to have money for this creature. The Company was looking for pilots who knew the river, and Vaudin had been one of the first to go over.

In Christian's eyes the man had shown himself a traitor by marrying this girl, by leaving Serrières where he had been born and where his ancestors had always made a living from the river; he had also shown himself a traitor by setting a bad example to the weaker brethren.

Christian thought for a moment. The idea of humiliating Vaudin was tempting. As he said nothing, Joseph went on: 'My first idea was to chuck their muck overboard. Into some quiet reach eight or nine feet deep. You want your consignment? All right, go and look for it, since you're so clever. But it's a consignment we accepted, it wouldn't look good – '

Christian interrupted him. 'My son accepted it. It's a consignment for which I'm responsible and it will be delivered.'

He was silent for a moment, then, surveying the crate from one end to the other, he asked: 'How much does it weigh?'

'I don't know,' Joseph said, 'but it's heavy.'

Christian got up slowly, went towards the crate, stooped, and lifted one end.

'It can't be much over two hundred pounds,' he said, lowering it.

'What do you want to do?'

'Nothing . . . You'll see . . . I think I've got an idea.'

He lay down on the canvas beside the blacksmith. 'Actually,' he said, 'it's not bad here.'

There was a long pause with only the wind's intermittent howl above them. From time to time they could just hear the river against the bulwarks, the slap of a wave which must result from the movement of eddies formed at the end of the dyke, at the point where the current met the stagnant reaches. Christian felt numbness steal over him. He forced himself to lie still, to put up a resistance to the thoughts which came to him. He wanted to clear his mind so that sleep might come. He was on the point of dropping off when Joseph asked: 'Are you asleep?'

'No.'

'Look here, Christian, there's something I want to say to you. I may not be the captain, but I'm sixty-three years old. You know me, and your father knew me. I've never stepped out of line. If the barge traffic dies, I'll be one of the first to suffer. At my age you don't find another job. And since my son died, I've had his two kids to keep . . . My God, they're a fine pair. And strong. And I swear they've got the river in their blood. The old woman and me, we wouldn't want them to go short . . . In other words, I've got more reason than most to hang on. I'd like to see steam go to the devil ten times over. If you gave up, it might mean beggary for me.'

'Me give up! But you know me well enough –'

'Don't get carried away. I said *if* you gave up. I know you won't do any such thing. For me, it would be the worst thing that could happen. Even so – well – it doesn't stop me from saying in all honesty, Christian, that in your place I wouldn't even go back upstream. For the rig you've got, with the horses and all, you'd get enough to give you a decent income. You sell, and let your lad sign on with the companies. They'll take him.'

'Of course they'll take him. They've already approached him.'

'They've approached all the young ones who're any good.'

'Swine!'

'Let me speak. Swine or not, if you don't want to give up, there's good money to be made with a single barge, transporting stone for dykes.'

'Dykes which are going to help the steamers.'

'Not immediately.'

'Perhaps not, but eventually. Besides, what sort of work is that for a true boatman?'

Joseph did not answer straight away. Christian heard him breathe deeply, then shift and raise himself on his elbow before saying in a voice difficult to hear: 'I know it's terrible, lad, but you know, sooner or later I think . . .'

He broke off. Deep down, he had perhaps accepted certain ideas, but to go as far as putting them into words – certain words – was beyond him. Christian understood. Nevertheless, though without anger, he said: 'Joseph, if anyone else were to say that to me . . .'

'I know. You'd knock his head off.'

Joseph said no more. He let a few long sighs of wind pass over them, then he repeated in a voice already blurred with sleep: 'You'd knock his head off, and you'd be right. My God, but you'd be right!'

That night the wind came to grips with the high mountains. It had already assailed them the previous night and throughout the day, but timidly, repulsed by the cold which streamed down from the glaciers into the alpine meadows and pine forests.

That night, bustling northwards, pressing the cold currents down against the opposite slopes, the burning wind had enveloped the mountains. The great walls of ice had begun to sweat as in springtime. This release of water in meadows and woods when autumn was already bronzing the land was unbelievable. Yet it was happening. The topmost peaks had not known such a warm night all summer.

This strong, steady wind blowing up from Provence and the

Rhône valley was drenching the lands of Provence and giving water to the valley and to the river. The inhabitants knew that a rise like that was only a foretaste of the rains which the wind would bring.

They waited feverishly for the first clouds. When the rains came work on the river would start again, and wiht it the battle between steam and the barges.

Christian Merlin had slept only a few hours. Awakened by the sun, he had got up at the same time as Joseph Cathomen. They had gone to wash at the end of the dyke, where the current ran fastest. The water was fresh. The river had risen several inches. Merely by looking at it, you could tell the south wind had reached the higher regions of the glaciers.

They had returned to the barges, where a few men were beginning to emerge from under the deck-tents, bleary-eyed, yawning and stretching, their heads still heavy with last night's wine.

Christian had asked M. Tonnerieu to bring the register of goods. Now the old clerk was there, his glasses on his nose, his big book open on a packing case, and his hands resting palms down on the pages which the wind wanted to turn too fast. The sun, already high, was crossing the Rhône, where its reflection unrolled a broad highway of light. On the left bank, Tarascon stood out in sharp relief. On the right, beyond the plane-trees, Beaucaire in full sunshine was yellow and pink with its Roman roofs and tiles.

Christian waited for his men. It was a day when they had earned the right to a little rest.

When they were all there, he turned to his son.

'We'll start by unloading the goods you took on from the *Triomphant*. You'll go down to the *Rhodan* and tell Vaudin that if he wants his crate, he can come and get it.'

On the quay there were a dozen porters. Among them was the tall, dark-eyed agent. This morning he was wearing his Company cap and a blue jacket with gilt buttons. He had heard what Captain Merlin said. He called out: 'It's not worth the bother, I'm here for that.'

Christian did not even glance at him. As his son had not moved, he said: 'Claude, you heard what I said to you.' His voice was firm. Claude looked around him. All the men were watching him. He shifted from one foot to the other a couple of times, then jumped on to the quay and hurried off.

The steamer was berthed much farther down, at a part of the quay where there were no other boats. From here she was visible head on, but partly hidden by a spit of land on which were warehouses.

As soon as Claude had gone, the men from the barges began to unload the consignments, which the porters loaded on to their trolleys, after verifying the names written on the canvas bales or on the wood of crates. M. Tonnerieu supervised, marking his register as the names were given to him.

When they came to the crate containing the connecting-rod, Christian said: 'No. Leave that one.'

'It can still be put ashore on the quay,' said M. Tonnerieu.

'No,' Christian repeated in his captain's voice. He felt surprisingly calm and strong.

His men had finished unloading when Claude returned, accompanied by Jules Vaudin, who was also wearing a blue jacket with gilt buttons and a cap of the same blue. He was a big, tall, heavily built fellow of about thirty, with a rather round face. He took up position on the quay.

Silence.

It was just as though they were all holding their breath to hear the wind sing. A few spectators had joined the porters, who had not yet wheeled away their trolleys. Men and trolleys all formed a big semi-circle around Jules Vaudin, who stood beside Captain Merlin's barge.

And overhead the sun beat down; the wind went singing on its way. That was all.

'I've come to take delivery of a crate addressed to Monsieur Beuker,' Vaudin said.

'I'm going to give it to you,' Christian replied.

'So I should hope. It's what I'm here for.'

Christian walked slowly towards the crate. He bent down. His hands slid under the corners, which were not lying flush with the deck because of the bands round the outside. He did not know how much the crate weighed, but he knew he was going to carry it. He braced his back; slowly his bent knees straightened. The crate rose. Once he had got his hands as high as his waist, Christian bent his knees again. Now, it was not just a matter of pushing, of holding back a little so that the crate was up-ended. Like that, it was almost as tall as he was.

Christian allowed himself time to draw three deep breaths. The others had understood; no one offered to help him. A quick glance told him that the crowd had grown still larger and that it included some men from the *Rhodan*.

He put his back up against the crate, bent his knees again, raised his hands over his shoulders and grasped the two corners. He filled his lungs with the wind which was blowing full in his face in great gusts, and, bending forward, he toppled the crate so that it leaned against his back.

He had judged it well. The load was perfectly balanced.

His legs straightened and he began to walk almost normally. He felt so strong that he said to himself: I could carry it to their filthy kettle in one go.

He crossed the deck, which resounded dully under his weight. When he had lifted the crate, there had been a murmur from the crowd; now there was silence again.

When he reached the bulwark, Christian stopped. The step required to reach the quay was a bit too long. He breathed in, allowed the weight to push him forward, and crossed.

Four steps along the quay, and he again bent down to deposit the crate gently in front of Vaudin. He was hardly out of breath. He stood up and said: 'There it is, you can take it.'

Vaudin's face was so red that Christian wondered if he was about to explode.

Vaudin knew that if he did not carry the crate, he would look ridiculous. But he also knew that Christian was much stronger than he was. Christian understood what was going on in that head under the Company cap. He was in the seventh heaven. Vaudin had to find a way of not carrying the crate and of not losing face either – that round red face of his.

'Glad to be rid of it,' Christian said. 'I don't particularly like muck like that on my barge.'

Vaudin sniggered. He said very loudly, for all the world to hear: 'But you're glad enough to get the money for transporting it. Everyone succumbs to the Company's money in the end, even those – '

In an instant, Christian forgot everything. Forgot his vows to keep calm and his wish to see the other collapse under the weight of the crate. These words seared him to the quick, like red-hot iron. 'Liar!'

His fist shot out at the same time as the word and shut Fatface's mouth. Vaudin was practically lifted off the ground. He would have fallen backwards, but Christian's left hand quickly caught him by the lapels of his fine jacket. Only his cap flew backwards and rolled like a biscuit along the quay.

Christian thrust Vaudin's back against the crate and punched him four times. And four times Vaudin's skull crashed against the planks.

When Christian let go of him, he was nothing more than a great puppet who sagged at the knees and sank to the ground, turning on its side.

Christian turned round. At a glance, he took in the circle which had broken up. Already there were men on the ground and others on top of them. Some were yelling and running away. The barge crews were jumping from the barges, fists at the ready. Everywhere men were rolling and punching. Four paces from Christian, Joseph was at grips with the tall dark agent.

'Let him have it, Joseph!' Christian shouted.

And as if that were all the blacksmith was waiting for, the tall dark man was plucked from the ground as if seized by the wind. But it was worse than the wind. It was Joseph who had managed to dodge the blows and the tall fellow's lunge, and who had caught his wrist as it shot out. No one could boast of ever having escaped Joseph's grip. Joseph twisted the man's arm behind his back, the tall fellow arched his body with a fearful yell, but the blacksmith was not soft-hearted. With his free hand he grabbed the seat of the other man's trousers and raised him high in the air. With a crash he landed on the quay, face downwards. The tall dark man was not likely to get to his feet in a hurry. And certainly not without help. The blacksmith had flung him down with all the strength of his mighty shoulders, and with a gasp such as he gave at the anvil when handling his heaviest sledge-hammer.

Above the oaths and the sounds of fighting rose the harsh voice of M. Tonnerieu calling from the barge: 'Stop! . . . Stop! . . . It's disgraceful. You'll all end up in prison. Stop it, you pack of hooligans!'

Christian knew perfectly well that it was for him to put an end to the fight. He kept repeating to himself: Christian, if your father were to see you. But two or three chins which came within reach of his fists were too much of a temptation for him.

It was no longer a brawl, it was a massacre. The men from the steamer were puny by comparison and there were too few of them. Christian got a grip on himself. Putting his fingers to his lips, he whistled.

Regretfully, his men stopped punching, letting go of their victims who made off, cursing. Only Joseph, who had just knocked out a mechanic by sending him crashing against the trunk of a tree, turned round and grabbed another man in passing.

Christian flung himself upon him. 'That's enough, Joseph! That'll do!'

The blacksmith's hand, already raised, fell back, useless. He let go of the man.

'You heard me whistle, Joseph. If the older men don't set an example . . .'

Joseph watched the man he had just released hurrying away; then, with an exculpatory gesture, he said: 'I never heard a thing. You know I'm hard of hearing.'

The barge crews were reassembling and going back on board.

There were a few black eyes and bloody noses, but nothing serious. Tirou had cut his hand while disarming a porter who wanted to lash out with an iron hook; Claude had a split ear, which was bleeding. They too had joined in the fight.

The crate containing the connecting-rod was still on the quay, just as Christian had left it.

PART FOUR

The Wind's Work

On the sixth day of the wind the clouds arrived. The sky's heat made them glisten beneath as well as above. Anything which did not shine with the fire of the sun gleamed with the burning reflection of the sea.

And when they reached the coast they scarcely darkened, for the land too was glowing and hot. When the first shadow touched the beach, a sigh ran all along the strand. The wind neither slackened nor freshened, but there was a change in the density of the air. All year long the hedges and windbreaks, planted to protect the crops from the mistral, lived bowed towards the south. And suddenly the south rebelled, breaking a habit on the threshold of the very season when in normal times the north made itself master of the land.

The shade moved forwards, covering mountains and plains, plunging into the hollows of the valleys without ever slowing its advance. And the shade was startling. People glanced from the remnants of clear sky to that fleecy mass fringed with dazzling light, and said: 'Such a wind at this time of year, did anyone ever see anything like it?'

'We must be going to have a cataclysm.'

The anxiety of waiting gave way to a fear which no one dared put into words, a fear which they would not admit to themselves, which they dissimulated beneath exaggerated expressions uttered as if in jest. They talked of cataclysms and deluges, and then added by way of reassurance: 'You're joking. There'll be some water and that'll be that.'

'It's a bit late for water for the crops.'

'It's never too late for water for the river.'

The boatmen also looked at the sky. They saw it reflected in the river even better than by raising their heads. They read its secrets more easily.

In all the ports of the valley, from Lyons to Beaucaire, life was starting up again. Barges were being loaded. The steamers began to spit forth black. They were not yet getting up pressure in their boilers, but they were lighting a preliminary fire which they would fan when the moment came. It was as much to kill time as to see if the machinery was functioning.

And this expectoration was like a warning to the barge-masters. It meant: Watch out. As soon as the river gives us a bit more water, that's it. We're off, and the war will start up again.

At Beaucaire and Lyons, the coming of this offensive, which the Companies wanted to mount in order to deal a mortal blow to the barge-trains, was felt more strongly than elsewhere.

At Beaucaire, at the port of La Couronne, in the squares, at the port of Beauregard, in Rue des Bijoutiers, Rue des Brasseurs, Rue des Quatre-Rois, the walls were plastered with big white posters which proclaimed in huge black letters:

RHÔNE STEAM NAVIGATION COMPANY

The *Sirius*, an elegantly and commodiously appointed packet, reaches Avignon in 10 hours and goes upstream from Beaucaire to Lyons in 2 days.

Passengers will find on board spotless cleanliness and every care and attention, together with an excellent table d'hôte at 5 francs a day.

The Company undertakes the transport of horses by means of loose-boxes, after the fashion of English vessels.

The barge hands who knew how to read read it aloud to the others, who said:

'It's not true. It's a try-on.'
'It is true. It's there in black and white.'
'Are the horses going to have the table d'hôte?'
'No, but they're going to learn English – it says so.'
'Impossible. Read the last line again.'
The reader obliged.
'What's "after the fashion of" mean?'
'Don't know. Must be English.'

They laughed and thumped one another on the back.

'Imagine cleanliness and coal!'

'So what? Perhaps the rest of us have dirty boats. Is that what their notice means?'

They joked and raged. Fights were in the air, but after the battle around the crate the steam men had kept to their boat or to the Company's hostel. They had collected their crate and were hard at it repairing their pump. As they worked, they glanced at the sky and then at the river.

And the river, which everyone watched constantly by day and night, had risen only a few inches.

Ever since the clouds had completely covered the sky, the water seemed to be the source of light. The river appeared motionless, made of icy but gleaming metal, ceaselessly polished by the wind.

On the day the sky began clouding over, Christian Merlin summoned his son and his prowman under the deck-tent of his barge. The barges had been unloaded and reloaded, and like the other barge-masters, he was waiting for the water to rise in order to give the signal for departure.

Since the barges could not always sail in the deepest part of the river on the upstream journey, it required a greater depth than for the journey downstream.

Everything was ready, all that was needed was the river's good will, and the sky proclaimed that that would not be long in coming.

When Tirou and Claude came in under the awning, it was already dark. Yet it was only the middle of the afternoon. To save lighting lanterns, they fastened back the canvas flap which the wind kept whipping. The wind hurried over the awning, fell before the entrance flap, and sent eddies as far as the bunks.

Christian pulled out his trunk and the other two sat down opposite him on two coils of new rope. Seated thus, lit from the side and caressed by the wind, they eyed one another a moment without speaking. Long moans travelled the length of the barge and sped away over the river. Christian could see the left bank, nibbled ceaselessly by foam-fringed, close-packed wavelets, which at times jostled and chased one another along the rocky spurs.

He had brooded a long time before reaching his decision. He had reached it alone, thinking only of what his father would have done in his place. The river's delay had set him on edge, but as regards what he wanted to say, he felt completely calm.

He took his pipe out of his pocket, filled it, then held out the tobacco bladder. Tirou rose lightly and leaned forward to take the pouch. He helped himself, then passed the pouch to Claude. When the three pipes were lit, Christian said: 'I didn't ask you to come here in any light-hearted frame of mind. I've given myself time to think about it.'

He had prepared his speech carefully. The words were all present and correct; he had weighed and measured everything, but when it came time to speak, he was in difficulties. He looked at the river again, then back at the men. The smoke from the three pipes lay between them. It billowed, trailed along the deck, rose, then allowed itself to be drawn towards the exit, where the wind dispersed it at once.

'Look,' Christian went on, 'steam, progress, everyone's free to believe in it or not. You know what I think about it. I thought you shared my views, and now all at once you don't. Perhaps you're right. The future will tell.'

He stopped again to inhale deeply. Everything he had just said was by way of a preliminary. Now he had to make up his mind to come to the real point. And that was the most difficult. Because the other two had understood already. Their eyes said as much. There was something in their expression which seemed to say: 'No. Don't go too far. Don't say it. You're going to ruin everything.' They were too proud to put their feelings into words, Christian knew, but to silence their looks was another matter.

He took a long time to make up his mind. At last he said, in a voice that was almost gentle and not at all like his captain's voice: 'I'm going to go upstream. You never know what the Rhône's going to do, but there's a risk it'll be hard going. And I only want men with me who really believe in what they're doing. I know

you'd do your work the same as you've always done it. It's nothing
to do with that. But the risk to be run . . . It's not just a matter of
going upstream, but of going upstream even if the steamer can't go
any farther. You understand . . . So your luck may lie on the other
side. With them. With the future and progress.'

His left hand rose slowly to indicate the direction of the port of
La Couronne where the *Rhodan* was berthed.

His voice had faded out on the last words. His throat closed up
tighter and tighter and refused to let out the rest.

There was a silence, broken by the howling of the wind and the
flapping of the canvas, then:

'Father, it's not possible . . . not possible . . .'

Claude's voice was quivering with half-stifled sobs.

Christian looked him straight in the eye and said with an effort:
'Yes, lad . . . Every man is free to go his own way. You've both
chosen and there's no going back on it. I was angry with you, but
I'm not any longer. Every man is free . . . You may even be right,
but I've a mind to prove the contrary. Only, you're not going to
work side by side with those who are straining themselves to prove
you wrong. It wouldn't be natural . . . You can't be on both sides
at once.'

The prowman had not said a word. His red face had flushed
redder. The veins on his forehead stood out, his eyes stared. His
clenched hands trembled on his knees.

Christian had the feeling they were still waiting for something.
He said: 'After what's happened, you'll understand that I can't
keep you. The men would think . . .'

He said no more. He had not envisaged speaking of that. He had
almost said that to retain on board two men who had consented to
help out the Steamship Company would represent a blow to his
authority. But he did not have to speak of that. It was not the crux
of the matter. The most important element was something in him.
It was hard to explain, but it was something that lay very close to
his heart and was not unconnected with the fact that his own son
was mixed up in the business.

Claude had lowered his eyes. His lips were pressed together.

Christian realized that he was making a considerable effort not to beg, not to implore his pardon. It was what he would have done himself in his place. From pride. Solely from pride. And it was just as much from pride that he, Christian Merlin, barge-master, refrained from taking his son in his arms and shaking him, saying: 'Come on, it's all right, I know you. And I know you too, Tirou. You've acted stupidly, but I know you're sorry. I need you for the upstream journey and you will show me what you're capable of. The Rhône's certainly going to give you the opportunity.' Pride restrained him, and the same pride restrained his son from saying: 'Flog me in front of the whole crew, but keep me with you.'

At the end of his tether, Christian got up. 'Go and see Monsieur Tonnerieu,' he said. 'You'll be paid. I'll go and tell him.'

He went out without looking back. He felt he would never be able to bear watching them collecting up their clothes and packing their kitbags and trunks.

He had just cut his own flesh to the quick. And the operation had been more painful than he had anticipated.

Now, standing on the poop, he looked at the barges of his train moored downstream. The wind whipped his face and chest. The wind which was bringing the long-waited rain. The clouds were on the point of breaking. A thousand signs betrayed that it would be soon, yet Christian felt himself emptier, lower in strength and hope than he had ever been.

Christian stood for a long moment, not really thinking but filled with the longing to go back to the deck-tent and tell his son and his prowman that he would keep them on. In the end, afraid of yielding, he felt he must act, take steps which would prevent him going back on his decision. He must be captain more than ever. The one and only captain, firmly at the helm of his rig. The captain whose sole concern was his struggle against steam.

His gaze, fixed on the far distance, almost on the dividing line between earth and cloud, returned to his barges. Some of the men were resting, others chatting in groups. Yet others were attending to horses; the cooks must be making soup in their galley, from which issued a good smell of cabbage and a white smoke which the wind blew in all directions. Outside the door, the deck-boy was munching a thick slice of bread on which he held down a small round cheese with his thumb.

Christian raised his fingers to his mouth and whistled, then went and stood on the bulwark of his barge, opposite the quay, his arms folded, head held high, waiting.

His men assembled very quickly. He had counted them as they came. When they were all there – except his son and Tirou, who had remained under the deck-tent – when M. Tonnerieu had taken up position beside him, Christian let his gaze range from face to face. The wind kept up its dance, billowing shirts and ruffling hair. They were all bare-headed because of this devilish wind, which would have blown their hats into the river.

Christian said in his firm, composed captain's voice: 'Well, now . . . You can see the sky as well as I can. It's going to piss down. As soon as the level's right, we'll go upstream.'

There was a murmur of approval. He had just voiced what all his men knew.

'I've called you together to tell you of my intention to go upstream regardless – '

As he was drawing breath, M. Tonnerieu touched him on the elbow and, rising on tiptoe, whispered: 'The prowman and Claude aren't here.'

'I know,' Christian muttered before going on. 'What with what the wind is bringing and what the glaciers have still to give, there could be a bad flood. And after the drought the Rhône's going to bring down a good deal of debris. You know that as well as I do.'

He paused again; then, slowly, in a voice which laid stress on every word, he went on: 'We shall go upstream even if the river is very high. Even when it's too high for the steam-kettle to pass under the bridges, we shall go on. So I want to tell you this: Claude Merlin and Honoré Baudry are no longer members of this crew.'

He stopped to allow the murmuring to die down, then went on, still calm and slow: 'If Baptiste Carénal accepts, he will be head prowman.'

He looked at Baptiste, who was exactly opposite him. Baptiste nodded.

'If you accept, come up here beside me.'

Baptiste obeyed, obviously uneasy.

'Does that suit you?' Christian asked.

'It suits me.'

'You know the risks?'

'I know.'

Christian turned back again to the quay. 'There are some old boatmen in this town whom I know well. They're ready to sign on with me for this upstream journey. I'm telling you this so that you know I shall never find myself in an awkward position . . . I repeat, there are risks. Let those who want to leave the rig say so before this evening. They'll be paid as if they had completed five days' journey upstream with us. That seems to me fair. It will enable them to get home. They don't even have to come and tell me. They should go and see Monsieur Tonnerieu, who will pay them. I'm not taking on anyone to replace the two who have left. The new prowman will reallocate duties. If anyone doesn't like his new post, he should come and tell me. If others go, I shall recruit. I repeat, I shall have no difficulty in finding people. Well, there you are, that's all I have to say to you.'

His throat felt as if he had been chewing dusty straw.

The men were already dispersing, talking among themselves about what he had just told them. Turning to Baptiste Carénal, Christian said: 'Thanks, Baptiste.'

The other stammered: 'It's . . . it's me . . . But Tirou . . . I mean to say. You shouldn't have.'

'You heard what I said to you? It was quite clear. I want only men who are totally committed.'

Still embarrassed, Baptiste scratched his beard. 'God above,' he said. 'Oh well, it's all right. I'll go and fetch my kitbag and box.'

Christian watched him go, swinging his bony shoulders a bit. He sighed. Baptiste came of a line of real boatmen, yet no one in his family had ever captained a barge. They belonged to those who serve without much questioning. There were three of the family on the rig. The father was the bailey – in charge of the horses. Baptiste, the elder son, was a deck-hand, and the younger was deckboy. Three men who risked everything with him. Three men whom he could be certain would accept. Three men, of whom one had just been promoted head prowman.

To tell the truth, he was sure of his crew, but that business of the crate had disturbed him so deeply that he was ready to suspect everyone.

When he turned round, M. Tonnerieu was still there. He had momentarily forgotten him and his everlasting books and figures. The clerk twisted his face into a sort of smile and asked: 'Now can I perhaps have a word with you?'

'As many as you like, Monsieur Tonnerieu.'

'First of all, what's all this nonsense about two men being dismissed?'

'It's not nonsense.'

'But Claude's your son.'

'Exactly.'

'Which means he's also your father's grandson.'

'An added reason.'

'What do you mean - an added reason? If your father was thinking of giving him his share of the outfit, he –'

'Don't make me laugh, Monsieur Tonnerieu,' Christian cried. The clerk was beginning to get on his nerves. 'It's true you've known my father longer than I have, but you don't know him well. If you imagine he would have confidence in someone who goes and works against us –'

'You're exaggerating.'

This time Christian lost his temper.

'Exaggerating? God in heaven!' he roared. 'All right, bear in mind that before taking this decision, I thought it over. My father would have done the same. I'm sure of it.'

M. Tonnerieu had let his eye-glasses fall; they were swinging on the end of their chain in front of his paunch.

'Good ... Very good ... But I hope too many of the men won't follow suit, because at five days per head I don't see how I'm going to pay them.'

He was turning on his heel to withdraw when Christian put a hand on his shoulder and held him back.

'What's this you're telling me?'

'If you want to see the books and the cash-box, that's easy. You're forgetting the men are paid and fed even when the Rhône is unsuitable for navigation.'

'But surely –' Christian fell silent, half stunned.

'Oh yes,' the old clerk quavered, 'you watch the river, live with it, you're a boatman. But you know, so far as I could make out, your sort used to be everywhere ... Everywhere, you hear me? And without clerks they were all finished in three trips downstream. But don't worry, I've seen the clerks of the other rigs, you're still far and away the soundest. You've got no more cash in reserve, but at any rate you don't owe anybody anything. The others are weighed down with debts. The Merlins have always won through. Real lords, the Merlins ... Lords.'

His little jerky steps were retreating, following the bulwark in the direction of the galley. Suddenly he stopped, turned round, and indicated a point on the esplanade.

'Ah,' he said, 'I was forgetting. There's a man who's been waiting to speak to you for over a quarter of an hour.'

Christian had joined the man who was waiting for him under the trees. He was just approaching him when the first drops began to fall.

'What do you want with me?' he asked.

'To talk to you about something important.'

The man was small and slight and rather poorly dressed. His face was bronzed and wrinkled. He held an old canvas hat in his hand. His head was half bald, and white.

Christian hesitated a moment. The rain which was pattering in big drops over the cracked earth was causing the dust to smoke. It gave off a good smell. He had waited so long for this moment that

he was annoyed with this man who was going to prevent him from savouring it to the full as he gazed at the river. He longed to tell the man that he would see him later, but the other was already wet and bowing his back against the downpour. His bald head was streaming.

'Put your hat back on and come and shelter,' Christian said.

They walked very quickly towards the barge, which they boarded. When they came in under the deck-tent, Claude and the prowman had already gone.

The rain whipped the awning. The eddies of wind sent the water in in bucketfuls through the open entrance. Christian unhooked the canvas flap, then, practically groping, he felt for a lantern which he lit and hung on the centre mast.

The little man was standing just inside the entrance. He had taken off his hat again and his bald head gleamed in the lantern's light.

'What is it you have to say to me?' Christian asked.

The man twisted his hat, hesitated, then said rather hoarsely: 'I don't trust steam.'

Christian began to laugh. 'And you've been waiting for me just for that?'

'Boilers have burst before now. It could happen again. I don't trust it.'

'Nor I,' said Christian. 'I don't trust it either, but I don't give a damn.'

'I made enquiries,' the man said. 'Everyone told me, "Captain Merlin is the strongest." '

'There are others.'

'Not as strong.'

'Good. So what?'

The man lowered his eyes, gazing at his hat which he continued to murder in his clumsy hands.

'I've got a kid . . . Little boy . . . Seven, he is. He's sick. They don't know what's the matter with him here. The doctor told me, "You'll have to take him to Lyons." I said yes, but I'm a mason . . . The journey. And my wife'll go with the kid . . . All right, the steamer'll take them. But I don't trust it. So I went to find your clerk. He told me no passengers. Not this trip . . .'

'No,' Christian confirmed, 'not this trip.'

'But my wife and the boy won't take up much room.'

'It's not a question of room, but of risk.'

The man began to laugh. A dry little laugh which took tucks in his face of a thousand wrinkles, and made him close his eyes. 'But with you I'd be quite calm. Everyone told me so, from the harbour master down. And he knows all the boatmen. He knows what he's talking about.'

It was on the tip of Christian's tongue to answer: 'This time the risks are as great with me as they are with steam.' But that was something he would never say. Such words would never issue from his lips. The little man's request embarrassed him. After all, if he travelled upstream, it was because he really thought he'd get there. He had never pushed off telling himself that he was running the risk of leaving his whole train of barges on the bottom.

He had never been crazy. Nor was he now. They would go upstream and, if the river required it, they would stop.

Christian looked again at the little man who was waiting. The man was no longer laughing, but his face had remained criss-crossed with wrinkles. His eyes, burning with a light of hope, asked the questions. Christian went to push aside the canvas entrance flap. The water was pouring over the planking of the deck. It was like a stream all pocked with hail. Huge bubbles formed and burst at once. The rain fell so heavily that it was barely possible to see a few square yards of boiling river. The banks had vanished, So had the sky. There was nothing but the rain, which was not managing to drown the wind.

Christian turned round and looked at the man, who had not stirred. He said calmly: 'No. It's out of the question. This weather could be with us all the way upstream. They wouldn't even find a dry corner for themselves on the barges.'

The man studied the deck-tent. He seemed to be saying, 'What about in here?' Perhaps he would have said it, only Christian did

not give him time. Pulling his purse from his pocket, he took two
five-franc gold pieces and held them out to the man, saying: 'I'd
like to help you, all the same. Let them take the coach. I know it's
expensive, but they'll get there faster.'

He remained with his hand held out.

'I didn't come to ask that of you,' said the man.

'I know. But I'd like to help you. Take it. If I could have taken
them I wouldn't have made you pay, so . . . Take it.'

'I didn't come for that,' the man repeated.

He hesitated again, but his right hand slowly detached itself from
his hat and opened to accept the money. It was a rough, cracked
hand seamed with whitewash. He was a mason. He had said so, and
it was obvious.

He said thank-you, and Christian had the feeling that it was
certainly the first time this man had ever accepted help. As he was
moving towards the exit, Christian said: 'You're going to get
soaked. This could go on a long time.'

'It doesn't matter,' the man said. 'I haven't far to go.'

He said thank-you again, shaking Christian's hand, then, pulling
his brown canvas hat well down over his white skull and hunching
his back, he went out unhesitatingly into the downpour.

Christian followed him out and watched him hurrying away
along the esplanade, where the water was sweeping down leaves
torn from the glistening plane-trees.

In Beaucaire, as in all the riverside towns, the rain had emptied the
streets. Doors had shut in the warmth of houses in which fires had
been lit for cooking dinner. The talk was all of the rain and the
river. Those under the same roof were drawn together by the rain
and darkness, but families were isolated from other families. There
would be no evening gathering on the chairs and benches, which
had been hurriedly brought indoors. The water which the sky
poured down played on the sills. It overflowed the gutters, cleansed
at last. Only a few rats slunk along the pavements, from one hole
to the next.

Some who thought of the river did so in fear that it would spread into the city and reach the kitchens after flooding the cellars. Others were terrified of floods, their only refuge being their houses. But there were others whom the river carried with it, and who carried the river within themselves. These were the men on the barges. The core of their existence was there, and they were not troubled by what they owned on land.

When the river was too low to carry barges, boatmen felt frustrated and betrayed. When they lacked what constituted their superiority over landsmen, they were stranded. They lived only in hopes of rising water. And the longer the wait, the greater their desire.

When at last the water came, they wanted it to be terrible because their own strength was renewed with the flood. The more the river terrorized the landsmen, the greater their contempt for the danger it represented. The river men needed the landsmen's fear as a yardstick of their own courage. And when they took out their boats to go to the help of villagers and farmers clinging to rooftops, it was because they were traditionally rescuers as well as boatmen; but it was also because their proud nature found satisfaction in it. For the men they went out to pick up were as weak and frightened as women. The boatmen saved them, but they looked down on them from the heights of their own coolness and courage.

Only the fear of a mysterious overriding justice which might give the Rhône the idea of punishing them, prevented them from wishing for the sort of floods which would enable them to show that they were the water's masters, the lords of the valley, the only ones who could pit themselves against the river.

Such men were found on the barges, but they were found indoors as well: boatmen who no longer had a vessel and who knew that only a flood could still give them the opportunity to show what they were made of.

And these were the men who were often least restrained in hoping the river would run riot.

On that watery night the mason's visit kept Christian awake a long time. The rain drummed continuously on the canvas and the deck.

The wind wailed and gusted everywhere. The lantern was out. There was thick darkness in the deck-tent, where Baptiste Carénal was occupying Tirou's bunk. Claude's bunk was empty. Baptiste was snoring, Christian listening to the rain. If the downpour was the same throughout the valley and in the Alps, the water would be all right in one day's time.

Before retiring, Christian had gone to prowl around the steamer. The rain had emptied the esplanade. It was barely possible to discern a few gleams on the side where the port of Beauregard lay.

There was light on board the dark, ill-defined bulk of the *Rhodan*. Christian heard a hammering on metal. The repair had not been completed. Once the part was in position, it would require at least a further six hours to get up steam enough for the *Rhodan* to depart.

All this – the poor little mason, the *Rhodan*, the rain on the river, the departure of Tirou and Claude – went round and round in Christian and kept him awake.

They were going to sail. Go up-river now that it was once more navigable, but what would the steamer do? If the water rose too much and too fast, it would be dangerously full of debris. The wise thing would be to wait a couple of days. Let all that the flood might rip from the banks go on downstream. Wait for calmer water. But suppose the river went on rising for days on end? And suppose the steamer left as soon as she was ready?

The other barge-masters whom Christian had met during the day reckoned that the flood might be a bad one. They did not yet know whether they would decide to leave, but Christian had sensed that they were inclined to caution. True, none of them had horses as good as his, but weren't they also a bit frightened? Frightened for their barges, of an accident which would finally ruin them? In former times a captain who lost his rig always re-established himself, but today, with the competition from steam, they all knew that to be impossible.

And then, formerly, one day was never a vital matter. If a captain decided to wait until the river was in a better state, the others waited too. There were enough clients for them not to need to take one another's. Now, it was not only a matter of getting there, but of showing that one could do it as well and even better than steam. Christian had demonstrated this on the down-stream journey, and now perhaps the river was going to allow him to do as much on the way back.

He could wish that the flood might be terrible. Strong enough to frighten the men from the companies and prevent their tall steamers from passing under the bridges. But no one would prevent *him* from going upstream. No one. And certainly not the river.

On the contrary, the more he thought about it, the more the feeling grew in him that the river was his ally, his staunchest friend. His own son had betrayed him, but the river would not. He sensed it in this night loud with the sound of water from the sky, water which was going to gather in the valley's heart to swell the river.

The more he thought about it, the more his mind became fixed on the Rhône. *His* Rhône. He saw it as clearly as if he were at the prow of his barge in broad daylight, battling against the current. He ended by forgetting everything else in order to see nothing but the Rhône. A Rhône powerful and insolent, tossing vast muddy waters southwards; waters which would set every living thing in the valley trembling – plants, beasts and men. Every living thing except himself, Christian Merlin, captain of the finest rig afloat. Every living thing except himself; he had a pact with the river.

These waters, which would make the boldest flee, would yield to him. They would bow to his will. If the current gathered strength, so would the cross-currents. It would suffice to know how to find them, to know how to manoeuvre the barges so that the water's very strength would aid them on their upstream jour-ney as it had downstream. A hundred times already he had made good use of those eddies which flowed behind the islands when the flood was strong, but tonight, in order to fix his attention on a river shaped more by his needs than by reality, he pictured himself borne on by obedient waters.

Half asleep, he continued to imagine a voyage which would

obliterate steam and all the rest of his problems. He had been welcomed here like a triumphant hero. When he reached the port of La Charité, the whole of Lyons would be waiting for him, to hail his exploit.

Not only would he sail upstream faster than anyone ever had before, but at the same time he would destroy steam once and for all.

The night howled, but Christian gradually fell asleep, pushing into the depths of his slumber this dream which he had begun while awake. And as it progressed, the dream emerged out of the greyness of doubt as bushes emerge from mist to sparkle in the sunlight.

This age of progress, of iron and fire, this age of machines and inventions was also the age of notices, proclamations, decrees and regulations.

In every port administration buildings were being built or enlarged. Every day the offices took up more and more room. All these pale, sickly, sedentary employees amused the boatmen, but it was they who laid down the regulations, and that was irritating rather than amusing. It was another invention of the steam men to complicate the task of river men and force them to pay additional taxes.

For even if sedentary employees did not have such large appetites as productive workers, they still had to eat. And it was the workers who fed them.

Not only had the boatmen to pay so that these idlers could eat their fill and wear starched shirts, but they were even obliged to do their work for them. For it was the clerks of barge-trains who had to fill in all these forms. And it was no good the clerks knowing how to read and write; as they were almost all very old, they had great difficulty in grasping the subtleties of these new regulations.

It was what was known as progress. Everybody's job was made more complicated after it had been shouted from the housetops that steam would enable men to live better and work less. A fine result! It was no longer possible to transport coffee, soap, wine, without filling in complex forms which the men in the navigation office and the weights-and-measures office had to verify and register.

Even the Prefect managed to poke his nose into navigational matters. As if that bladder of lard would have known the difference between a barge and a port! Notices three feet high had been stuck up, saying:

POLICE REGULATIONS
OF THE PORT OF BEAUCAIRE

Every helmsman, captain or clerk of a vessel, boat, barge-train, etc., arriving at the port of Beaucaire is required to berth, according to his type of vessel, in one of the places designated in the Regulation of the Prefect of Gard, dated April 29, 1840, and in the position which the Harbour Master shall indicate to him...

Article 10. During heavy flooding of the Rhône, and so long as the navigation of steam vessels is not interrupted, the berths of all boats in general being submerged and un-approachable, the said steam vessels will be berthed up-stream from the suspension bridge to the Porte de l'Hôtel de la Tuilerie, to the exclusion of all other vessels, known as savoyardes, which can easily tie up at the Porte de La Couronne upstream...

Anyone found guilty of swearing, threatening or taking action against the Harbour Master in the execution, or on the occasion of the execution, of his duties, will be ar-raigned on the sworn statement of the aforesaid and punished according to the penalties laid down in the Penal Code, depending on the gravity of the case.

The harbour master, who had captained a rig for more than fifteen years, was the first to laugh at these notices. When he saw the boatmen busy reading them, he would clap them on the shoulder, saying: 'You've got the message. If you want to knock me down, just don't do it when I'm on duty. Afterwards, you can lash out as much as you like, but on duty, no.'

He too was obliged to discharge his duties while applying the regulations, and with these blasted blockheads of boatmen, it wasn't always easy.

'Your regulations aren't worth their weight in farts,' raged a barge-master.

'Go and tell that to the Prefect, leather-breeches!'

'Fuck the Prefect!'

'You do that. You won't be the only one.'

Everything always sorted itself out in the end, for the harbour master was at heart on the side of the real boatmen. The boatmen knew it, but they knew too that the all-powerful companies could apply pressure on the bureaucrats. So in order not to risk causing a friend to lose his job, they brawled for the pleasure of it and to show that they still had it in them, but they always ended by obeying orders.

The day was still far distant when Christian awoke. Several times during the night he had roused from sleep just long enough to listen to the river and the sound of the storm.

Only towards morning did the river's voice begin to predominate. The storm still drummed as loudly, the wind blew as strongly, but amid the roar there was a new sound which Christian recognized at once. A regular, rounded sound, well supplied with lighter notes skipping over a solid bass depth. It was the upstream dyke, the one which protected the quiet reach of the port where the boats were moored. This time the Rhône was running bank high. In less than two days it had grown from a skeletal state to fullest depth.

This morning the dyke was growling like an animal which wanted to bite, although it was not yet clear whether it wanted to bite in play or in earnest. There were friendly gurglings within the river's deep sound, but they would not last long. Before mid-morning the dyke would be entirely covered, and the water would make only a heavy sound, loud with menace.

As soon as he was on his feet, Christian thrust aside the entrance flap. A slap of icy water whipped his face and chest. He shivered, but more with pleasure than with cold.

'Good God!' he growled. 'Just the Rhône I wanted.'

Behind him, Baptiste, who had just got up, was startled. 'Just the Rhône you wanted! God above, it's going to cause a flood to end all floods.'

'Baptiste, when you go and find us a mouthful, will you tell the bailey and the blacksmith to come here.'

Baptiste pulled on his boots, put on his coat and his leather hat, and went out. Christian let the soaked canvas fall back and lit a lantern. No rain seeped into the watertight deck-tent, but everything within was already humid, sticky and cold.

Christian dressed. He fastened his belt around his loins. He made ready his axe and his coils of cordage. Every gesture was a source of joy to him. He had gone to sleep with his idea of dominating the river; of showing everyone that he was indeed the strongest, the master of the valley, and the idea had only taken firmer root in him during the night.

Baptiste was not long in returning, followed by his father and Joseph Cathomen. The three men came in and took off their dripping coats, which they hung on the mast nearest the entrance. Everything glistened in the lantern-light, and the men's beards were sprinkled with droplets.

'Morning,' Joseph called. 'We've done it this time. We've been wanting water and we're going to get more than we need.'

'Right enough,' the bailey agreed. 'It doesn't look too good. But we had to wait for it. And it's still preferable to a drought.'

'It may not look too good for the steam men and for outfits which aren't at full strength, but it's a different matter for us.'

Christian paused to give weight to his words. 'I told you we'd go upstream. We shall go upstream.'

The others looked at one another. Then Albert Carénal said: 'Fair enough. As the river is this morning, we can go upstream. But tomorrow...'

'Listen to me, Albert, we're not going to argue about what we'll do tomorrow. I asked you both to come here because the bailey and the blacksmith are primarily concerned with the horses. You know the animals better than I do.'

'There's nothing to worry about in that quarter,' said the bailey. 'Ours are the strongest, that's for sure.'

'You can never be too strong,' Christian said.

'No, but there's no other outfit to match ours.'

'Has old Tonetti got horses?'

'Of course he has,' said the bailey. 'He even came to see me to suggest some exchanges.'

'It's not a question of exchanges but of reinforcements.'

'Reinforcements? But you've got twenty-eight magnificent animals.'

'I want thirty-six.'

The number fell between Christian and the other three. And then for a long moment there was only the sound of the rain and the wind and the river.

The other three looked at one another, shaking their heads, then they looked at their captain, and then back at one another once more. In the end it was the blacksmith who said, almost timidly: 'With another four couple we'd certainly go upstream like the wind, but at more than a thousand francs apiece, all the same . . .'

Not knowing what else to say, he scratched his head.

'All the same what?' Christian snapped. 'I'm out of my mind, perhaps?'

'No,' said Joseph. 'More horses mean fewer risks, you're not out of your mind, but more than eight thousand francs . . .'

Christian began to laugh. 'You must have heard Rapiat telling me the cash-box was empty. But there's no question of asking even the first sou from him . . . I shall pay for these horses. And I want good ones. That's why I'm sending you to find them. Keep your eyes skinned.'

Christian bent down and pulled from under his bunk a small brass-studded black wooden box, from which he took a coarse canvas bag. He patted the bag, which gave forth a musically metallic sound. He gave the bag to the bailey, saying: 'There's plenty in there.'

The bailey took the bag. It was obvious that he wanted to speak, but he could only stammer: 'I'll be damned! You're the captain all right...You'll see.'

'You'll go as soon as we've had a mouthful,' said Christian. 'I want to leave at dawn.'

The bailey and the blacksmith had gone out into the downpour, the new prowman had also just left the deck-tent to go and rouse the men, when Christian heard someone hailing him from the quay.

'Ahoy! Captain Merlin! Open up a bit so that I can see to come aboard.'

Christian lifted the entrance flap and went out, a lantern in his hand. There was a sound of hesitant footsteps on the deck, then the gleam of a leather coat in the lantern's beam, which penetrated barely a couple of yards into the moving curtain of rain.

'I think I've arrived just in time for a mouthful.'

Christian recognized Old Surdon's voice.

'Come in,' he said. 'I've already eaten, but there's some left.'

The old man, who was even taller than Christian, stooped to come in under the canvas. He was carrying a big bag made of oiled black canvas which he set down before removing his coat.

'First of all,' he said, 'how's your father?'

'Well.'

'Is he ageing as well as I am? I mean, as little?'

Christian looked at the old man, who was watching him and smiling. Old Surdon was what the barge crews called a mountain. He was over six foot tall, and he must have weighed over two hundred pounds. He had no paunch and was as straight as a mast; he was a year younger than Christian's father. He too had retired. Having no children, he had sold his outfit to come and settle with his niece, who had married an ironmonger from Beaucaire. Everyone knew that his private drama had been to see his successor wreck the whole business inside two years. He merely said: 'Some people are unlucky.' But he thought: Some people are as suited to captaining a rig as I am to being an ironmonger. Christian knew the old man was bored to death in this district where people spoke a dialect he didn't understand and emptied their slops in streets where no child destined to become a boatman had ever played.

The old man had sat down. He had tossed his soaking wet hat on to a bunk and shaken his head like a long-haired dog. His white hair fell over the nape of his neck and over his ears, where it merged with his beard. Only a glint betrayed the gold rings in his ears. His beard too was long and white. It encroached on his face as far as the cheekbones. The tanned nose and brow seemed almost black against such whiteness. His red-veined, watery blue eyes glistened.

He began by eating the anchovies and drinking the brandy which Christian offered him. He smacked his lips.

'It's good,' he said. 'And at my age one's entitled to a nip.'

Christian poured him another glass. He was watching the old man, and from time to time he cast a glance towards the black bag placed near the entrance.

'Ha,' the old man said, 'are you looking at my bag? It's been up and downstream a few times. As often as your father's, certainly ... And suddenly last night the wanderlust gripped it. And this morning it said to me: "Jules, we're going to make another trip upstream. A fine trip with Christian, who has the strongest outfit at the moment." And here we are. Me and my bag.'

Old Surdon spoke calmly, as if he were announcing that he was going to buy a few sous' worth of tobacco. Christian was too taken aback to answer.

'I'm not asking you to pay me,' Old Surdon went on. 'I'm doing it for the love of it. For the sake of doing it one more time. Because, to tell you the truth, and you know it anyway, I'm sick to death of that fool of an ironmonger. He's a good fellow, but he's not one of us, and he's an ironmonger.'

'It's a trade like any other,' Christian said stupidly.

The old man's eyes crinkled, forming a network of tiny lines on his cheekbones, which disappeared into his beard. 'Well,' he said, 'perhaps it is. But then, it's ours which is not a trade like any other. I'm glad. It puts all the others in the wrong and we're alone in being right.' He laughed again, then said: 'All the same, you're a

bit put out to see me here. All right, I'll explain . . . I've been itching
to for a long time, but I said to myself: You'd look such a fool. Well,
you know how it is. And then, I know this is going to be no ordinary
voyage upstream . . . I know it. You've only got to see the river and
know how obstinate you are. Obstinate as your father. Well, I was
hesitating. Yesterday at nightfall I came to see you, I watched your
rig from a distance, and then I said to myself: It's impossible, it
won't work. And so I went home.'

Christian listened without saying a word. He seemed to hear his
own father speaking. The old man filled an enormous red clay
pipe with an iron lid, lit it, tamped the tobacco well down with his
thumb which covered the whole top of it, then went on: 'You
know where my ironmonger hangs out?'

'Yes, beyond the Place Vieille.'

'Well, I was crossing the square. It was dark already, and what did
I see? A couple of fellows settling down to sleep on the ground,
under the arcades. Boatmen. I could tell that even in the dark.'

He broke off for a moment and looked hard at Christian before
going on: 'Well, I see from your face you've guessed who it was.'

Christian had guessed. And he was furious that the old man
could read him so perfectly. He thought: Good God, he's like my
father.

'Well,' the old man went on, 'you can imagine that when I
recognized your lad I didn't say: "There's Christian's boy." No, I
thought: "Good Lord, it's Félix Merlin's grandson. And there on
the ground like a down-and-out . . . Hell! And with Tirou, a damn
fine prowman if ever there was one." And there I was thinking he
was like to marry Félix's daughter. Ah well, that's no concern of
mine.'

The longer the old man went on in his even tone, the more
Christian felt uneasiness well up within him. He took another nip,
poured out another for the old man and filled his pipe, more to
gain time than from any desire to smoke.

'I couldn't do anything else,' he growled.

'I'll bet you couldn't,' said the old man. 'That's what I thought.
And if I'd have been Félix I'd have thrashed the pair of them and

brought them back on board with a few kicks up their arses. I said
so . . . Because they told me all about it. And that they'd been
wrong and they were sorry. And all the rest of it. Practically
bawled like kids. So what could I do? My niece gave them some
soup and they slept in the ironmongery.'

He said no more. Christian was waiting to hear him say: 'They're
out there in the rain, hoping. And you're going to tell them to
come on aboard.' He was waiting for it and there was a warm glow
within him. But the old man didn't say it. And as soon as he began
speaking again, Christian had the disagreeable impression that he
had guessed what was going through his mind and that he had
deliberately allowed time for his imagination to get to work.

'The ironmongery isn't the port of Beauregard's hotel,' the old
man continued, 'but it's better than the pavement. Drier.'

He was taking his time. He took at least four pulls at his pipe,
whose bowl was glowing, before going on: 'This morning I shook
them awake. I told them there were carriers going up to Aramon.
And I said to them, "So long as the road hasn't become a quagmire,
you'll certainly arrive before Christian's rig. And if you wait a bit,
you'll see it going upstream. And you'll see a very fine rig. Well
captained. And a good voyage upstream. And you'll see too that it's
something very different from a smoking heap of metal."'

His eyes shone with pleasure. He gave a series of little chuckling
laughs. He held himself erect on the crate where he was sitting. He
winked, raised his forefinger to his ear, then pointed to the back
of the deck-tent.

Beyond the wind-whipped canvas the team-drivers could be
heard at work.

'Humph!' he said. 'It's a long time since I heard that except from
the quay. It does something to you, I swear it. If your father were
here, he'd tell you the same.'

'If my father were here, he wouldn't allow you on board.'

The old man had risen. His metallic gaze had hardened. He
measured up to Christian, whom he overtopped by half a head.

'My God!' he shouted. 'Put me ashore? Me? Send me packing to
the ironmonger's back shop. Hell and damnation, do you want to

kill me? I'm not asking to be second-in-command. I'll go where you tell me. But here I am and I'll show I'm still worth my place. Never mind what place.'

Christian could not take his captain's tone with this man. Calm, planted stolidly before him, Old Surdon gazed at him through the pipe-smoke which had filled the deck-tent.

'Stay with me,' Christian said. 'I've only replaced Tirou, but I need a tough old devil like you with me.'

Surdon coughed and knocked out the bowl of his pipe against the sole of his boot. To do so, he had to lower his head. Not quickly enough, however, for Christian had time to see two big tears fall on his beard.

Christian had left the deck-tent and Old Surdon was at his heels. The day was having difficulty in piercing this drenched universe to pour down on river and barges a glaucous light which cast grey reflections everywhere. Beneath these reflections the water of the Rhône was clay-coloured.

'There's the devil of a flood building up, Christian,' the old man said. 'You've taken on additional horses, that's a master stroke. Your father would tell you so. Or rather, no, he wouldn't say it so as not to spoil your character, but he'd think it. Ours will be a memorable voyage upstream, I can tell you.'

The old man was overflowing with good humour. He laughed under the squalls. The rain soaked his beard, and when he spoke his breath sent droplets spurting before him.

With Baptiste Carénal, the three of them prepared the main cable fixed to the foremast and checked the auxiliary ropes. Then, having reached the last barge, they joined the men who had just detached the ferry horses to tether them on the outside of the stable barge, where the team-drivers were giving the animals oats. While he worked and gave orders, Christian observed Old Surdon. The old man was rediscovering the gestures which he had repeated a thousand times in the course of his long career. His hands did not hesitate. He did not have to seek a firm footing on a rack or a rowing bench.

The others were watching him also. The news had quickly spread from one end of the rig to the other, and it seemed as if Surdon's presence had obliterated in the twinkling of an eye the shadow which the departure of Claude and Tirou had cast over the whole crew.

When the men heard the horses stamping in the mud of the esplanade, they stopped work and stood up to see them.

In the town as well as on the river, trees, barges, men were wrapped in a mist which trailed from the clouds. The horses were less than twenty yards away when they began to emerge from it. They moved forward, a warmer shade than that of the trunks of the plane-trees. Sturdy, heavy, slow, they were two mighty hammer-blows, followed by two more, then another two, and two more after them. The bailey was holding the bridles of the first pair. He too seemed broader and heavier in this mist, made ever thicker by the sheets of rain which gusted from puddle to puddle.

Standing silent on the bulwarks of the barges, Captain Merlin and his men watched.

When the two men and the animals reached the quay, Christian went down. The others followed, and formed a semi-circle around the newcomers.

The horses in the stable barge neighed when they scented the additional beasts. The new arrivals answered. Erect, heads high, soaked manes scarcely lifted by the wind, steam issuing from their nostrils, they called, stamping the mud and pebbles with their hoofs.

Christian and Old Surdon went up to them. They ran the palms of their hands over the animals' warm flanks; the steaming skin responded to the caress. 'Yes,' the old man repeated. 'Yes, yes . . . They're strong. My God, they're strong.' And all were thinking: He's right. They've chosen well. They're strong animals. With them, we can risk the voyage upstream.

Christian merely asked: 'Have they done any ferrying?'

'Certainly they have,' the bailey answered. 'There was a good choice, I assure you. Two outfits were sold last month.' He hesitated. 'Two from Serrières: Rosenol and Duprat.'

'I'd heard as much, but I could hardly believe it.' Christian sighed.

'I thought they'd at least have been taken on for transporting stone.'

He turned towards his men, squared his shoulders, and assumed his captain's voice: 'Right. We've only got to harness them and we'll be ready to go.'

His throat was a bit tight, but when his gaze ranged over his men, when he again patted the splendid animals which the blacksmith and the bailey had just bought, when he heard the first shouts and the first whip-crackings of the team-drivers who were bringing the other animals out of the stable barge, when finally he looked at Old Surdon, who was smiling and lifting his face to the rain and wind, he felt a fine, firm joy rise glowing within him.

Turning downstream, from which direction the squalls caught him full face, he breathed in the air in little sips. He could neither see nor hear what was going on around the steamer, but the wind told him that the funnel had not yet started to spit.

There are mornings made expressly for the departure of those who know how to dare. Mornings when the day comes up so slowly that the milky gleams impregnating the clouds are barely distinguishable.

These mornings bring no hope. From beyond invisible distances they drag in painfully a sad and lifeless dawn. No birds spread wing on such mornings, and the sky's sole life is that of wind and rain. Everything breaks slowly, as if day were too weak to dispel the remnants of night.

And because, on such mornings, men themselves must spin the hope of departure out of night, only the strong dare embark. But they will go far, these men who bear within them a more luminous dawn than that which struggles to light up the river. They will go all day without tiring, towards a twilight which they will seek to prolong into the very heart of night.

The boatmen were among those who cast off on mornings when any departure is a challenge. Their faith was firm, they believed in their calling, and they knew how to make the effort to hope. Something told them that machines can give man immense power, but they retorted that this power was as nothing, because it transcended man. They sensed that machines transform those whom they conquer, and they were anxious to remain free. While others forged machine parts which would make cogs of them, they rose very early in unlit dawns to forge a hope which they propelled before them on the river.

Despite the heavy rain, when Captain Merlin's boatmen and team-drivers set about their tasks there were more than fifty spectators on the esplanade. They were mostly older men, who regretted not seeing the spectacle of a fine barge-train as often as formerly, and did not want to miss this departure. Perhaps also the news of Old Surdon's signing on had already gone the rounds. For it was an event. Christian sensed it. He realized too that he was giving the signal for a voyage upstream unlike any of those he had already experienced under his father's command and later under his own.

This morning everything was exceptional. The stormy weather, the river whose level was rising hourly and which would soon be up to the tow-paths, the additional horses, and above all this desire which he felt growing within him to reach the end of the course whatever it cost.

The bailey had already positioned the horses. He had his usual mount, a chestnut stallion in his prime and well accustomed to work. On his right, his mount's team-mate was not much younger, but he had been teamed with the other for the past eighteen months. As the second pair of this four-in-hand, he had placed the strongest pair of the batch he had just bought. Thus these two animals whom he did not yet know could give their utmost by letting themselves be led, even if they were not perfectly trained for the work.

He had proceeded in the same fashion all along the line, giving his team-drivers as mounts the older animals of the outfit, and positioning the newcomers in second place.

Fourteen horses were harnessed to the first barge, whose load was almost sixty tons. Eight were harnessed to the second barge, which carried approximately thirty tons. The remaining animals were divided among the three following barges which were much less heavily laden, until the last two had no horses at all. Linked in line, one to another, by a main cable the thickness of a boatman's arm and by two slimmer ones which acted as safety ropes, the train of barges was so long that from his post at the tiller of the leading barge, Christian could not even see the half of them.

Orders, oaths, whip-cracks, the stamping of the horses' shoes on the cobbles, were carried upstream by the wind and informed the river folk that a rig was preparing to leave. The muddy water which now covered the topmost stones of the dyke was bringing down branches, bundles of straw, and huge piles of undergrowth wrenched from the islands.

'All ready on land!' shouted the bailey, thrusting his hands into the harness as he mounted and bestrode his horse.

He raised his right hand, brandishing his whip.

Two land crew, axes in hand, were already going upstream along the bank and disappearing into the murk.

Christian raised his fingers to his lips and whistled downstream three times.

The wind brought back the cry six times repeated, coming nearer every time.

'All ready on river!'

The captain of each barge had just checked that everything was in order.

Before uttering the prayer and the order for departure, Christian turned round to look upstream. Baptiste Carénal was at the prow, the willow-rod in his hands, ready to push out to midstream. His brother the deck-boy stood beside him, also clutching a rod.

A few paces away from his post at the tiller, Christian saw Old Surdon watching him. In his right hand the old man was also clutching a willow-rod, whose tip rested on the quay, but in his left he held aloft a small boatman's cross bleached almost white.

'Yours?' Christian asked.

'No, better than that, it's my father's. It's forty-seven years since it last saw the river. It's been waiting for a great occasion.'

Christian returned the old man's smile, then, kneeling on the offshore bulwark, he dipped his hand in the river, stood up, turned towards his rig and crossed himself, crying: 'To God and the Virgin Mary, lads, and to the Rhône! And may Saint Nicholas be with us!'

He glanced again at Old Surdon, who, leaving his rod leaning against the bulwark, had also crossed himself and was sliding the crucifix under the canvas of the deck-tent. The old man's face shone with an inward joy and a vast confidence.

Turning back to his prowman, Christian shouted: 'Ho, prowman! Push towards the Empie!'

With one concerted movement, the prowman, the deck-boy and Old Surdon leaned on their rods. For a moment it seemed that the arching wood was going to break, or else spring back and hurl the men to the other bulwark. The heavy barge remained motionless, pressed against the quay by the force of the whirlpools still forming at the tip of the submerged dyke.

Compared to the feeble strength of a man, a greybeard and a boy, the heavy barge was a huge block. A mountain to be moved, with its tons of timber, olive oil, raw silk and wine.

The barge did not budge, but the men were unsurprised and continued their efforts. They knew that with water there is a long moment before movement at last becomes apparent.

They strove. The sweat on their faces began to mingle with the rain. Their breath issued in frail threads of steam which the wind at once caught up into the trailing cloud-mass. At last, slowly, imperceptibly, the arc of the rods decreased and straightened. A triangle opened between the bulwark and the quay. To make the most of the strength of the water which would flow into it, Christian leaned on the tiller, keeping the stern pressed against the bank. The barge formed a dam. The water rose between its side and the quay. The men pushed again, but already the Rhône was doing more of the work than their arms. It was there, between them and the land, all harrowed with wrinkles, all racked with nerves ready to relax like thousands of imprisoned reptiles. The prow moved through a good ninety degrees. Already it was a few yards from the end of the dyke when Captain Merlin, leaning his full weight on the tiller, thrust the stern into midstream.

Slowly, smoothly, still broadside on, the barge drew away. The cable paid out, whipping the water, emerging dripping. Already on the other barges captains and prowmen were busy following the manoeuvre. When the prow of the leading barge began to bite into the current, Christian shouted towards the bank: 'Ho, bailey! Haul on the ropes!'

Whips cracked on the bank. All the team-drivers began swearing to urge on the horses. So all the animals of the outfit moved off upstream, the leading fourteen first, then the others, four by four. Hoofs rang, slipped, scraped the stones and made the mud fly. Despite the rain, the iron shoes struck sparks. A terrible force was getting under way. For a moment, it seemed that the thirty-six horses would never manage to battle against the river's rage. Caught in the full force of the current, the barges were drifting, but all the ropes were taut.   The horses stopped. They pawed the ground. Under the lash of the whip they strained forward, necks outstretched. Steam rose from the flanks and nostrils of the whole team. At last the barges held steady. Slavering foam, the muddy river parted growling before their prows. The foremasts creaked The tillers and rudder planks moaned under the opposing efforts of water and men. On the esplanade, where more than a hundred people were now gathered, shoulders hunched against the rain, there was silence. They waited, holding their breath.

The barges were still motionless, but already the horses were beginning to move forward, tautening further the ropes whose hemp, long out of action, began to shed water like washing being wrung out. The ropes vibrated as if they were going to snap, the barges wavered a little, righted themselves, and the convoy got under way, working a bit more deeply into the muscular body of the Rhône.

Then a great shout went up from all the onlookers. Land crew and boatmen replied. Farewells and cries of encouragement rose above the hubbub. From all sides voices called:

'May Saint Nicholas be with you!'

'Long live the river men!'

Christian felt something contract within him. His hands,

clenched on the soaked wood of the tiller, did not tremble, but the strength of the river which made the rudder vibrate shook his arms and a long shudder ran all down his spine.

He looked behind him. Three barges were following, well in line. The fifth was scarcely visible, and the others were swallowed up by the ragged sky which continued unceasingly to drown the river. But they were following. He sensed it. Moreover, he knew that on each barge a helmsman was doing as he was, keeping an eye on the barge behind as well as on his own. If anything were to happen, he would be alerted at once.

Old Surdon had come up to Christian. He too had heard the shouts from the esplanade, and Christian guessed that a few tears had mingled with the water-drops glistening on his beard.

'It's a good departure, lad,' the old man said, his solemn voice trembling slightly. 'And it'll be a voyage upstream such as hasn't been seen in a long time.' He paused long enough to relight his pipe, then, having also glanced at what was coming behind him out of habit, he added: 'I'm going up to the prow. The river's bringing down a lot of stuff. Two men won't be too many. And the boy'll do all right with you.'

Christian's throat was too constricted for him to speak. He nodded instead. Then he watched the old man with his long rod over his shoulder walk calmly off along the bulwark, against which the turbid water ran.

He was going to keep watch with the prowman, straining his eyes through the murk, ready to thrust aside from the prow the tree-trunks and roots which the river was carrying down.

PART FIVE

The Voyage Upstream

Life had changed a great deal in the last twenty years. In the early days of steam navigation people came from far and wide to see these fiery monsters go by with their appalling din.

The first to be seen going upstream in July 1829 was the *Pionnier*. She still had a wooden hull – wood with carvings on it and built in the shape of a sea-going vessel. It had been quite an event. And then, two years later, the first metal-hulled vessels had appeared on the river. They were still infrequent. No longer an event, but a spectacle lasting half an hour which amused some and revolted others.

Gradually these monsters had begun to replace the fine horse-drawn barge-trains which grew rarer from year to year. So it was now the passing of a rig which was becoming an event.

It was sad to think that the rigs were likely to disappear one day, and their upstream voyage aroused emotion in even the most stolid. It was well known that the men who voyaged thus would have to wage war against the current for twenty-five or thirty days, and even more.

More than thirty days to travel up a hundred and fifty miles of river, whereas the same stretch downstream took only two or three – that gave some idea of the river men's task and of the effort they required of their horses.

On the upstream journey land crew and team-drivers had to act as quickly as prowmen and helmsmen on the way down. An error of judgement, a hesitation, and disaster followed. Horses with broken legs who had to be shot, team-drivers injured and half drowned who had to be cared for and taken on board, these were the least of the evils.

On board, captains and prowmen, keeping one eye on what lay upstream and the other on the team, severed the cable with an axe-stroke to save the horses. The barges, unattached, began to drift. The men tried to land without too much damage by mooring where they could, or else they dropped huge chains weighted with pigs of iron which acted as brakes as they dragged along the bottom.

And afterwards it took hours of work to restore the rig. Line up the team again, raise the chains with the capstan, resplice the ropes, pay out the cables, and push off again for midstream.

In this minute by minute battle, going on for days and days of the upstream voyage, boatmen, land crew, team-drivers, all knew from deck-boy to captain that it was necessary to have head and nerves as strong as one's arms.

The beauty of barge-trains lay in the perfect harmony between horses and men. The strength of one linked to the strength of the other. Linked by cracks of the whip and shouting, but forged by effort which ended by becoming a kind of fellow feeling.

And with steam this was precisely what was lacking. On the steam-boats there was nothing suggestive of life. They had power all right, but what was its source? A boiler which roared like the mistral under a porch. It was sufficient to lift a lever as big as a trowel-handle to release that power. There was too much mystery about it. There was nothing there that the eye could watch with pleasure, evaluate, estimate, linger over lovingly. Whereas the great horses, deep-chested, deep-cruppered, more than thirty of them all pulling together, were a sight to bring the spectator out in goose-flesh.

People did not linger to watch them pass out of mere curiosity. Curiosity was what they felt for the steamer. They watched the boatmen with the emotion born of tense struggles, battles whose issue was uncertain. For sometimes the Rhône proved the stronger. It capsized a barge before the boatmen had been able to cut the cables, and swept away the horses entangled in their harness.

If a steamer sank, it was only so much metal lost.

Besides, the horses and team-drivers were the links between the land crew and the river folk. People felt closer to the boatmen while their animals trod the towpaths, slept in the stables of the waterside inns, munched hay bought in the villages.

When the horses were too old for their harsh calling, the farmers bought them back if they were not too utterly worn out, if the attacks of marsh fever had left them any strength. The air of the high ground soon restored their vigour, and they were then splendid beasts, well schooled, to whom ploughing was merely an amusement. When they were in the orchards or vineyards and a barge-train went by on the river with its team-drivers swearing and cracking their whips, the farmers had to keep a tight hold on the bridles. Neck outstretched, nostrils flaring, ears pricked, the animal would send a long neigh in the direction of the river.

Some had been seen to kick up all four hoofs, overturn plough and ploughman, and kick over the traces in order to gallop down to the bank.

The horses, like the men, found retirement terribly dull. The Rhône exercised a constant hold over them, maintained secret bonds which nothing could finally sever.

The water was just right for the upstream journey. Full and proud and flowing bank high. A water good enough to make one forget the water falling so heavily from the sky that from the barges travelling up on the right bank it was almost impossible to make out a few grey forms of trees on the left.

Immediately above Beaucaire the towpath was in good condition and well suited to a Rhône at this level. The paired horses were pulling easily; they had ample room and were on firm ground consisting of close-packed pebbles and sandy soil which allowed the rain to drain away.

Christian watched his animals move forward, pulling confidently and steadily, just flicked from time to time by the whips of the drivers, whose shouts carried ahead of the team, borne upstream by the squalls.

Within the first hour M. Tonnerieu left the galley three times to come to the tiller. Behind his eye-glasses, which the rain misted and the wind set quivering on his nose, his small eyes darted anxiously from the muddy river to the captain of the rig.

'We're going up well,' he said, 'but it does seem to me that the level is rather near the towpath. If it rises farther, we're going to have to stop, you'll see. Do at least try to let it be in a place where we can get hay at a reasonable price. And not too far from a village, so that we don't have to hire a cart to fetch the provisions.'

Christian promised with a nod or a wink. He knew the clerk would not stay long in the rain, with his oiled canvas jacket and cap, equally waterproof but much too big, which he had to hold in place. He promised, but he knew he would go on upstream. It was in him. A splendid certainty. A firm mortar which nothing would dislodge. And those who had agreed to make this trip would go on like him to the end of the adventure. At present there was no question of either retreating or giving up. So why talk of it? He let the clerk go on talking, and his words slid off him like the rain off his coat. He held the tiller firmly in his hands, and the upstream journey was so easy that he had even sent the deck-boy into the galley, advising him to go and get in the dry with the cooks, who would certainly find a job for him.

Astern, all was going well on the other barges. The hand signals given him when he turned round indicated as much. Against the rudder, the river water sang clearly, freed from the barge's weight and churning merrily before opening up ten yards downstream against the stem-post of the stable-barge.

Two hours after departure they passed the castle narrows where the current was swifter. The water dashing against the bank threw up a trail of foam which licked the rocks a bare six inches from the path. Christian had to lean hard on the tiller to keep his rig in line, for the bank seemed to be as attractive as a lover. Shouts and whip-crackings redoubled. The iron horseshoes clattered and crunched on the pebbles, and the cable, strained to the limit, made the foremast creak.

For more than ten minutes the barges hesitated, barely advancing, drifting broadside, righting themselves, while the horses, halted in their advance, pulled with all their weight. Beneath the black and chestnut coats glistening with water and sweat, the tensed muscles rippled like the eddies of the river. The bailey and his drivers had dismounted. They pulled on the bridles with the left hand, while walking backwards with right arms raised, cracking their whips now in the air, now on the horses' hindquarters.

At the prow, Old Surdon and Baptiste Carénal, redoubling their vigilance, fended off anything which might come battering against the stem-post with the iron tips of their rods.

The water along the bulwark was flowing so fast that if Christian looked only at that, he had the illusion that his barge was going full speed ahead.

Those were tense moments. The air seemed filled with vibrations thrown up by the locking of current and rudder-planks. The deck-boy, realizing from the barge's motion that battle was joined, came out of the galley and ran along the bulwark to join Christian. His boyish face was serious, frowning with anxiety, a deep line creasing his forehead beneath the hat pulled well down at the nape. Without the captain having to say anything to him, he passed the auxiliary rope round the soaked wood of the tiller and, wedging himself in, hauled on the end. Relieved, Christian breathed easier and smiled at the boy, whose face lit up.

The barge still wallowed from side to side, then, almost brutally, it leapt forward as if suddenly unloaded. It had just cleared the exit of the narrows and reached calmer water above the bottle-neck. Christian began to laugh at sight of the deck-boy looking astern.

'That surprised you,' he said. 'You thought a cable had snapped and we'd lost half the rig. I know. It always feels like that when you're not used to it.'

Relieved, the boy began to laugh as he hauled in the rope and coiled it in its place. 'You should have called me before the narrows,' he said.

'I could have done. But I'm glad to see you realized we were at the exit from the barge's motion. That proves you've got the feel of the water.'

The boy was happy. Christian nodded towards the prow. Baptiste had turned round. 'You see, your brother heard you running.'

Baptiste cried into the wind: 'She's riding as if on oil.'

'You saw the boy,' Christian called. 'He felt the river like an old hand.'

'Felt it, did he? Father will be pleased.'

Christian glanced towards the bank, where the bailey was astride his mount again. 'For the moment,' he remarked, 'he's got other things to do than admire a chip off the old block.'

All three laughed, and Old Surdon turned round to laugh with them. It was good to laugh now and talk. Nerves were relaxed and breathing easier.

'Ho, prowman!' Christian called. 'If you can manage with the boy, let Old Surdon take the tiller a bit. And on his way, tell him to look in on Canut. He'll know what he's got to do there.'

The deck-boy, lithe despite his boots and his over-long coat, was already running towards the prow. The old man handed over the rod and went tranquilly as far as the wooden hut where the kitchen fire was purring away. Before stooping to enter the low door, he gestured with his hand, thumb towards his open mouth, and called: 'Your good health, Captain Merlin!'

As the barges in the rig cleared the exit from the narrows, the team picked up speed. At this point the river broadened out. In less than half a mile it doubled its width, dividing into three arms around the islands just beginning to be discernible in the murk. At low water it was necessary to ferry the horses across to the other side and go upstream where the current's depth was greatest. When the river was bank high, it was possible to remain on the right-hand bank. It was a double gain in time and effort, for though this arm of the river made a slight detour, it was practically stagnant. Below the islands there was even a cross-current which would push the barges and give the horses a rest.

When Old Surdon joined Christian, his breath carried a good smell of coffee and spirits. 'Well,' he said, 'we got through the narrows.'

'More easily than I expected.'

'With animals like yours, we'd get through worse ones.'

'Here, you're going to take the tiller for a bit.'

'Think I still know how?'

'Are you making a monkey out of me?'

The old man clapped him on the back with his heavy hand. He was laughing. 'You're not going to tell me you're tired?'

'No, but I want to have a drink.'

The old man paused. He ran his hands over his beard, from which the water squeezed out as from a sponge, then he said: 'You want to give an old fellow pleasure ... My God, but you're a good sort, Christian. You're Félix's son all right. Not a doubt of it.'

He grasped the great wooden tiller, worn by the fretting of hands and ropes. His glance went from the barge's prow to the bank, where the horses were pulling well. In a voice tight with emotion and without looking at Christian, he said: 'You can't know, lad ... You can't know what this is doing for me.'

Christian withdrew and walked as far as the galley door before turning round. When he looked astern, he had the feeling the old man had already forgotten him. Feet astride and solidly planted, his body scarcely bowed, he was firmly grasping his tiller, his face uplifted, his eyes wide, and his gaze flitting ceaselessly from the prow to the surface of the river, from the river to the bank where the team was toiling away.

On a barge the river was everywhere. It was present even in the fire of the huge black stove on which the cooks heated the food. The wood which it burned was always wood from the river, or driftwood gathered on the banks, or trees which had been felled because they were in the way of the tow-ropes. From the barge itself tree-trunks and branches were fished out with a boat-hook when the work allowed of such distractions. The timbers, straight and curved, of an old barge might also be burnt to heat the soup. And these often made the best logs. This wood which had spent years in the water after the end of its life on earth was done to a turn. It had been nourished with all the strength of the river. Its pores were sealed, it did not burn away too fast and it gave out a good heat. And then, for anyone with the time to listen to it, the wood had tales to tell. Tales of journeys upstream and downstream. Of the never-ending struggle with the water, muddy and limpid by turns. Of years of navigating while observing the river bed, of which it knew so much more than men who were content to let their gaze skim over the surface.

And the boatmen, when they had time, were much given to

listening to the wood's stories. For it was not only in the galleys of the barges that the stew-pot was brought to the boil with wood from the Rhône; it happened in the boatmen's homes as well. And there, there was nearly always an old man spending the evening of his days in recalling his best years aloud.

He did so for the benefit of his grandchildren who would be boatmen in their turn. He talked to them of what he had seen, heard, endured on the river, but sometimes he forged ahead a little and told of things he had not seen. He spoke without any change of tone and forgetting to indicate that he was outrunning reality. And thus the children learned of that whole fabulous and terrifying world which peoples the river's depths and haunts its most secluded banks. All the strange beasts which the river-wood had seen pass began to come to life, and in the evenings the flames which rose from the wood took on terrifying faces, projecting shadows on to the whitewashed walls which proved beyond a doubt that these creatures really existed and that the old man did not lie.

It was stiflingly hot in the galley, where a big black stove on legs and with four draught-holes roared away like a forge. The steam which escaped in long trails from beneath the lid of an enormous iron stew-pot gave out a strong smell of marinated meat, garlic, onions and bay-leaves. Canut and his assistant were standing in front of a little table fixed to the wooden bulkhead and lighted by a smoke-blackened window through which grey day crept in. With sleeves rolled up and hands sticky with congealed blood mingled with the green juice of chopped herbs, they were rolling meat balls.

'You're going to be boiled alive like crayfish,' said Christian, who was suffocating.

'You can't leave the stove open,' Canut said, 'it roars away too much with this bitch of a wind.'

The cooks were sweating and were as wet as the men on deck.

Christian unhooked from the ceiling a pewter mug which he half filled from the tall coffee-pot kept on the stove behind the stew-pots. Then he picked up the gourd of brandy and completed the filling of his mug. Sipping, he went to the door which separated the galley from the provisions store-room where the clerk worked and slept. M. Tonnerieu was sitting on his stool in front of his black desk. Elbows apart, head lying to one side on a big register on top of which his two hands lay clasped, he was fast asleep. Through the narrow, low window the squalls could be seen scudding past, whipping against the glass and pattering over the planking of the deck. Daylight cast a grey reflection on the old man's gleaming bald head; his eye-glasses had slipped on to the page of the register.

Christian thought: It's no life at his age. If an accident were to happen, he wouldn't even have time to wake up before he went to the bottom, trapped in his cabin. He closed the door noiselessly and said to the cooks: 'Rapiat's asleep. Try not to wake him. So long as he's asleep, he can't get on anyone's nerves.'

The two young men looked at each other, smiling. 'With what we put in his coffee, he'll be out for the count.'

The advantage of the master-barge was that one could come for a hot drink at any time in the shelter of the galley. Before casting off, the cooks carried on board each barge a gourd filled with coffee and hot wine. The boatmen covered these with rags and straw, but when it was very cold the drink was tepid within the hour. The men knew this and drank it all within the first hour, after which there was nothing to do but blow on their hands and stamp their feet. As for the land crew, their work warmed them sufficiently, and they therefore filled the gourds hanging from the flanks of the leading horses with cool wine.

Christian drank his blend of coffee and alcohol slowly, and a comforting warmth glowed within him. He thought of Old Surdon, and of the great joy this man from an earlier era felt at finding himself once more at the tiller of a barge leading six others upstream, fine barges and so heavily laden that from a distance it looked as though crates and barrels had been piled up and deck-tents spread on the surface of the river. And Christian repeated ceaselessly to himself: We shall go upstream. And it'll be the old man's great pride. And we'll stop as we pass through Condrieu. And perhaps, when he sees this old hand with us, my father will decide to join us to finish the journey upstream. The Rhône will rise and rise. All the steamers will be halted by the bridges and ferry-cables. Not a single one will get through, either downstream or upstream. And that will prove machinery's no good. Absolutely no good, except to play around with passengers and lightweight cargo, but never to handle heavy freight.

He repeated this to himself as he listened to the fire singing. The river was all around the barge. Its caress could barely be felt on the wooden flanks; yet ever since entering calmer water, the rig moved easily, the contented horses stepped out briskly and were ready to break into a trot. But there were tons and tons to be towed, and the current's brief respite would not last.

Christian hung up his mug, shook his oiled hat before putting it on again, and went out.

Old Surdon was so happy at the tiller that he did not want to rob him of his pleasure. Walking towards the prow, he went to take Baptiste's place.

'Go and have a drink,' he said, 'and take time to get warmed up.'

'I'm not cold,' the prowman said.

'Maybe not, but look at the old man and you'll understand why there's no point in hurrying.'

Towards the end of the morning the wind slackened and the rain changed to a kind of icy mist which fell close-packed like very fine snow. High in the sky, the wind must have climbed suddenly and opened a gash in the clouds through which light oozed, diffused by the mist but warming neither earth nor men. Everything grew pale, transparent, and in this cottony world which muffled sounds and blurred outlines the horses, who were scarcely discernible from the barges, seemed to go forward without apparent movement.

As they were now between the right bank and the last island downstream from Vallabrègues, Christian Merlin made the most of a moment when the mist lifted slightly to give the signal to halt. Three men from the stable barge embarked in the runabout and came alongside the master-barge. The deck-boy jumped down into the runabout and made it fast to the ends of the two auxiliary ropes.

'Straight upstream,' Christian ordered. 'And see that those ropes hold.'

The bailey had slowed down the horses, and the rig was making less and less way, its cable thrashing the water. Rowing strongly in the runabout, the three men went up the arm of the river and beached on a fairly high spit of land planted with huge pollard willows. The mist was no longer falling. It had lifted level with the tops of the poplar trees, where it seemed to spread a veil.

The men belayed the ropes round four stout willows, stretched them across the water, and made them fast. Once the barges had stopped, Christian and his prowman paid out the main cable and let it unwind from round the foremast, while the horses, no longer towing anything except this light cable, walked right up to the willows. The bailey and his team-drivers made fast this cable too before unharnessing their horses. Halted thus, the rig remained in the middle of this arm of the river, in line with the current's flow.

The runabout was already returning. The boy got out, making room for Canut, who jumped in after handing the oarsmen one of the stew-pots, two big baskets, and a small keg. The first runabout had no sooner pulled away from the bulwark than the second, also crewed by three men, took its place. Six sacks of oats had been loaded between the last oarsman and the stern bench. Caillette also handed down a small keg, baskets and a stew-pot before jumping into the little boat, followed by Christian, who called to Old Surdon: 'I'm going to see the bailey. Eat straight away and don't bother about me.'

'Don't worry. I'm always ready for it,' the old man said, smacking his lips.

As soon as the runabout grounded, the team-drivers fell upon the sacks and began pouring oats into the canvas nose-bags which they would affix to their horses' bridles. It was only when all the horses were fed that the men came to the stew-pot, mess-tins in hand. Caillette's big ladle performed on land the task of Canut's on board. But here the men had to eat standing up, backs to a willow, blowing into the air the boiling hot steam of the stew, redolent of meat and wine.

The bailey ate too, while listening to Christian.

'Good. It's gone better than I'd have believed possible. But the river's still rising. I think we'll lose time if we keep to this bank beyond Vallabrègues. We'll have to ferry the horses and cross over to the Empie. What do you think?'

Albert Carénal was holding his mess-tin in one hand, and with the other was tearing hunks of bread from the piece he had wedged in the crook of his elbow. He swallowed, lifted the gourd high, took a swig of wine, and shook his head before answering, taking time to reflect. 'It's true, we'd lose time. And we'd be blundering about in the scrub. There are some risks . . . Only, if you cross over, it won't be for more than a mile or two.'

'I know, it's maddening, it's a tough spot, but it's too risky to stay on the Ryaume –'

The bailey stopped munching. His face froze. Christian broke off. All the men had simultaneously stopped eating and talking. Turned towards the river, mouths full, or about to close on a steaming morsel which remained speared on the end of the knife, they stood there gazing upstream and towards the middle of the river.

A steamer!

They had all recognized the sound of the engines. Muted at first, it mounted rapidly, becoming clearer, more distinct, together with the spitting of the boiler, the clatter of connecting-rods, and the protests of the river rent by the paddle-wheels.

They peered between the trees on the island which separated them from the mainstream of the Rhône. Soon the big black vessel came in sight, with its slicing bow which sheared through the water and lifted it into huge cushions of foam. Several horses reared, others uttered long neighs stifled by the canvas of their nose-bags; and it was like an expected signal. The men began to swear and to curse the steamer and those who piloted her.

'She's a big one,' Christian growled.

'Yes,' the bailey said, 'she's one of the Bonnardels. We haven't seen them often as yet, but they must have made the most of the high water to release them. It seems they're out for heavy freight with these. There's as much in one of those boats as you can stow in a whole rig.'

'She's high out of the water. She'll never make it upstream if the river continues to rise.'

'She's not fully loaded. She'll surely take on more for the voyage upstream.'

Christian felt a dull rage come over him. He clenched his fists. His nails bit into his palms. He said again between his teeth: 'She won't make it, by God! I'm telling you she won't make it.'

The steamer was coming downstream very fast. They could see her passing behind the barrier of tall stripped poplars. Even in the arm of the river the water-level dropped, the ropes holding the whole rig whined round the willows, which began to shake. An anxious moment followed. Would the arm empty and leave the barges stranded on the bottom? No; directly after the steamer had passed, the level rose again, while great waves swept over the earth of the island, foaming and whirling between the trees, sweeping up bundles of red and yellow leaves which coloured the troubled water in the river arm. Now the whole train of barges was dancing at the end of the ropes which lashed the water. The monster's smoke, black as the low sky, was white, spreading outwards, forced down by the mist. It sank back over the water, over the islands, and even over the banks. The men swore more violently.

And the steamer had scarcely disappeared behind its filth when the racket of a second was heard. As big, as black, as furious as the first, she went past, shaking the river anew, drowning the island and fouling the valley.

'God in heaven!' the bailey swore. 'We shan't be able to risk it much longer. Here we're sheltered by the island, but if we'd been caught as we were this morning, with two of them one after the other, it would have been another matter. It's enough to make the most placid animals take fright.'

'Two,' said Christian. 'Two of them together. That must be so that they can come to each other's assistance in case of trouble. They're not very sure of themselves, you see. They're scared.'

'Scared, yes, but they're still risking it.'

The bailey had spoken sadly, then, having emptied his mess-tin, he went off towards the horses. Christian watched him go. What did he mean by that; that they were all the same, all scared but still risking it?

The keg, the empty baskets, sacks and stew-pot were already aboard the runabout. Christian again took his place there and the men began to row towards the rig.

After the shouts and insults, land crew and boatmen had lapsed into silence. After the steamers had gone by, the river had grumbled a moment, then had gone quiet too. And there was something out of the ordinary about that blanketing silence, something which gave rise to anguish under the lowering sky, made still heavier by the smoke.

The runabout reached the rig without a word being spoken. The men's faces were like the sky, in which the smoke had left a vast sadness.

When Christian regained his barge, he was struck by Old Surdon's expression. The old man's whole face indicated great excitement. There was a gleam of hatred in his clear eyes, but there was also a gleam of joy. He rubbed his huge hands together; the sound they made was that of a hempen rope rasping over a wooden bulwark.

'Canut's kept yours hot,' he said. 'Go and eat. I'll be fine until we get opposite Vallabrègues.'

'It's all right,' Christian grunted. 'I'm not hungry for the moment.'

'What's the matter? You all look as though those bitches of steamers had gone over your bellies. But, God above, you wanted to fight! You wanted to show that we're still the stronger, and now, because those two have gone downstream, do you mean you think you're licked? That means three of them will be going upstream instead of one, and what difference will that make? None whatsoever. There could be six dozen of them and it wouldn't raise the bridges one inch. What will it profit them or diminish you when they're blocked and you sail past spitting in their eye? Personally, I'd like to see hundreds of 'em blocked all along the river. And I'd like to see the river stay high so long that the companies all go bust.'

A shout came from upstream. 'Rig ahoy! Ready for the upstream journey!'

Christian looked downstream. His men were at their posts. He turned upstream and shouted: 'Haul away!'

He returned to his post at the tiller. Baptiste Carénal and his brother the deck-boy were at the prow. Beside the galley, Caillette was drawing water from the river in a big bucket. Farther off, Old Surdon was at the foremast, where he was beginning to haul in the ropes. Christian admired the precision of his gestures, his confident glance, and his way of standing on the bulwark.

When everything was in order and the rig was under way normally again, the old man joined Christian.

'It's years since I've enjoyed my victuals so much,' he said. 'That Canut of yours is a real cook.'

He was calm. He was standing near the helmsman's place and his gaze was going slowly from the team to the barges, from the bank to the islands, as if he would have caressed the river. He filled his big clay pipe, lit it, and said: 'During the evening I had the chance to get your lad talking a bit. He's what he is, but he's very far from being a fool. So far as the river's concerned, he knows it inside out. Well enough to make a good captain, only . . . .'

He hesitated. He looked at Christian, then he looked again at the river before going on: 'Only he's got ideas which aren't quite those of a captain.'

'He's got the ideas of an imbecile who's let himself be duped by other imbeciles from the companies.'

'Perhaps. But there's something else. He said: "The machine can improve man's lot." Well, we don't see eye to eye with him on that. But let's discuss it. Let's allow that he's right. Only, he also said: "It's got to improve the lot of the workers. Not just that of the bosses. The bosses mustn't be able to make use of it to kill the workman and deprive him of his livelihood. If you had steam, you'd earn more and work less, and you'd keep your men because they'd work less and earn more." '

'Have you ever complained of overwork?' Christian cried. 'Do I complain? Have you ever heard my men complain?'

Old Surdon smiled – a smile which seemed to indicate that Christian's anger amused him, like a child's tantrum.

'You're upsetting yourself as if I'd reproached you for something,' he declared. 'But you know nothing will make me change my opinion. Only, I'm trying to understand others. And what you're saying to me is exactly what I said to your lad, and do you know what he answered? He told me that if your men never complained, it was because they were afraid.'

'Afraid? Afraid of what?'

'Of you,' the old man said.

Christian lost his temper. 'Oh, shit! But you know me! Haven't I always treated my men correctly? Just as my father did?'

'Of course. But what was correct in your father's time may perhaps not be so today.'

'I'll be damned! And you've come along to tell me things like that?'

'Not me. It's – it's our era. The weavers revolted. The boatmen never have. Yet they toil even harder than the silk workers.'

'My God, it's the first time –'

'It's the first time anyone's spoken of it to you. The first time you've begun to think about it. Fair enough. You go your way with your eyes fixed on the river. It's quite enough to keep you occupied. But you only look at men to see if they're doing their work properly.'

The old man said no more. Christian did not know what to reply. Surdon's words were so unexpected that they left him stunned. The old man took a few steps along the bulwark as if to return to the prow, then, thinking better of it, he came back and planted himself in front of Christian, saying: 'Tell me honestly, if one of your men came and complained that the hours were too long, for instance, or that he wasn't paid enough, what would you do?'

Christian sighed. Tight-lipped, eyes fixed on the first pair of horses, he refused to open up to this old man who seemed able to read him as well as his own father.

'You don't want to answer me, eh? All right, I'll tell you what you'd do. You'd tell him to go and find a berth on another rig. And he'd be lucky if you said it without smashing your fist into his face.'

Stung, Christian looked at the old man, whose eyes were still smiling. 'Well?' he said. 'When you had your outfit, wouldn't you have done the same?'

'Of course I should, and I'd do it today. But that doesn't mean to say I'd be right. It may well be that steam has begun to put an end to those days as well.' His voice grew graver. Without giving Christian time to answer, he drew closer to him and went on: 'Come on, lad. You and I are cut from the same cloth. The same cloth as your father. And if it's true that steam must put an end to barge traffic, you know very well it would finish us too. But we must be honest. There's the river. It's our calling and our life. But what gets us is the existence of the companies quite as much as their ships. Steam is the preserve of huge capitalist groups, not of artisans like us. It isn't only going to kill off horse-drawn barges, but a whole way of life – a way of life in which we're our own masters.'

There was a long moment of silence between them. Now the river was curving in a bit and the narrowing of the arm compelled the rig to sail close in to the island which tailed to a point upstream. The water was singing as it cascaded over the low-lying parts of the island; they formed a dam which the river was attacking broadside on.

For a moment the old man watched the increasingly muddy water carrying down drifts of dead leaves and dry grass blended into long, supple rafts waving on the surface.

'It's still rising,' he said. 'The Durance must have yielded plenty.' He paused, then added before moving off towards the prow: 'I was able to sell my outfit for a good price. That will surely see me out without my having to ask help of anyone. Because I'm not a charge on the ironmonger, believe me. But I know those who haven't been so lucky. And do you know how much the poor relief gives? Seven pounds of black bread every fifteen days. Seven pounds. You can see how much that is . . .'

He broke off. He had been speaking low. He hesitated as if he had something else to say, then turned and moved slowly away. His step was heavier and he had ceased to smile.

The passing of the two steamers and Old Surdon's words over-shadowed the afternoon. At first Christian felt utterly crushed. It seemed to him that everything was closing in on him. That the valley was going to be snuffed out by this sky which grew darker as the day wore on. Despite the hard and dangerous work – for they had had to change banks twice – he continued to mull over his son's words and those of the old man, and all that neither had dared say but that was implicit in everything.

Then, imperceptibly, something crystallized in him which ended by forming a kind of block on which nothing would ever make an impression. Everything sensitive in him had closed up and tightened, like his lips, on the anger which had not ceased to seethe within him. Perhaps it was true that the whole world was in process of changing utterly. Perhaps it was not only steam and what went on in this particular valley, but it was none the less the valley which counted.

The valley and his river.

The river was his universe, and it was to this universe that he wanted to cling. He did not give a damn about the rest. The world could change its aspect, be overwhelmed by revolution, it had no importance.

In 1831 the weavers had revolted, there had been uprisings, end-less troubles, but had they hindered him from continuing his work? In 1834 it had all started up again. Had the massacres in Paris or elsewhere changed anything whatever in the boatmen's lives?

No, what counted was simply and solely what happened on the river. Even the hillsides above its banks were only a side-issue of no interest. They would still yield enough wine for the boatmen and wood for the barges. There was still silk to be transported and a thousand other goods which men would have need of under any régime. For the last four years the papers had been talking of peasant unrest and the rural exodus. The valley had been in a state of chronic upheaval and the towns were transformed by the influx of workers. But he, Christian Merlin, barge-master, carried on his life. The peasants and workers belonged to a different world.

At this moment he was voyaging up-river just as he had always done. And he would go on to the end whatever happened. Perhaps there were young men confused enough to allow that the barges' days were numbered; well, they would see about that! He, Christian, would prove the opposite. He would rub their noses in their own filth. As for his men, content or not content, paid adequately or otherwise, he could do no more for them. His whole fortune was in this barge-train which was enabling them all to live – his men as well as himself. After all, they had not been compelled to follow him. If they were there, it was because they had chosen to accompany him, and since they had signed on, they would go on to the end. All boatmen in all ages had always acted thus, neither flood nor steam would overtopple that.

The more he forged ahead, the more he bit back his anger, the more Christian felt a strengthening of his desire to arrive, and to arrive as fast as possible.

Now the river was again beginning to seem nearer, more alive. He felt it was his ally. He began to be at one with it once more.

When Old Surdon came to help him at the tiller for the crossing, he smiled at the old man and said: 'A good upstream journey, Grandpa, and I've an idea the sky has more rain in store.'

The horses had already crossed, shipped six at a time in the run-abouts. The boatmen would haul in the two ropes which had been stretched from one bank to the other and had enabled them to cross without drifting while making use of the current's force.

'I've seldom seen such a swift crossing when the river's so high,' the old man observed. 'It was well done, lad. The horses pulled strongly and the men knew what they were about.'

He had regained his open expression. His face only hardened now when he thought of the steamers, but it was no longer sorrow that clouded his gaze, nor anxiety. He had complete confidence in this rig which he had just watched execute the most delicate manoeuvre there was. There was only joy and anger in him. Like Christian, he was overjoyed by the sight of the river rising hour by hour. Like him, he cursed the black monsters whom he hoped to see held up on the upstream journey, blocked by the bridges.

And Christian guessed that without difficulty. He was comforted by the presence of this old man, whose words had momentarily disquieted him. When he agreed to take him aboard, wasn't it the river itself whom he had taken on? As a result of having lived with the river and loving it, had not the old man become the Rhône itself? Hadn't he succeeded in penetrating to the heart of all the secrets of the waters, banks and depths?

It seemed to Christian that an unknown force, a power like that attributed to the gods, had taken over everything. It was this which had led the old man to come aboard, and Christian knew now that nothing would have been strong enough to force him to remain on land.

Christian was still Captain Merlin, sole master of his rig, but the old man was there, and without giving a single order, he could inspire everything, bring everything to pass.

The rig continued upstream till nightfall. The water was too strong for them to be able to reach Aramon that evening, but when they stopped they were not much more than a mile away from it. There too there was a long island, still more than three feet out of water. It was covered with scrub and pebbles, and enabled a narrow and rather deep arm of the river to run along the right bank. The relatively calm water allowed them to moor easily, and the horses could be brought back without difficulty to the stable barge, where they would spend the night on dry straw.

They were just finishing tying up when a narrow gash opened in the sky, like a horizontal lightning-flash caught between two clouds. Rays of pale yellowish light shone down, like a transparent pyramid in front of the mountains. In this unexpected light, which lasted the space of three oar-strokes, Old Surdon, busy coiling the main cable, looked even taller and broader. His beard and his wild hair formed an aureole about his head, and his slow movements seemed to take on a boundless amplitude.

Christian gazed at him for as long as the light lasted, and it seemed to him that something strange, something surpassing man's understanding, had just passed swiftly over the valley, now suddenly in the grip of a night cold and violet as the presage of a storm.

On the river the nights are often hard to get through in times of flood. The most hardened boatmen sometimes needed to escape a moment from the darkness and the cold. Those who proudly believed they were supermen were men none the less. And like all human beings, they needed warmth. Men of the water, of the wind and sky, children of nature though they were, they were yet made of sentient flesh. Not one of them could have brought himself to recognize such a truth, but they all by instinct had the galley on their master-barge. And the galley was not merely the kitchen, but the warm and living heart of the rig. A heart nourished on the night's blood, that is, on a good fire of wood. The men came there to eat and drink, but unaware of it though they were, they came there also for the fire. It was the fire's job to dry soaked clothes, dry out boots, warm hands numbed by the icy water, keep hot the wine and soup. A job which everyone recognized. But there was something which penetrated via gazing eyes and the pores of the skin, something which chased out the dark, cold, wet night from the depths of a man's being. The hours spent at the prow enabled night to seep into a man's very core, where it left a black slime like that which the Iseron, bringing down the filth of factories, left at its confluence with the Rhône.

Only fire could purge this filth, dissolve it in its living warmth and light.

And whoever had cooked the night before nursed this fire from evening dusk to the half-light of dawn, unaware in the depths of the dark night that he was the one who made it possible for the others to go on without despairing until day broke once more.

In the early hours of darkness the rain began again. The wind had sprung up once more, but it was a steady wind, not particularly violent, and the sound of the downpour on the canvas of the deck-tent was continuous. It sounded like a well-fed rain, in no hurry to come down, and settled in to last.

Christian was not asleep. He listened to it a moment, then, abruptly shaking off his weariness, he got out of his bunk. The lamp on the first mast had stayed alight. It was burning slowly and its small flame was barely visible behind the smoky, greasy glass. Old Surdon stirred in his bunk. He had not been able to sleep either.

'You're like me,' he said. 'When your rig's moored in the open river and the water's altering, it's no good your having men on watch, you still can't get to sleep.'

As the old man was raising himself on his elbow and throwing back his blanket, Christian said: 'Stay where you are. If I need you, I'll come and call you.'

'You can hardly stop me going for a leak.'

The two of them got dressed and went out.

The night was very dark. The rain was icy. The wind was not driving it, it was rather that its close texture had a cold air inter-woven, which seemed to move slowly and spread over the ground as the drops struck.

Near the lantern in the prow, which cast a quivering reflection over a few feet of streaming deck, Baptiste Carénal stood stock still, his back rounded and his head hunched into his shoulders. The brim of his oilskin hat lay directly on his coat of the same fabric.

'All right?' Christian asked.

'All right. But the water must have risen eighteen inches in the past two hours. It must be over all the islands, it's bringing so much down.'

He turned, picking up a short-handled boat-hook with a big iron hook. Christian went close and looked at the surface, lit by the lantern. In front of the prow, branches and dried grass had piled up. The current holding them against the barge's stem-post lifted them, kneading them like fermenting dough. A yellow and white scum was forming; bubbles kept bursting.

The prowman thrust his hook into the mass and drew it towards midstream. A rent opened, revealing water which seemed black beside the eddies catching the light.

'Is it all like that so far?' Christian asked.

'Yes, but it's not much good my keeping a look-out. If a trunk or a root were to come down, I don't know if I'd see it in time to fend it off before it struck. I've cleaned the lantern glass three times already, but with the rain it blackens over quickly.'

'I'll do a stint. When I come back, I'll take over.'

Christian moved off towards the galley, whose dirty window was lit. He overtook the old man, who was walking slowly along the bulwark.

'Had your leak, have you?' he said. 'You ought to get back to bed.'

'You can hardly stop me going for a drink.'

In the galley Canut was asleep with his elbows on the table. The sound of boots on the boards woke him. He sat up, rubbing his eyes.

'Hell,' he said, 'I must have dropped off.'

'Go and lie down,' Christian said. 'Those who come in for a drink can easily put another log on the fire.'

'Rapiat said to me: "On a night like this you want to have hot wine and soup ready for the men on watch." He wanted me or Caillette to be here.'

Christian lifted the lid of a stew-pot drawn into the corner of the stove. The hot soup smelt pleasantly of bacon. To one side, in a big bucket, were ten litres of hot wine.

'Everything's in order, go and lie down. We'll help ourselves.'

The cook went into the pantry where M. Tonnerieu and Caillette were sleeping. When the door had closed, Old Surdon remarked: 'Your clerk snores like he talks – in the voice of an old maid who's never been satisfied. He's an old pest, but not bad at heart. And he's certainly looked after your and your father's interests.'

'True enough, and yet he's never understood the first thing about barges.'

'You know what clerks are.'

They each drank a glass of hot wine. When Christian went

towards the door, the old man followed him, saying: 'You going on your rounds?'

'Yes, and you're going back to bed.'

'No, I'm coming with you.'

'But what's the point? You'll just get more tired.'

'No,' the old man said slowly. 'I'll just get happier. You can't understand, lad. You can't understand.'

Christian understood perfectly. The old man had managed to get a berth for a last voyage upstream. It was a matter of prime importance to him, and he did not wish to lose one iota of the happiness the journey gave him.

As the river level was liable to change very quickly, they had moored the rig downstream from a spit of rock which acted as a breakwater. The barges were placed one against the other in order to offer more resistance to the debris the river was sweeping down and to reduce the number of men on watch. Beginning upstream, there was the master-barge, then, amidships, the prow of the stable barge, whose forward port side was close up against the stern half of the master-barge's starboard. The others followed suit, forming a long, firm articulation which still retained a certain flexibility.

On leaving the galley, the two men crossed to the stable-barge. Joseph Cathomen was on watch at the prow, fending off bundles of branches which the current jammed between his prow and the side of the master-barge.

'In another hour there'll be tons of it,' he said.

'I feared as much,' Christian said. 'When the water rises after such a long drought it makes a clean sweep of the banks.'

Joseph laid down his boat-hook and stooped near the lantern. 'See what the river's brought me,' he said.

He had spread out on the deck a pair of velvet trousers, wringing wet, but seemingly in good condition.

'I fished them out of a heap of muck. I pulled, I said to myself: "That's not scrub." So then I spread them out. The rain'll wash 'em. If I trim the bottoms, they might have been made for me.'

'Try fishing for the waistcoat,' the old man advised. 'And if you see a large size, bear me in mind.'

They moved off laughing, going now towards the stables, whose open doors wafted a pleasant warmth and strong smell of straw and urine. The horses were sleeping in the darkness, stamping a hoof from time to time, shaking a chain, making a ring clink.

They proceeded to the last barge, where they found Félicien Revolat. Since the barges were positioned one behind the other, there was a man at the prow of the first two, and thereafter a lone boatman was on watch, going from one to the other, lantern in hand. He checked that the ropes were holding, and that nothing was catching on those which trailed level with the water.

On the way back, Old Surdon sought to insist on taking Joseph Cathomen's place. 'I'll only stay an hour,' he promised, 'and afterwards I'll go in the galley and look after the soup. Let me do it. If I go back to bed I shan't sleep and I'll exhaust myself.'

Christian went to relieve the prowman. The night was just as dark, and the rain continued to fall, steady, obstinate, well and truly determined to drown the valley.

Christian thought of Old Surdon. When his hour was up, he would go and settle in the galley to serve out soup and hot wine to men relieved on watch. To each of them he would retail an episode from his long life, the whole of which had been spent on the river.

The drenched dawn revealed a valley in which the night had passed like an unending nightmare. Those inhabitants of the low-lying quarters of towns and villages who had gone to sleep awoke to find themselves marooned in their houses; those whom the water had roused from sleep had fled in the darkness, half dressed, splashing and groping, or thrusting before them the light from a lantern which made this liquid movement between the houses terrifying. Everywhere it was like thick ink. Slippery mud and viscous slime. The cold of the river and the cold which rained down from the sky and cascaded off the rooftops. They carried whatever they had been able to take of their most precious possessions. Or what they considered the most precious. In fact they had snatched up at random in the darkness whatever came to hand.

'I've brought this bag of linen, and it isn't what I ought to have brought. There were other things more useful.'

'The money?'

'I've got it.'

'The money from the cupboard?'

'No, from the kitchen. Did you think of the cupboard?'

'No, I was looking after the boy.'

'I'll go back.'

'No. Stay with us. I'm scared on my own.'

And they set off into the night, going wherever the land rose. Without really knowing what street they were in.

The town crier went round with his loud-hailer. He announced the approximate height of the river, at a guess, more to arouse the river folk than to give a precise indication.

The height of the flood in feet was not important. The Rhône was at the door, in the cellar, in the kitchen where it was over the stove, in the bedroom where it was going to cover the bed. Never mind the feet and inches. Everyone was on the move without even knowing where they were moving. To get away from the flood.

No one remembered having seen the river rise so quickly. And the old people who were dragged into the dark groaned for their homes and the belongings which they had not been able to save. They groaned and cried repeatedly that it was the end of the world.

The boat-builders' yards were reminiscent of the biblical flood. A flood in which Noah, warned too late, had not had time to finish his ark. The boats already started began to drift, filled with water, rolled between obstacles before being caught by the current. And the boat-builders watched their boatyards die and their store of dry timber scatter. For years there had been hardly any boats to build, and now the few they had under way had vanished.

And the boat-builders, together with the other river folk, climbed towards the hills and the higher parts of the town, saving what they could of their tools and wondering whether they would ever make use of them again for anything other than the rebuilding of their own homes.

And this distress was added to that of the night.

At dawn on the second day of the voyage upstream, the rain, though coming down just as heavily, allowed a grey light to filter through which seemed to ooze from the river quite as much as from the sky. The water had risen more than three feet since dusk and the departure was extremely hard on men and beasts.

The horses, embarked six at a time in the runabout, refused to jump into the turbid water when they reached the bank, where the river now flowed among the trees. They reared up, beating their hoofs against the planking of the prow, which resounded dully at surface level. The drivers shouted, cracked their whips, pulled at bridles, while the boatmen tried to hold the wildly rocking boat steady by boat-hooks secured to rocks or branches.

Twenty times the runabout almost capsized, but the skill, coolness and strength of the boatmen, who were soaked with sweat quite as much as with rain and river, was proof against everything.

It took more than an hour to disembark the horses and couple up the teams. The bailey and his men, thigh deep in water and battling with the current, floundered about on the treacherous bank where each step was an adventure.

When the teams were ready and the tow-ropes fixed and taut, Christian gave the order to haul a little to try and recover the mooring-ropes whose knots were under water. The men in the runabouts reluctantly had to bring themselves to sever some of them at water-level.

From the galley door M. Tonnerieu watched everything, saying not a word, pulling a face each time an axe-stroke touched a rope at the runabout's bulwarks. Every yard of hemp thus abandoned to the depths of the river wrenched a little groan from him; it made the cooks laugh and caused Christian to shrug his shoulders.

At last, when the runabouts were once more alongside the two leading barges and the men were all back at their posts, Christian dipped his hand in the muddy water, crossed himself, said the prayer and gave the order to depart.

Preceded by two members of the land crew who went on foot, in water up to their knees, thighs, sometimes waists, to sound out the path and cut the branches which dammed it, the horses began to move forward. Christian knew that these pathfinders risked falling into a hole at any moment. He hardly took his eyes off them, and he had seen to it that the first runabout was ready to be launched. The two men in it kept an eye on what was happening on the bank. In this icy water the land crew would not be able to hold out more than an hour. It would be necessary to relieve them without halting the horses, and the runabout's oarsmen would have to pull strongly to pass under the main cable heavy with water, reach the river bank at a point upstream from the pathfinders, set down two men in water, take on the other two and bring them back on board. Once there, they would change boots and clothes in the galley, where Canut would give them a big bowl of hot wine.

Old Surdon, who had just made fast the runabout alongside the master-barge, came up to Christian at the tiller. The old man's bright eyes were smiling under his hat, pulled well down. 'Another eighteen inches,' he said, rubbing his hands, 'and not a single steamer will pass under a bridge.'

'That's true. But, my God, the men are going to be frozen.' Christian gestured towards the land crew, who were toiling, struggling against the current, clinging to scrub which the river bent and twisted.

'When I crewed with my father,' the old man said, 'even when I was head prowman, as soon as it was necessary to go wading, I was the one he sent to the bank. And in those days we weren't relieved so often. You can be sure I spent days and days paddling. Which didn't prevent me from sticking it out. And if you want me to take the place of one of your men, I'm ready to start again.'

'No,' said Christian. 'Go and dry off. In a moment you'll come and take over the tiller.'

Before departing, the old man said again: 'Don't worry. Only another couple of miles and your horses will be walking in the dry. Above Aramon the towpath is much higher.'

Christian knew it, but he knew also that it was difficult to foresee how long it would take them to cover those two miles. Impeded by the water, nervous, constantly compelled to pull harder on the tow-ropes which kept catching on bushes, the horses were making much less headway than on the previous day. And the river was beginning to look truly menacing. On several occasions the prow-man and the deck-boy had to fend off with their boat-hooks huge tree-trunks which were being rolled down by the current, lifting skyward the dripping tangles of their roots and branches.

'Hey, prowman!' Christian shouted. 'D'you want an extra man as reinforcement?'

'It wouldn't come amiss,' Baptiste called. He had taken off his hat and his waterproof waistcoat.

Christian called to Old Surdon, who left the galley and came hurrying up, struggling into his oilskins.

'What's up?'

'They need another man up front.'

'I'll go,' the old man said.

'No. Take the tiller.'

'That's your post.'

'No,' Christian shouted. 'By God, I'm still captain here!'

The old man gestured as if to say: So you are. I'd forgotten.

He took up position at the tiller, and without offering any further explanation, Christian went off. When he reached the run-about, he turned round and shouted to the old man: 'You're captain now, until I return aboard.'

Old Surdon, who had undoubtedly guessed Christian's intentions, cried: 'You're crazy. Your place is here.'

But Christian had already jumped down into the bottom of the runabout, which he pushed out from the bulwark.

'We'll take advantage of it to relieve the two men on land,' he told the oarsmen. 'Paul Barillot, you'll stay with me on the bank. Albert will come back here with the two men who've been relieved. They'll go and get changed. Then one will reinforce the men at the prow, and the other'll go in the runabout with Albert.'

The two men were rowing rhythmically, pulling hard on the heavy oars whose tallowed straps whined. Between two pulls, Barillot said: 'Whatever you may want, it's not a captain's place.'

'Row on,' Christian growled. 'The captain does what he wants to do. And if I've a fancy to take a dip, no one's going to stop me.'

When Christian let himself slide into the water, he reflected that it was years since he had done this job. Without the presence of Old Surdon on his barge, it would never have occurred to him to replace one of the land crew in this fashion. But as soon as the old man had spoken, the necessity of doing so had come home to him.

Now, he was on land where he had to test each step before going forward. The icy water reached above his knees. In places it flowed so strongly that he had to cast his boat-hook with its recurved point ahead of him, hook this beak on to a branch or plant it in a tree-trunk, and pull on the handle to enable himself to walk. At every step he had to make a considerable effort to lift his feet from the mud because of the water filling his boots. And yet without boots it would have been impossible to walk and to keep his balance on pebbles and in sand which flowed almost as fast as the river. However, the path was fairly level. To the left, it skirted a row of poplars some twenty years old. Clumps of alder and dwarf willow had grown up under the tall trees. They bristled with reeds and caught in passing the grass and leaves which the river carried down. Bowing gradually beneath the weight, they leaned into the current. When the deposit was too great, they gave way suddenly, ducking under the water which then carried their burden a little farther down. Once freed, they emerged slowly, battling against the current like exhausted swimmers, until at last their dripping heads broke surface and tossed under the rain. On the river side no tree impeded the tow-ropes, only lightweight bushes, buffeted by the current, which Christian or Paul Barillot hacked down with one blow of the axe. The most serious obstacles were the big branches which the water had thrust against the bank and lodged between two trees. They sometimes blocked the path completely, and if they had been there for any length of time, the men had to beware of that moment when the dam they had formed gave way. While one of them wielded the axe, the other pushed with all his might on the handle of his boat-hook, ready to turn the freed mass aside.

Making full use of the force of the current, he thrust it as far out to midstream as possible, so that it should not tangle in the horses' hoofs.

Despite the cold of the water which numbed his feet and hands, Christian felt the sweat streaming down his back. The work was hard, and the first pair of horses were relentlessly on their heels and they had to keep their distance from them. When an obstacle rather more firmly lodged took too much of their time, they heard the animals approaching. The harness rang, the nostrils blew hard. The drivers' whips cracked ceaselessly. Several times the bailey shouted from his mount: 'Move on there! Move on! We can't stop here.'

Redoubling their efforts, chests heaving, arms flailing, Christian and Paul hacked away, sending flying chips of white wood the size of two hands; these drifted away on the current, dazzlingly white in this leaden, clay-coloured world.

At the risk of being knocked down by the trunk when it yielded suddenly, the men worked in unison to cut through it faster. And as soon as the wood began to crack, the one working downstream planted his axe with one mighty stroke in a tree-trunk, grasped his boat-hook hooked on to a branch, its handle floating within reach, and quickly, quickly thrust out to midstream with all his might. Sometimes the load thus released sent up fountains of water full in the men's faces. The branches turned, rolled over, righted themselves. If a bad eddy drove them back too quickly towards the bank, a driver might be forced to dismount to push them in his turn out to midstream and protect his horses.

Christian and Paul had been battling thus for more than an hour when the wind brought the rumble of a steamer. From barges and horses a cry went up, heralding the steamer that the men were insulting even before she hove in sight. Christian turned round, but the rain was falling too heavily and they heard the steamer for more than a quarter of an hour before they could begin to make out her bows. She was going up in midstream. Slowly, but in-different to what the river might be bringing down, for no man stood at her prow.

'Those bastards are keeping themselves dry,' Christian growled.

'Let be,' Paul said. 'They won't get farther than Avignon.'

The steamer was now recognizable. She was the *Rhodan*.

'God above!' Christian gasped. 'To think that without that blasted crate we brought down...'

'You're joking. Those we saw going by yesterday would have brought her scrap iron. And what would you have gained then? Nothing. On the contrary. Now, you're going to watch her pass, but tomorrow you'll have the pleasure of returning the compliment. We'll go through and she'll be blocked by the bridge.'

'The way she's going, that's not certain.'

'If it isn't that bridge, it'll be another.'

Christian thought so too, but he needed to hear it said. Needed to know that he and his men shared a common hope and kindled to a common cause.

As he continued to advance and to hack out a path, he turned round from time to time to take a quick look at the steamer. The red and black vessel raised huge waves which continued to surge among the trees long after she had passed.

'We're going to have a basinful,' Barillot said. 'We'll have to pick a young tree to hang on to.'

They pushed on farther, then, when the steamer had passed some fifty yards ahead of them, flung themselves simultaneously on the branches of a mulberry whose top was level with the water. A few yards downstream the drivers were swearing and cracking their whips to keep the frightened horses in line. The waves buffeted the horses' flanks and the biggest broke over their backs, soaking the drivers. The horses tossed their heads, neighed, and occasionally reared up, pawing the water with their forelegs. In midstream the barges in the rig were dancing. Water swamped their low decks, streaming everywhere.

'God in heaven!' Christian raged. 'Everything's going to be soaked... Shit! Swine!'

Barillot also shouted.

They had raised themselves as high as they could, weighed down by their wet clothes and water-logged boots. Despite everything, the biggest waves swamped them completely. Coughing and blowing, they continued to insult the steamer.

On the master-barge, Old Surdon clung to the tiller and shook his fist from time to time at the steamer, which went on her way as if no one was on board to steer her.

Driven downwards by the rain and the wind, which was still light, the thick heavy smoke spread out over the river like black mud over a road. It lingered a long time – long after the steamer which it cloaked had ceased to fill the valley with her rumblings.

Then, as if the Rhône wanted to avenge itself on men and horses for the passage of this steam-kettle which had broken its banks and sullied its surface, everything became more difficult.

It was impossible to moor the rig at midday and only the men on board could eat the boiling stew brought by the runabout without leaving their posts. Horses and drivers had to pursue their route without having anything.

After two hours of exhausting effort Christian and Paul were relieved. They returned to the barge, where they stripped in front of the galley stove. Waistcoats, shirts, trousers, boots, were already drying, hung on wires stretched from one bulkhead to the other, or laid out on benches. The air was thick with steam and with a strong smell of sweat, intermingled with the smells of coffee, stew and wine.

Caillette put log after log on the stove, which roared away, reddening the cast-iron boiling rings.

Christian had asked for three men to take over on land, for the increasingly uneven path and the ever-rising water made progress dangerous and difficult.

As soon as he had eaten, he put on dry clothes and went to the tiller. Old Surdon still wore his slightly hard smile. His eyes gleamed fiercely.

'It's more than fifteen years since I've seen the Rhône rise so fast, lad . . . We shall go up. And that'll leave them stuck. We'll be the only ones to go up . . . God in heaven, but it's hard work. Bloody hard work.'

Christian took over the tiller and the old man went off towards the galley.

Wasn't there something a bit disturbing in the old man's gaze? Hadn't he suddenly become a trifle mad? Christian looked at the river, at the men and horses, and something contracted within him. Something which frightened him a little.

He knew the river well enough throughout its course to know that the water was already in his house. His father and sister would have had to take what they could up to the attic and settle there as best they could without fire in the cold and damp. If the flood continued, his father would certainly decide to abandon the house, whose foundations, shaken by the water, would no longer offer any security. He would take a boat and leave with his daughter, run ashore at the bottom of the slope, and they would both climb up to the hut among the vines from which the valley was visible for miles and miles. They would concentrate on the clearings where they could see the river. They would be in an agony of apprehension for the house and for the rig. They would think of him, and of Claude, who was not even with him any longer. Would the lad and Tirou manage to get back to Condrieu quickly? What would his father say when he learned what had happened?

Christian mulled over all these questions, then forced himself to put them out of his mind in order to concentrate on the idea that what was happening on land was nothing compared to the permanent threat to barge traffic represented by steam. Nothing was more important than the survival of their calling, and only a flood of vast proportions and long duration could vanquish steam.

That, and that alone, was what he must think of.

That morning many barge-masters gave up all thought of leaving. They had looked at the river and the leaden sky and said: 'It would be madness. You don't risk an outfit on a river which is no longer human.'

So they had moored their barges more firmly. They had pitched the pigs of iron overboard and even fastened big stones to all the ropes they had left. The drivers had gone with the horses to seek stabling safe from the flood, or pasturage on the heights. There they would stay with their animals until the river was back between its banks.

Once all this was taken care of, masters and men put themselves at the service of the river folk. Those boatmen would be long remembered in the villages! Those at Montfaucon, for instance – the brothers Etienne and François Robert and François's son Jean, known as Gabien. They risked their lives constantly on their runabout. So long as man or beast was in danger, they were in constant demand. They did not know what weariness was. They scarcely took time for a swig of wine and a slice of bacon between trips. Seldom had such humanity and courage been seen. People first, then livestock, then furniture.

Montfaucon was one of the worst hit places. More than twenty houses with water up to the roofs. Two barns swept away like matchwood by the waters. Six tile foundries with their ovens ready for firing completely destroyed. Through the torn vines, among the olives and mulberries uprooted like thistles, the Roberts rowed their runabout to pick up poor wretches sitting astride their roof-trees and calling for help. Poor wretches completely paralysed by fear, numbed by rain and cold, who had to be lifted down from the roof-trees to which they clung, hanging on to chimney-stacks. The boatmen literally tore them from their refuge and passed them from hand to hand, like children.

Once the boat was full, they returned to the bank through the currents, where they had to dodge tree-trunks which moved at the speed of the river and would have cracked open the runabout like a nut.

The stockmen marooned in the midst of submerged lands were the most difficult to rescue. The stockmen and their animals, maddened by the water. The cows and bullocks plunged so much that the runabout rolled and pitched to the point of shipping water. And the more the animals were beaten, the more restive they became.

The Roberts were at Montfaucon because their rig happened to be there, but in other ports there were other boatmen.

In the boatmen's villages – Condrieu, Sablons, Vernaison, Givors – the flood shook the houses. And often the women were on their own. 'If only our men were here!' they raged. 'The one time when we need boats in the port, and there's nothing. Not a man nor a barge. And everything's going to be left in the water, furniture, wine from the cellar, bacon from the salting-tub.'

'And when they do get back, they'll complain that there's nothing to eat or drink.'

'They'd damn well better not let me hear them!'

The women were strong and as foul-mouthed as their men. They performed prodigies in an attempt to save everything portable. The old men took out some old tub of a rowing-boat and rediscovered their rowing skill. The boys also began to do the same – lads who had dreamed of going on the river and now found the river coming to them.

Women, children, old men – they were all people of the Rhône. When the river ravaged their gardens, cellars, rabbit-hutches, homes, they did not view its entry in the same light as a farmer or a shopkeeper did.

The women loudly berated their men, but it was primarily to conceal their own anxiety. They did not even know where their men were. Like the other villagers, they climbed to high ground and took refuge on the hill slopes. But once they were in the dry, it was not their flooded homes they looked for, it was the passing of a rig.

The innkeepers were often the first affected by flooding. Their floors were flagged and the solid walls had seen the water rise many times. The most terrible thing for them was when the river prevented boats from going up and down. And a flood had to be really bad for the boatmen to give up. The innkeepers knew it. Very low water, on the other hand could halt the traffic completely, and that meant the death of the inn. The worst flood never lasted for weeks, but drought could go on and on.

And the waterside innkeepers knew how to handle a boat almost as well as a boatman did. They all had a boat. There was no need

for them to climb on the roof and shout or fire off a gun to summon help, they were men and could look after themselves.

Once the water had receded, their staff began washing off mud
and sweeping out the sand which the river had carried into kitchen,
stables, rooms. It was the occasion for a tremendous spring-clean-
ing of the whole house.

A mark would be scratched on the wall with an iron point and
the da᷄ inscribed. This year, the way things were going, it looked
as though a mark would be scratched higher than that which bore
the date 1827. And in a dry season, when innocent travellers looked
at the mark, then turned to see the low river far behind them, they
would say: 'Impossible! The water couldn't have risen as far as
this.'

And the innkeeper would take a certain pride in explaining: 'Oh
yes, sir. It was up to there, you ask anyone round here. And we
others didn't leave the attic. And every day I went out in that
cockleshell you see there.'

And it was not only with strangers to the valley that they dis-
cussed the river's rages, but with the barge crews also. What was
terrifying at the time took on great beauty when recollected. To
river folk and those who sailed, floods were battles. Like soldiers,
they told their war stories and the only thing never mentioned
was fear. To hear them, they had all behaved like heroes.

So nights of dread were forerunners of certain long, dreamy
evenings by a fire of wood the river had left behind. And those
downstream would unhesitatingly burn on their regained hearths
the bed or table of a river dweller upstream who had lost his all.

That evening Captain Merlin's men had to halt two hours before
nightfall. They had barely covered half a normal stage, but men
and horses were exhausted. They moored the barges at Aramon.
The water had not yet reached the first houses of the village, but
the quays were already submerged. Despite everything, it was
easier to come alongside here than alongside deserted river banks.
The horses could be lodged in the inn stables, and so could some of
the men, who would be drier there than under the deck-tents

where everything was humid and damp. Besides, the waves raised by the steamer had swept in under the awnings and the top bunks were soaking wet.

When they had finished mooring and the horses had been taken in and shut up, the three men who had relieved Christian and Paul Barillot on the towpath went to change their clothes in the galley. Christian joined them.

'How goes it?' he asked.

'All right. The last hour's even been a bit easier than the rest.'

'That's how it struck me,' Christian said. 'There weren't so many obstructions.'

The men looked at one another, hesitating to speak. At last the most senior said: 'It wouldn't surprise me if someone hadn't cleared a path for us.' He paused, then, since Christian said nothing, he added: 'There's a rig ahead, I'm sure of it.'

'No such luck. Besides, where d'you think it would come from, if not from Beaucaire?'

'Then Saint Nicholas has got himself a hatchet,' said the man. 'Because everything was freshly cut down. And I swear it was no apprentice's work. It had a master's touch. It was just as you might have done it yourself.'

The man said no more. Christian stayed looking at him a moment, then went out.

Old Surdon, who had listened without moving a muscle, followed him. When they were alone, the old man asked: 'Well, what d'you make of it?'

'I'd like to know for sure.'

'All right. I'll come with you.'

They took the smaller of the two runabouts, and with the old man at the oars and Christian upright in the prow handling the pole, they reached the river bank above the village, at the beginning of the path they would have to take next day. At that point the towpath ran along the top of a fairly high dyke which was still some eighteen inches above the Rhône. There were just a few lower places where the river was beginning to encroach on the path of earth and stones.

'It'll still be all right tomorrow,' the old man said.

They walked on until they reached the first bushes growing on the side of the dyke, between the water's edge and the path. All were chopped down, and the axe-marks were still fresh.

'It's not more than an hour since that was done,' the old man observed, rubbing his thumb over a notch.

Moreover, some of the cut branches were still on the bank, held in position against the dyke by the current. The two men stopped and listened. Nothing. Nothing but the steady sound of the rain in an evening falling from a sombre sky.

They quickened their pace, and covered a good mile. In several places the soft ground showed the imprint of soles which the river had not yet blurred. They were the soles of bargemen's boots, and it was clear that there were two men. After a long moment, Christian understood. But he did not speak, and it was the old man who said at last: 'God in heaven, if it's them, I wonder where they're going to spend the night.'

'Pig-headed,' Christian grunted.

'Pig-headed like you. No more and no less.'

Cupping his hands to make a loud-hailer, Christian called upstream: 'Claude!...Tirou!'

Nothing. Not even an echo.

The two men went on, lengthening their stride to win time from the night. Christian was no longer conscious of fatigue. A strange kind of warmth was coming to life in him. It was a sensation he was certain he had never experienced before.

At last they reached the point where the cutting ceased. They saw enough there to look for tracks, and found them leading off among the scrub into open country, part of which was already submerged through infiltration.

'A proper swamp,' the old man said.

Christian called again. But the only response was the cawing of a flight of invisible crows.

'Not worth going in there,' said Old Surdon. 'As soon as you get to the water, you'll lose the tracks.'

Stiffening, stifling momentarily the warmth which he felt rising within him and which would have driven him to search the whole swamp, Christian growled: 'Oh, to hell with them! I've asked nothing of them. They can go to hell.'

'Don't fret,' the old man said. 'They know what a river bank is like in flood. They're not daft enough to go and get stuck fast. Smart lads like that'll know how to find somewhere dry.'

'You're imagining things,' Christian said, turning back. 'I don't give a damn. If it *is* them – '

The old man interrupted him. 'Who d'you want it to be? The Tarasque, the local monster?'

'I've asked nothing of them . . . They're not doing any more – '

The old man broke in again. 'Don't talk daft. I know perfectly well what you're thinking. Maybe you don't give a damn, but you're bloody glad for all that.'

Christian didn't answer. The old man, out of breath, kept quiet for the rest of the way back, then, when they were taking their places in the runabout, he said simply: 'All the same, when the river gets into a man's blood, it's quite something.'

That night Christian found it hard to get to sleep. Before returning to the deck-tent, he had visited the inn on the pretext of making sure the horses and men lodged there had been well looked after. He had been right through the two big stables, where a boy of about ten was keeping an eye on the animals. He had questioned him about passing travellers, but the boy, a bit retarded, had not seen anyone that day except the crew of the rig.

Yet without any possible doubt, his son and his head prowman were there. They must have spent hours freezing in waist-deep water, to assist the progress of his rig. This thought, at once maddening and comforting, nagged at him. There was the picture of these two battling on his behalf against the river, with no boat to bring them help in case of accident, and there were also the words of the old man: 'When the river gets into a man's blood . . .' What had the old man, with his ability to read men's inmost thoughts, meant by that remark? That Claude had done this because he could no longer cut himself off from the river? Had he done it for the river or his father? Hadn't the old man said it to punish him for being too hard on Claude and Tirou? And yet he had approved the decision to dismiss them from the rig. Wasn't it for the rig, out of loyalty to their calling, that Claude and Tirou had worked like this?

Christian slept little and got up several times to check the state of the river and see that the men on watch were at their posts.

The river had risen farther, and when the dreary dawn began to tinge the incessant rain with grey, the water was entering the lowest houses. It was at the door of the inn stables and was already creeping into the main room, from which the innkeeper and his serving-maids were removing tables and benches.

'It's made up its mind to last and to rise high,' he said to Christian. 'It wouldn't surprise me if it gets up to the first floor.'

Christian dared not rejoice openly. He forced himself to say: 'That's not much of a prospect.'

'No,' said the man, 'but it's not the first time.' He paused and asked: 'Are you going on just the same?' He had a big red face and huge grey moustaches stained yellow with tobacco.

'Yes,' said Christian. 'I'm going upstream.'

'You'll have trouble. The towpath is going to be –'

'I know,' said Christian. 'But I'm going upstream.'

'You're just like Old Félix,' the innkeeper said. 'I've seen him go upstream at times when no one else dared risk it. No one. But he went up. And it always turned out all right. All the same, there are big risks this time.'

The runabout returned from carrying supplies of vegetables bought at the inn. The clerk was aboard. He was carrying his money-bag and was coming to pay the innkeeper.

'Quite right,' said M. Tonnerieu, 'there are too many risks. But this blockhead doesn't want to hear anything . . . Only, his men will end up by deserting him. There's already one who's been to ask me for his wages.'

Christian reacted to this statement as if he had been stung. 'What?' he yelled.

'Yes, his wages,' the clerk repeated. 'He says this is madness.'

'Who is he?'

'Young Marcelin.'

'And you've paid him?'

'Not yet.'

'God above! Get down from there!'

It was brutal. Suddenly overcome by a rage that set him trembling, Christian dragged the clerk from the boat. The old man jumped into the water beside the innkeeper, while Christian leaped aboard the runabout and shouted to the oarsmen: 'To the barges! Quick!'

Christian stood in the bows, swaying backwards and forwards with every pull on the oars, his fists clenched. His gaze raked the barges, drawn up at the limit of the deep water. He saw Marcelin waiting at the entrance to the galley on the master-barge. The oarsmen had understood and made straight for the galley. The prow had not yet touched the bulwark when Christian leaped aboard. Marcelin, seeing him arrive, must have recognized the fury in his face.

M. Tonnerieu had said 'young Marcelin' because he was, but he was a great tall strapping fellow with a beard already well grown and a dark and lively eye. He put down his kitbag at the entrance to the galley and took a few steps back along the bulwark. In two strides Christian was on him.

'Want your wages, do you?' he shouted. 'I'll see you get 'em.'

Marcelin was nimble and managed to dodge a couple of blows, then, making the most of a respite, he leaped from the barge to the flooded quay. The water splashed around him, and he began to run, lifting his feet clear.

Pulling hard on their oars, the men in the runabout quickly overhauled him, and the man who was ahead of him held out a boat-hook at water level and caught Marcelin's foot in it. He tripped, flailed the air with his arms, and fell full length. There were shouts and laughter from the barges and the inn. Christian, who had jumped out behind him, arrived just as he was picking himself up. Grabbing him by the lapels of his waistcoat, he shook

him, shouting: 'You rotten little bastard, I couldn't half teach you
a lesson. You'd see even less than you do now. But I don't want to
teach kids.'

Blinded by the muddy water, Marcelin was spitting and blowing.
He no longer had the least desire to fight or flee.

Lifting his arms to protect his face, he stammered: 'I've got three
small kids . . . You must understand . . . My wife died of a fever . . .
It's my mother who looks after them. If I . . .'

'Shut up!' Christian said, releasing him. 'You undertook to
make this upstream journey and you'll make it.'

Christian was no longer shouting. His voice was heavy and hard.
Marcelin had lowered his hands. There was still fear in his face, but
Christian noticed that he was looking at the men who had gathered
along the bulwarks. There was perhaps more shame than fear in
his gaze.

'You'll go upstream,' he repeated. 'Like the others. And when
you get there, you'll come and thank me for having allowed you
to do it. Anyone can feel like chucking it momentarily . . . As for
the kids, you've got to work for their sake.'

Marcelin looked down and mumbled a few words which Christian took to mean something like: 'Forgive me . . . don't hold it
against me.'

'Go and put your kitbag back in its place,' he said. 'And as you
go past, ask Canut to give you a drop of hot wine. It'll do you good.
And it's not worth getting changed this morning, you'll be on the
towpath with me. Since we're both wet already, we might as well
be the first.'

They went back on board, where the men had already begun
work again.

Once the horses were coupled up, the rig moved off, captained
by Old Surdon, who said the prayer and gave orders in his voice of
former years.

Christian went ahead of the team, axe in belt and boat-hook in
hand, in water up to his ankles, then up to his knees, then up to his
belly in the low-lying parts, followed by Marcelin whom he heard
splashing along behind him. On this path where the branches had

already been cut, it was hardly necessary to do more than sound out the ground and make sure it was firm.

When he reached the point where they had turned back the previous evening, Christian confirmed that Claude and Tirou had gone on. Not only had the scrub on the right been cleared, but everything which the river had brought down in the night had been cut or swept away. The other two could not be very far ahead, for several times he saw the current carrying down branches whose white cut ends protruding from the water indicated that they had only just been chopped off. Wood chips also floated here and there. Christian stopped and turned round.

'You see,' he said to Marcelin, 'this is a voyage upstream the like of which has never been seen. It is Saint Nicholas who goes ahead and clears our path for us.'

'No,' said Marcelin, 'everyone knows it's – But I wonder how long they'll keep it up.'

Christian forced himself to walk a good quarter of a mile farther, then he turned to the rig and summoned the relief.

The runabout put out from the rig and overhauled them. When it was level with them Christian told the two relief men to stay on board. 'By poling up along the dyke,' he said, 'you'll quickly overtake the two fools a bit higher up. They're the ones who need relieving.' And he added for the benefit of the oarsmen: 'You can pick us two up on your way back.'

Christian was chilled by the water which turned his feet and belly to ice, yet deep within him there was still that comfortable warmth that made him a little breathless.

When Claude and Tirou came aboard the runabout which Christian and Marcelin then boarded in their turn, no one said a word. The oarsmen pulled in the direction of the master-barge, and drew in alongside the galley. The four men entered the galley. Christian and Marcelin stripped in order to change. Claude and Tirou made for the fire, took off boots, waistcoats and shirts, and remained standing there, warming themselves. Their velvet trousers steamed on their bodies.

'Perhaps you ought to change,' Christian growled. 'You're not going to stay there until you've dried out.' When the other two did not budge, he added: 'Where are your kitbags?'

'At a farm below Aramon.'

'Bloody fools.'

Christian hardened himself. He looked at his son, stripped to the waist. Handsome, solid, firmly modelled, like all the males in his family. He wanted to take him in his arms and say to him: 'Oh lad, it does me good to see you again. I thought it was impossible . . . If your poor mother was here . . . And the old man . . .'

A whole flurry of such phrases whirled round in him. He kept them at bay by barricading himself behind a rage which he must have had some difficulty in sustaining.

'Canut,' he said, 'stir yourself and find them some dry clothes. For him – ' he pointed to his son, whom he did not want to call Claude – 'you can look in my box. For the other one, ask Félicien. His ought to do.'

The cook went out. The door swung to, driving a blast of cold air inwards which formed arabesques in the steamy atmosphere.

'That was bloody silly,' Christian repeated.

The warmth within him was affecting him more and more, and he needed harsh words to keep his ill-temper going. As soon as he was dressed and had finished his boiling hot soup, he said: 'When you're ready, you'll go and assist the head prowman. As for him, the runabout will take him down to the first savoyarde and he'll put himself under the captain's orders.'

He had again said 'you'. He did not want to say Tirou and Claude. That constituted affection. A few words among themselves were good when all was going well. But he could no longer call them by their names; he felt it would have been ridiculous; so he said 'him' and 'you'. And he was furious at this anger, which he none the less continued to stoke.

He returned with pleasure to the rain and the cold air. At the tiller Old Surdon welcomed him, saying: 'So those two bright lads are back. I hope you're going to make them sweat blood.'

'You can bet on that,' Christian answered.

'Besides, the Rhône's going to see to it that we're all on our toes. Them and us. I never remember seeing it bring down so much and rise so quickly. And the Durance must be pouring it in; look over at the Empie, the water's almost white.'

And indeed, on their right the river was sweeping greyish water along. Bundles of branches and reeds were floating everywhere. Some of them were like long rafts. A great many bottles, boxes and rags were caught up in them, and even broken furniture, planks and fence stakes. Whole trees, sixty feet in length, their roots and branches thrusting out of the water, were becoming increasingly frequent. Sometimes they bore straight down on the stem-post and Christian had to lean hard on the tiller to avoid them. Despite this, Tirou, Baptiste and the deck-boy, who were all three at the prow, had great difficulty in fending them off with their iron boat-hooks.

On the bank, where the horses, well rested, had been able to forge ahead at a good pace during the first two hours, progress became more and more difficult. First, there was an enforced halt. A hut had collapsed and was lying across the path. A twisted mass of beams, planks and big stones formed a dam. The bailey halted his horses.

'Let go the anchors!' Christian shouted.

The chains rumbled as they scraped over wood. The capstans began to turn, clicking, while the anchors fell to the water with dull splashes amid a fount of spray.

The drivers had leaped down from their mounts to unfasten the ropes and tie them to the stoutest trees. Four of them had gone forward to help the two members of the land crew. As soon as the rig was made fast, Christian and the three men left aboard the runabout joined them. Even with nine of them, it took them over an hour to clear the path.

They had to chop down two huge poplars which were holding the roof-beam fast. This in turn was holding back all the intertwined material.

A second tree lay on the bushes, and when the roof-beam gave way suddenly, rearing up some eight or nine feet from the river and falling back, it raised a great fount of water and waves which knocked over several of the men. When they got to their feet again, one of them had lost his axe and two their hats. Albert Boissonet, the last to rise, was groaning, his face twisted with pain. He was holding his right arm with his left hand.

'My God, his arm!'

Christian went towards him. Blood had already soaked through his waistcoat, visible through a great rent in his waterproof.

'Get him into the runabout,' Christian commanded. 'Let Bonnetin and Marthou take over on the towpath. The rest of you back to the rig, fast.'

The men helped the injured man to clamber into the boat. His face was pale and his teeth chattering.

'I can't move my arm,' he was yammering.

Standing in the stern, Christian shouted to the bailey: 'I've an injured man aboard. Couple up. We'll leave again as soon as you're ready.'

On board, the men carried the injured man into the galley. He had fainted.

'Give him a nip of brandy,' Christian ordered. 'Canut will look after him. The rest of you to your posts.'

He himself returned to the tiller. This accident had hardened him still further.

'The trouble's starting,' Old Surdon growled. 'But it can do whatever it likes, God damn it; we're going upstream.'

The old man had hardened too. Christian could tell from the sound of his voice, which whistled between his clenched teeth. It was no longer will-power which drove him, but a kind of rage.

Once again the rig began its difficult advance and slowly reached the point where the yellowish waters of the Rhône overflowed the right bank, assailed on the left by the furious onslaught of the Durance. Whirlpools several yards in diameter were formed at this juncture, drawing into their waltz and dragging down towards the bottom everything which the river and its tributary brought down. It was a kind of primitive struggle, all crested with foam, where the yellow and grey intertwined without really intermingling, where there was no longer any discernible direction to the current.

Checked and then diverted from its course, the Rhône over-whelmed the already submerged country on the right. The island downstream from the rocks of Les Essarts had already disappeared. Its presence was betrayed only by a movement of the water, which hesitated, bristling with choppy wavelets and small swift eddies which were relentlessly swallowed up by the larger, slower ones.

To get past, the horses would have to be diverted into open country beyond the surf-line of the waves breaking over the rocks, whose highest points were still just visible.

'It must have built up some almighty piles of debris,' the old man said. 'Otherwise, even in a flood, it wouldn't be so churned up.'

It was true. Christian had never seen the confluence of the Rhône and the Durance so violent. And it was just at this point, where the waves rose highest and the whirlpools hollowed out enormous funnels, that it was going to be necessary to lengthen the ropes. For if the horses were to skirt the rocks, the barges had to remain at least ten yards from the point where the surf-line betrayed their presence. To pass closer inshore was to run the risk of being caught in a cross-current and flung against the rocky barrier. Christian gave the order to pay out the ropes just at the moment when the first couples emerged from the water to climb the hillside, follow-ing the two men who were marking out a path through the brush-wood and loose earth.

Stones rolled beneath the horses' hoofs. Some remained caught in clumps of thorn, but other, heavier ones bounced as far as the river.

Christian never stopped murmuring: 'O God, don't let a horse go down.'

Grasping his tiller firmly, keeping a constant eye on the move-ments of the water and the distance between him and the rocks, he also watched the horses. The drivers had all dismounted and were firmly clutching the shortened bridles. Christian was so busy surveying it all that he did not even notice he had stopped praying.

The higher the horses climbed, the worse the earth underfoot became. Christian hardly took his eyes off them, fearing all the time that an animal would fall, which would certainly have brought down a good part of the team, thus making it necessary to cut the ropes and abandon the barges to the fury of the waters.

His whole attention was concentrated on the bare hillslope where streams glistened, but it was the cry that went up from the prow which sent a shudder through him – an inarticulate cry, followed by:

'Man overboard!'

Christian saw at once that it was the deck-boy. A great tree was alongside the bulwark. A boat-hook was planted in its trunk. The deck-boy's boat-hook. In trying to withdraw it, he had been dragged overboard by the tree when it rolled over.

'Hold the tiller!' Christian shouted.

The old man grabbed it. The boy had just surfaced some ten yards from the bulwark, but he seemed semi-conscious. Christian bent down to wrench off his boots, but Tirou had already plunged in.

'You bastard! That's my job!' Christian raged.

But, practical above all and knowing that the prowman would need help, he ran along the bulwark and got a rope ready. Baptiste, the boy's elder brother, one foot bare, the other booted, ran up with tackle. No doubt he too had been beaten to it by Tirou.

Thrashing the water with his powerful arms, the prowman had already reached the boy. He held him with one hand and raised the other to show that he was waiting for help.

Simultaneously, the two men whirled the weighted ends round and threw. The ropes uncoiled and snaked across the deck, and both landed within three feet of the swimmer. Tirou made for Christian's, which was downstream, clung to it and turned over on his back. His head disappeared under water as the rope went taut, but he surfaced quickly and shouted: 'Haul away!'

Christian was about to pass the rope round a butt on the bulwark when the old man yelled: 'Look out! The prow!'

A beam, scarcely lifting above the water, was coming slantwise like a battering-ram. Christian gave the rope to Baptiste and leaped for the prow. He was barely in time. Hardly had he snatched up a boat-hook when the great plank was on them, driving straight for the barge's flank. He planted the hook's iron point in it and heaved with all his might. He was able to keep it from striking end on, but none the less the current swung the heavy piece of oak so that its full length crashed against the barge's side. There was a vibration, a dull shock which ran through all the ribs, then a cracking.

Now Christian was forcing himself to hold off the plank, realizing that if he let go it would shoot like an arrow all along the bulwark. 'Be quick!' he shouted.

The two cooks who had emerged from the galley joined in. Canut seized a boat-hook and added his strength to Christian's, while Caillette helped Baptiste to haul in Tirou and the boy.

Due to the fierceness of the current and the utterly haphazard nature of the whirlpools, the rescue took a good five minutes. Five interminable minutes.

At last, when the two men were on board, Christian and Canut were able to push the beam towards midstream, where an eddy whirled it away. The cook's normally rosy face seemed drained of blood, yet great drops of sweat stood out on it.

Baptiste had taken his brother in his arms and carried him into the galley where Boissonet was groaning, stretched out on Caillette's bunk. A glass of spirits revived the boy, whose greenish face regained a little colour. He put his hand to his head and said: 'I saw it . . . It knocked me out . . . And then nothing.'

'What knocked you out?'

'I don't know.'

Tirou, who was stripping down, explained. 'I saw the blow, but too late. It was a classic case, the log which rolls over and the lad who wants to hang on to his boat-hook. Only he went arse over tip on to the trunk. That's what knocked him out. And it was an eddy reversing which brought him to the surface. If it hadn't been for that, he'd have stayed under.' Then he added, as if to excuse himself for having jumped in first: 'It's lucky I was wearing shoes. I went in with them on. But they've stayed in the water, and I don't even know whose they were.'

'Let the boy lie down,' Christian ordered. 'And try to get him warm. The rest of you hurry up. We need all hands.'

As he was going out of the galley he heard the clerk saying: 'These things always go in threes. It's madness ... Madness.'

Christian wanted to turn round on the spot, but he controlled himself.

'Let him babble,' he growled. 'The rig before everything.'

And having made sure that Old Surdon was all right at the tiller, he returned to the prow where a man from the runabout was already at work.

In the little hamlets and isolated farms the tragedy of the sudden flood was heightened by solitude. People felt themselves surrounded by water and the sky was so close to the earth that it was no longer possible to tell where the river ended. It was necessary to call and keep on calling throughout threatening nights and days when the house shook under the water's assault.

In the big cities the sheer number of people to be rescued added to the rescuers' difficulties. As soon as a boat drew alongside, clusters of people clung to it. At Lyons an overloaded boat smashed into a tree during the night, and seven people were drowned. An old boatman, Huchard, saved three soldiers reinforcing a dyke who were being swept away by the current. A doctor spent more than an hour clinging to the branches of a tree, with two women hanging on to his garments. On the Cours Bourbon, another boatman, Old François, was alone instrumental in saving seventeen people before being dragged under and drowned by three others who paralysed his movements.

In the city centre the river reached a height of almost twenty-five feet above low watermark. No one had ever seen anything like it. Opposite the Cours du Midi, five factories lay under several feet of mud and water. The earthen dyke had given way, and the water had penetrated streets, arcades, and the lower rooms of the Hôtel-Dieu. Between Les Charpennes and the Port Henri IV, more than twenty houses had collapsed and were blocking the streets. Beams floated haphazardly. The force of the current turned them into battering-rams, and they eviscerated other houses which collapsed in their turn.

No one was even sure if there were people under the debris. They looked for them in vain. The river scattered the debris and in the darkness families were split up.

Everything happened very fast, in dusk and half-light, by the gleam of a lantern or in pitch darkness. The authorities no longer knew which way to turn, where to lodge these transient and hungry fugitives. And those who lived on the high ground were reluctant to open their doors, for flood meant famine, and the hungry flung themselves on well-stocked cupboards.

Men are as selfish in bad times as in good. They gazed from their windows on the wretchedness of others and bemoaned their own fate, imploring heaven's protection equally against flood and a refugee invasion.

Those who opened their doors widest were the poor. According to the middle classes, this was because they had nothing worth stealing. In actual fact, they were so used to wretchedness that they had a better understanding of it in others and they did their utmost to relieve it.

Night was the worst.

Night spent in houses whose ground floors were under water. Night spent in other people's houses, wondering if one's own still stood.

Night was the worst, even for the boatmen who watched the river, wondering constantly if their mooring ropes would hold.

There were barge-trains halted in the ports, which were no longer places of refuge because the water was breaking in great waves over the dykes. There were boats and crews trapped among the islands. They had tied up there in expectation of a flood like those they had known in the past. But still the water rose, and the poplars around which they had passed their mooring-ropes cracked. The roots lifted the undermined earth, long trunks suddenly struck the barges, killing horses and men and smashing the runabouts. Kicking off their heavy boots, the survivors leaped into the river, swimming in darkness with no idea of the direction of the bank. Spun round by whirlpools, dashed against rocks, held under by roots, they shouted but their shouts were hardly heard by the river folk. And each one of them battled alone.

For some it was their last trip downstream. For those whose strength and luck brought them ashore, the night was a nightmare which left them exhausted, half naked, mentally drained, their bodies moulded and battered with weariness, stretched out in pouring rain on the sodden earth of the fields.

They possessed nothing now but their lives. When at last they were able to stagger off through the mud, they reached their villages only to learn that the flood had destroyed their homes as well.

Ruined, they cursed the river. Yet because they were of the river's breed, beneath the black ash of this night of mourning, there still lurked in them a spark of love which the first spring sun would rekindle. Because they were of the river's breed, they would begin all over again to live with it.

During these nights and days which were like no others, a great battle raged up and down the valley. Sky, wind, light, darkness, water from heaven and water from the earth, men, horses, barges, trees, rocks and flooded land, all took part in this campaign. And no one knew which side he was on. The trees contended with the wind as much as with the river. They held out against men and against the barges moored to their trunks, which, with the force of the current, pulled twenty times more strongly than the strongest teams. The land did battle with the water and the water with the land. The sky rent the clouds and the clouds besieged the hillslopes. It was one vast upheaval of Nature's forces. And amid this fury man also fought. Tiny yet towering, he battled for his modest possessions and his mighty pride.

Captain Merlin's crew had spent a very bad night. Caught by twilight less than two miles downstream from Avignon, they had had to moor the barges to some mulberries which held little hope of lasting the night. Christian had therefore insisted that two men should be permanently on watch on each barge. He himself had hardly lain down; he had gone often to the galley, where the deck-boy had recovered fairly quickly from the shock he had had, whereas Albert Boissonet was still suffering terribly. The wound had stopped bleeding, but it was almost certain that the arm was broken.

M. Tonnerieu had been insistent that they should take the injured man ashore, but it was too risky to do so by night on board a light and fragile runabout, and Christian knew that at any moment he might have need of these boats.

Three times during the night the men had had to raise the mooring-ropes on the trunks of the mulberries because they were under water. It was exhausting and dangerous work.

In the galley, a cook had been permanently on duty, keeping a hell-fire going to dry clothes and keep the soup hot.

At dawn Christian had given the order to move on.

The clerk, who up to now had hardly left his office, came often on deck. He was anxious, peering short-sightedly at everything and harassing Christian with his ceaseless 'It's madness. We must halt at Avignon and wait for more favourable conditions... Madness... And the best proof is that we're the only barge-train on the river.'

As if to prove him wrong, about mid-morning a train of five big barges, heavily laden, came in sight upstream. The rain had lessened slightly and Christian saw it coming from a distance, travelling fast in midstream. The men at the prow shouted: 'Rig going downstream... Five barges to pass!'

The river was so wide that passing presented no problem.

When the leading barge was no more than a hundred yards away, Tirou shouted from the prow: 'Rig from Serrières. Captain Marthouret.'

Christian handed the tiller over to Old Surdon and went up to the prow. Marthouret, opposite, had also delegated his post to a second-in-command in order to come to the prow of his barge. As soon as they were within hailing distance, Marthouret shouted: 'Ahoy there, Christian!'

'Ahoy, Adrien!'

'How's it downstream?'

'All right for going down. When you get to the Durance, steer for the Empie, it's fierce on the Ryaume.'

'Thanks. Upstream, in Avignon, avoid the Empie, the current's less on the Ryaume.'

'And the wooden bridge?'

'We got through coming downstream, you'll get through all right going up. Take the second arch.'

'And the steamer?'

'Stuck below the bridge. If the flood lasts as long as I'd like it to, she'll be there ten years! I'll be going upstream too. And I hope I see her still tied up there when I sail past.' Marthouret laughed as he said it.

As the barges passed, the two men had walked aft, and stood face to face for a moment. But the barges were already drawing apart even while they were conversing from the stern. As the barges went by, other men exchanged local news.

'How're things at Condrieu?'

'Not good. The low-lying parts are flooded up to the first floor.'

'And at Serrières?'

'Quay's under water.'

'And the chapel?'

'Flooded.'

'Damnation! That means my house is too.'

Marthouret had recognized the old man, who had removed his hat and was waving it high in the air, letting the wind blow wildly through his long grey hair.

'God in heaven!' Marthouret had cried. 'You've signed on Grandpa Surdon.'

And the old man had shouted: 'And why not? Don't I have the right to get out and about a bit?'

'You've picked a good time.'

'It's a river after my own heart, lad.'

And the men on the rig going downstream cried: 'It's Grandpa Surdon.'

And the old man laughed and waved his hat.

The voices criss-crossed the river, which bore the downstream rig rapidly away. Its last savoyarde was melting into the greyness.

'To go downstream in conditions like these also takes some doing,' Old Surdon said. 'And if you don't drop your anchor a bit, you shoot the arches of the bridge at the speed of a cannon-ball.'

'I'll bet Marthouret didn't drop his anchor.'

'No fear! He's quite a lad, that one. And his father was just the same.'

The water continued to rise, and progress grew ever slower and more difficult. Christian sensed that his men and horses were at the end of their tether, but the certainty of being able to beat the hated steamer spurred him on. Old Surdon exulted.

'I told you so,' he kept repeating. 'That dirty bitch of a steamer's going to watch us sail past. And she'll never have seen an upstream voyage as good as ours. And we'll be at Lyons while she's still rusting there. And the others in the same state . . . I tell you, lad, steam's had it. It'll never recover, after a blow like this. They've put too much cash into their scrap iron to be able to pull out of this.'

Such talk served to harden Christian's determination still further.

Now he was no longer conscious of fatigue or danger. There were no more risks, no further questions to be asked of anyone, no further advice to be taken; there was only the river. He had known its language and communed with it direct for so many years that he was sure he had nothing to fear from it.

Like Old Surdon, was he not himself in some measure the river? Ever since his departure from Lyons, was not everything in league to promote his triumph? A steamer aground on the way down, another halted by a bridge on the way up. Since he had begun sailing, this was the first time he had gone up like this with the near certainty of being the only one to do so. Marthouret, perhaps, would go up in two or three days' time, but for the moment he was alone. Alone in daring it. Alone with a team whose like he had never seen. To acquire it, he had even dipped deep into his own savings, but it was for the river. And the river, which had no more liking for steam than he had, would help him to the limit of his undertaking.

Besides, was there not a deep-seated reason why everything should thus be on his side? Had not a supernatural power charged him with a mission? That being so, what could he have to fear? Nothing. Nothing save the weakness, the feebleness of certain persons. But he would know how to bring them to heel. He had done so already. He would do it again, and more brutally, if it were necessary.

They could call him selfish, say he was heartless, he did not care. Great undertakings were not brought to fruition without crushing underfoot whatever might be in the way.

He had his path to pursue. He would pursue it.

And if his son had rejoined him, it was not, perhaps, out of affection, nor out of respect or devotion, but quite simply because he wanted to bear his part in what he, Christian Merlin, was alone capable of carrying through.

No one had ever seen an upstream voyage like it. Even Old Surdon, with so many years of navigation behind him, said so.

Gradually, as the hours passed and fatigue lay heavy on men and horses alike, Christian sank farther into his dream. He himself no longer felt weariness nor anguish. He no longer felt anything except that shiver of delight which the tiller's vibration sent through him, putting him in close and direct communication with his river.

A voice was in him. A mighty, secret voice which spoke the river's own language and ordained his route.

Only he could hear it clearly. He grew more convinced of it with every difficulty overcome. Only he could hope that this voice, whose message would be incomprehensible to other ears, would accompany him to the very end of his marvellous road.

The clouds continued to travel up the valley and to carry the rain still higher, on to the flank of the mountains from which the water streamed down towards the Rhône and Saône. All the tributaries poured in, the whole region was flooded, and great lakes criss-crossed by currents were formed among the mountains. The slopes were torrents and the plains were lakes.

Towards the end of the morning there was a break in the clouds to the north, but it was only a trick of the wind.

The river had reached its highest point, though no one knew it.

And that day there were so many dramas all up and down the valley that the newspapers gave up reporting them all. Even in the low-lying districts far removed from the river, where water penetrated only by infiltration, some houses collapsed. The foundations gave way because the earth was loosened and slid from under the weight of the stone.

Three suspension bridges had water up to the wooden traverses maintained in place by wire cables and were swept away. Huge planks reared stiffly up on end in the midst of whirlpools and spun round as they went under, only to erupt farther down and fall flat, sending up founts of yellowish foam. Wire cables trailed in the current, others writhed like snakes caught in a snare.

No one knew what was happening upstream or downstream; there were other things to do than exchange news.

Isidore Cuminal, one of the best barge captains, had halted upstream from Le Theil. But the position became untenable. Isidore therefore decided to push on to Ancône, where his barges would be able to find shelter. He was not far from his goal when the horses harnessed to the forward cable slipped. Those behind were still pulling and the stable barge turned broadside on. It filled with water straight away, capsized, and dragged the other barges with it. The captain cut the tow-ropes to save his horses. Almost all the men managed to reach the bank, but the barges were smashed against the pier of the bridge.

The water rose as far as Rochemaure, where the road from Les Fontaines seemed like a canal. Barns and farmhouses continued to collapse. The current swept away carts which the peasants had abandoned in mid-field, for only a few days earlier they had been busy with their autumn sowing.

Avignon also did battle with the river. The Prefect telegraphed appeals for food for the destitute. But no one heard anyone else's appeals any longer, for everyone was clamouring for aid.

The laundry-boats and boat-mills were swept away. Torn from

their moorings, they sped over this river which for so many years they had watched flowing southwards, but the river had run riot. It capsized the boats or broke them up on the rocks. The removal of these boats would clear the banks, and barge crews going upstream would be able to get their tow-ropes past much more easily. So what was high drama for some made life much easier for others.

But the drama was to end by involving all of them, and almost all of them felt it. Only a few boatmen believed that this flood had come expressly for them, and that the disaster it caused was of little account. Only a few of them felt like this, and the best of them spent their days and nights in rescue work. They did so out of natural generosity, out of love for their fellow men, but perhaps also so that St Nicholas and all the river gods whom they had never seen but whose presence they were well aware of, would protect the old barge traffic and destroy steam for evermore.

The crews of the steamers, who were almost all former barge men, also did their share of rescuing villagers. And some told themselves that St Nicholas was watching them and would not hold it so much against them in future that they had left the barges for iron ships.

At Lyons, the Companies' offices were like military headquarters during a battle. The buildings on the peninsula were flooded, so they had abandoned their offices for some houses built on the slope of Sainte-Foy. From their windows they looked out on the confluence of the Rhône and Saône, the one as turbid as the other. They had their meals and the latest news brought in. They assumed a serious mien when talking of the distress of the river folk and of all those whose living depended on the river, but every announcement that a barge-train had been wrecked delighted them, though they did not let their satisfaction show.

Around noon, as the rig was coming in sight of Avignon, the rain stopped and the sky lightened a little, though it was still covered with soot-coloured clouds. To the north, long rays of grimy light appeared, as if the sun had suddenly changed position in the sky to point their road.

The city came in view, with its massive walls and its palace. But it was not the city that drew the boatmen's eyes. Christian and his men gazed upstream, between the southernmost point of the island of La Barthalasse and the right bank. That was where their route lay, and no doubt that was where the steamer was moored downstream from Villeneuve. In fact, the *Rhodan* had anchored downstream from an islet hugging the larger isle, where she was sheltered from the worst of the current. Tirou, the first to see her, turned and shouted: 'Steamer upstream, against La Barthalasse!'

'Our luck's in,' Old Surdon said. 'If she'd been on the Ryaume, she'd have got in the way of our tow-ropes.'

'Our luck's in,' Christian repeated as he watched the sky clearing. Now the horses could go forward more easily, for the towpath was raised a little just outside Villeneuve. There was barely a foot of water on it, and it was in good repair and much wider.

Already the two members of the land crew who went ahead of the team had started running to gain an advantage and to make ready, while they were still downstream from the bridge, the holding ropes which would enable them to keep the tow-ropes in position while the horses were getting on the upstream side.

Marthouret's information had been accurate. The river was running strongly on this side of the island, but straight and without too many whirlpools. The wooden bridge reared its threatening interlacing of beams, but it was obvious that nothing untoward lurked under the second arch, with its long triangle of water. It afforded a clear passage, where the current was exceptionally fierce, but regular and without surprises.

The clerk emerged from the galley and went to find Christian. Standing foursquare in front of him, he said: 'You're going to halt before you get to the bridge. While the men are eating, I'll go and find a doctor for Boissonet. His arm's swelled up like a drowned dog.'

'I'll halt at nightfall,' Christian said. 'Below Villeneuve.'

'You've no right,' the old man cried, flourishing his eye-glasses.

Christian felt oddly calm. 'I decide what's right,' he said. 'I'm the captain.'

'It's disgraceful,' the clerk squeaked. 'Your father would blush for shame if he knew.'

'Get out, you make me sick.'

Old Surdon advanced on the clerk, whose head came scarcely half way up his chest. Taking him by the arm, he spun him round and gave him a push towards the galley, as if he had been a badly behaved child. 'Back to your books, you damned scribbler,' he roared, 'or I'll duck you, clothes and all.'

The clerk withdrew, waving his arms and crying that he was on a barge run by madmen.

Old Surdon came back, excited, and smiling more broadly than ever. 'That black rat would like to spoil our upstream voyage. Blast his eyes, he ought to be shut up in his cage!'

On the towpath a dozen men were coming to meet the horses. When he drew level with them, Christian saw that they were talking to the bailey. They were walking along beside his horse, still talking. After a moment the bailey turned towards the rig, cupped his hands to form a loud-hailer, and shouted: 'Ahoy! Christian! Men from Villeneuve. They say we can't go on. We might smash their bridge.'

'We're going on.'

Two of the men had gone to the horses' heads and were lifting their hands to catch the bridles.

'Use the whip!' Christian shouted.

The bailey's whip began to crack about the men's ears. They drew back. Then the group retreated, shouting threats and shaking their fists.

Old Surdon laughed. 'They're crazy,' he said. 'It's not the first time they've done it. They've already got themselves well and truly licked.'

'I know,' Christian said. 'Crazy but dangerous.'

The rig had drawn level with the steamer. Several men were leaning over the rail, watching. There was an exchange of insults, but the boatmen had more important things to do than watch the steamer. The team had reached the bridge, and, aided by the drivers, the two land crew were quickly making the holding ropes fast to the rings in the quay. The runabout with its six oarsmen had already joined them. The main cable was attached to the runabout, which made for the second arch. Pulling rhythmically, the six men struggled for a moment with the current, then, making the most of a whirlpool's reversal, they forged upstream.

While watching them at work, Christian and Old Surdon leaned on the tiller to keep their barge postioned exactly opposite the arch.

When the runabout carrying the main cable got above the bridge, the horses were already waiting. Numerous spectators had gathered along the bank, and a few bold spirits had even ventured on to the bridge whose wooden frame shook under the river's assaults. The main cable, made fast and fully uncoiled, hardly rubbed against the supports of the arch. The bridge acted as a dam, and the sound of the water going through was too loud for orders to be shouted, but Christian and the bailey never took their eyes off each other.

When the bailey raised his arm, Christian raised his in answer. The blood was pounding in his temples. The prowman, who was watching him, cast off the holding ropes which it was the land crew's responsibility to collect. The main cable grew taut. The barges backed slightly, paused, then began very slowly to proceed upstream.

Tight-lipped, chewing on his beard, hands gripping the tiller, Christian knew perfectly well that he was gambling with the river. Perhaps no one before him had attempted what he was now going to try. He tried to see everything simultaneously. The team. The Rhône beneath the arch. The whirlpools round the piers. The cable stretching against the massive upright and disappearing sometimes beneath a wave.

The nearer the rig approached to the bridge, the faster the current raced and the louder grew the terrible noise of the water. It was at once terrifying and marvellous. The Rhône was so strong that nothing could be finer than mastery. And Christian was indeed the master. He could feel it.

The barge quivered. The cable was strained to breaking point.

Ahead, standing on their horses, the drivers lashed the whips for all they were worth.

There were perhaps a thousand persons gathered on the high ground to watch Christian Merlin's triumph over the river and his victory over steam. When he reached Lyons, there would be tens of thousands. Far more than when Jouffroy Steam-Pump went up the Saône for the first time.

The master-barge passed through. One by one the following barges crossed this dividing line in the river, which continued to roar and spew forth foam. The river parted before the bows of the barges. The bow waves rose so high that they sometimes broke over the decks.

'We're through, lad! We're through!' Old Surdon cried, his strong voice choked with emotion.

Christian did not answer, but his heart swelled with a mighty pride.

He turned round. The last savoyarde was already under the bridge. It was going through when, in the same instant that he heard the shouts of Baptiste Carénal and Tirou, Christian felt the deck shudder under an almighty shock. A tree with all its branches reared up ahead of the barge. A tree running with water, which had just risen straight from the river as if conjured up by heaven. For two or three seconds the tree remained motionless. At the prow, the two men trying to fend it off with their boat-hooks seemed like two dwarfs attacking a giant with straws. The tree wavered to the right, straightened again, then came down like a sledge-hammer on the barge's prow, snapping off the barge cross and tearing open the bows.

On the bank, the horses were dragged back by the cable which no one had had time to cut. They staggered towards the river, and their fall brought down the drivers as well. After a few seconds' silence, a long cry went up and sped across the flood.

Christian turned and shouted: 'Cut the ropes!'

Too late. Already, while the barge was going down by the bows, the stern was lifting. Old Surdon sliced through the cable with one blow of his axe, but the barges he released had already turned broadside on and the men could not steer them through the arches. Christian saw them heading straight for the piers.

His own barge, with her bows stove in, was already plunging head first.

'My God, Boissonet!'

Christian ran along the bulwark, already partly submerged. Canut and Caillette came out of the galley, dragging the old clerk. He had lost his eye-glasses and groped blindly, hands held out in front of him.

'Jump!' yelled Christian.

The two cooks gripped the clerk and leaped into the current, still holding him.

Christian went into the galley.

'Save yourself!' Boissonet shouted to him.

But Christian did not heed him. Grasping him round the waist, he emerged just in time to avoid being sucked under by the barge as it went down. Without releasing Boissonet, he let himself go under. He could feel the current propelling him downstream and he knew it was vain to struggle. He must let himself be borne along and save his breath.

At last he surfaced. He had not let go of Boissonet. They were still some way from the bridge.

Christian spat, and drew in air. As he swam, he kept Boissonet's head above water. Boissonet was unconscious.

There was now nothing but planks and debris on the river, and the heads of men swimming as he was. There was no longer a barge-train; Christian had nothing to save but this one man, and he was not sure if he was still alive. Yet he clung to the idea of saving him, whatever the cost. He swam economically, saving his breath, but he had to fight to free himself from the terrible power of a whirlpool which had gripped him and was dragging him towards the piers of the bridge. He swam, but the river was racing faster, ever faster.

'Father, make for the Ryaume!'

His son's voice came from downstream. Claude was safe, he had managed to get through the bridge. He would have ample time to reach the bank.

'The Ryaume, Father! Make for the Ryaume!' Claude's voice broke.

Christian made a desperate effort to free himself from this whirl-pool which the river was driving at full speed towards a massive beam which formed the angle of a pier.

Then, realizing that he would not make it and seeing his son's head bobbing on the water as he struggled to remain downstream from the bridge, he shouted: 'Over to you, Claude!'

And with the last of his strength he hurled Boissonet towards the triangle of supple water which was shooting under the arch. If he succeeded, Claude might perhaps be able to grab the injured man as he went past and get him to the bank.

But Christian would never know if he succeeded. Already the Rhône had him in its grip. It spun him round like a child, and smashed his head against the pier of the bridge, which had with-stood, unmoving, the shattering of all the fine barges in his train.

CHÂTEAU-CHALON
17th August 1970 – 17th July 1971